The Poor Shall Inherit

~ A Family Saga ~

Daff Noël

SEAFLOWER BOOKS

Published in 2006 by
SEAFLOWER BOOKS
16A St John's Road
St Helier
Jersey   JE2 3LD

www.ex-librisbooks.co.uk

Origination by Seaflower Books

Printed by Cromwell Press
Trowbridge, Wiltshire

ISBN 1 903341 37 X

*For Julia,
without whose legacy
the childhood of many thousands,
mine included, would have
been the poorer*

About the Author

D aff Noël was born, the seventh child in a family of ten children, at the beginning of the German Occupation of Jersey. Her first book *Remember When...* was published in 1995, followed by the biography of Teddy Noel (no relation) *Barefoot to the Palace* in 1998. A sequel to her first book, entitled *We too Remember When...* was published by Seaflower Books in 1999.

Acknowledgements

Liz Ottaway, descendant of Annie Westaway and sisters Robbie Colledge and Vicki Clouston, descendants of Henry son of John Nathaniel Westaway Junior, have been so generous in their help and warmth of friendship that I will be forever indebted to them. I especially hope that they will enjoy this novel based on the lives of their ancestors who I am sure would have been very proud of the wonderful women they have become.

To the many local historians, the facts from whose works remained in my mind more so than their name or the title of their books, I give my sincere apologies at not acknowledging them personally. Thank you for aiding my imagination to flow.

To Anna Baghiani, Librarian at the Société Jersiase, Linda Romeril and Trudy Foster at the Jersey Archive and Colin Smith Secretary to the United Club I give my humble thanks for their help in my research.

To Dave and Jean Walter of the Surrey Lodge Guest House, Belmont Road, who welcomed me so warmly into what was once John Nathaniel's home, thank you.

To Dora, a writer whose talent far exceeds mine but who generously gives up her time to read through my scripts, my eternal thanks. I bless the day we became friends.

To Ray and Annette Le Pivert of the Channel Islands Family History Society – while helping me with a particular line of research you recalled the surname of my maternal line and in doing so reunited me with a long lost cousin. For that you have not only mine, but also my family's sincere thanks.

And finally to Roger Jones, editor and publisher, my grateful thanks for accepting this new genre to your list of books on the Channel Islands; your help and input has been greatly appreciated.

INTRODUCTION

To many thousands of Jersey men and women of my generation and earlier, the name 'Westaways' will always evoke memories of the shoes and boots that were distributed each year to poor, Protestant schoolchildren. Clothes were also given out – knickerbockers, liberty bodices, combinations (an undergarment with legs, sleeves, two or three buttons at the neckline and a row of unreachable buttons across the waistline at the rear), besides other assorted items – but it was the footwear which left an indelible impression. Always uniformly styled in black, the shoes for girls and boots for boys were a badge of the poverty we all experienced.

Early every September the mothers whose families had come through the means test would form a queue outside a shop called 'The Old Soldier' in New Street with their children who were to be kitted out. Many understood that they were benefiting from the Westaway Trust Fund from whom the application forms they'd filled in had been sent but few knew of the generous benefactress Julia Westaway, whose legacy had originally set the charity in motion.

2006 marks the centenary of that Trust which was established five years after Julia's death in 1901. However, today's parents no longer have to endure a means test, neither is the footwear evidence of the family's unfortunate circumstances as vouchers are now given out enabling a choice in footwear. Yet many remain ignorant of Julia's legacy.

The distribution of children's shoes and clothing formed only a third of Julia Westaway's magnificent £92,000 bequest to the island's poor, an amount which over the years translates into millions of pounds of today's money. The other two-thirds was to provide a crèche and day nursery for babies and a fund for the *pauvres honteux* (poor who never applied for parish relief). The Westaway Crèche stood on the corner of the Royal Parade and Saville Street in St Helier for over fifty years until ideas on institutional child care changed and the building was pulled down and replaced with accommodation for hospital staff. The fund for the *pauvres honteux*, given out at the discretion of the twelve Parish Constables, gradually depleted, as did the supply of clothing so that only the provision of footwear now remains.

Throughout the hundred years that the Trust has been formed the number of islanders who have been helped through Julia's legacy has surpassed any estimate which might have been made at the onset of its foundation. And though it has been generally accepted that both the recipients and the coffers of the States of Jersey would have been poorer without it, the only monument that recorded Julia's existence was in St. Saviour's cemetery. As one of those past recipients and now a Trustee I began this book as my own personal tribute. But I am greatly heartened to know that the public oversight will now be remedied with the acknowledgement of the Trust's Centenary.

So who was she, this magnificent benefactor? The official records make very poignant reading, including bitter family divisions over their father's estate leading to Julia being thrown into prison by her own brother; avaricious sharks circling around her and a great nephew claiming the estate by accusing her of being mentally incapable, and ending with a small local incident which led to the Privy Council Judgement in London. The more I read the more I wanted to know what lay between the lines.

Julia's story had captured my imagination many years ago and became a tale that I often enjoyed relating but, though I made several attempts to write it as a biography, the words would not flow. The characters that surrounded her were so strong that I soon realised that I could not dismiss the parts they played in influencing the outcome of her final decision, to leave her fortune to the island's poor. Fiction writers will tell you they just love it when their characters take over and insist on telling their story. So it happened with the Westaways. Their family story has evolved into a saga.

Having grown up in the town, I was familiar with the streets the family had inhabited and felt driven to walk them time and time again as if in their shoes. As I did so our town of the nineteenth century reappeared in my head and in the writing I was led to mix fiction with fact and real people with non-existent to bring it all to life again. Through it all I hope I have succeeded in taking you back with me to an earlier age and to an island so different to that presented to the world today.

Daff Noël
Jersey
October 2006

Nathaniel Westaway m. 1811 Anne Alexandre w Edward Mourant

- John Nathaniel m Anne Guillet
  1812-1870   1910-1856
  - John Nathaniel (jnr)
    1835-1879
    m
    Emma Tregear
    - John (Tregear)
      1863
    - Henry
      1872
    - Emma
      1877
    - Nathaniel
      1878
  - Annie
    1837-1896
    m
    Frederick
    Hedger
  - Charles
    1839-1854
    & Henrietta
    1839-1862
  - Nathaniel
    1841-1871
    & Maria
    1841-1857
- Harriet
  1814-1892
- Charlotte
  1816-1833
- William
  1819-1819
- Julia
  1820-1901
  - James
    1844-1877
  - Alex
    1846-1900
  - Charlotte
    1847
    m
    Roger
    Miles
  - Susan
    1848
    m
    Ernest
    Collas

1

WHEN THE SMALL PROCESSION came to the end of the deeply rutted track that passed through the sand dunes the man driving the leading cart brought his horse to a stop. Removing the buckskin glove from his right hand he undid the top button of his greatcoat and, reaching inside, took out a small telescope and placed it to his eye. Satisfied that the information he had received had been correct, that the ketch he was expecting had docked at the end of the new quay, he replaced the instrument and, buttoning his coat again, quickly restored the glove to his hand.

A scowl began to furrow his brow as he continued to stare at the swarming mass of men and conveyances of every description on the pier ahead. Several ships had arrived on the tide and bedlam filled the air as porters and tavern waiters besieged disembarking passengers in their lust for business, hawkers clamoured to ply their wares and traders loudly made claims on their incoming cargo.

'Really!' he complained silently. 'Why on God's good earth had the master of the *Gazelle* chosen to put in here instead of St. Aubin? Though it would have meant a long trudge there and back I would have preferred it to making my way through this rabble! The ride in the bracing sea air would have cleared this aching head but now, amid the racket, it will surely grow worse.'

As this grievance went through his mind Nathaniel Westaway swung slowly around in the saddle, his eyes skimming the rugged outlines of Elizabeth Castle as they searched westward past the Fort of St. Aubin to the destination of his preference. The two ships lying at anchor at the far side of the bay, clearly awaiting vacant berths within the shelter of the small harbour, explained the captain's decision.

'Yet do my eyes still see ships lying in wait outside the harbour of St Aubin, when there is a new quay in St. Helier? This loudly heralded Le Quai des Marchands, paid for out of the pockets of long suffering town merchants and tradesmen like myself? A pier not only supposed to do away with that ill-equipped creek of a landing place at La Folie but save us the tedious journey to and fro' the bay? A scant harbour that can only be entered on a high tide?' Nathaniel snorted with derision. It was as he had foretold at the early meetings, when plans for the building of the new quay were being discussed and deliberated over. It was simply not good enough!

'Jersey's trade will continue to grow and we must build with the future in mind. Tarry a small while so that we may all invest more and then construct a harbour of merit,' he had proposed. But the businessmen were neither prepared to put more of their money into the scheme nor to delay any longer. They voted against his advice and gave permission for the commissioned architect of harbours to begin work.

Nevertheless, at the quay's completion he could not help but be caught up with the celebrations. The finished work, lined with its smart row of granite stone merchant buildings, was very pleasing to the eye. Also trading was quiet at first and for a short time he was misled into throwing off his earlier misgivings, conceding that his fellow businessmen might have been right after all. However the traffic soon increased until it exceeded even his expectations and the initial sense of gain was soon lost under the heavy frustration that began to beset them all once more.

'That those dunderheads of politicians have finally been lobbied into constructing another pier at the island's expense is no consolation. Their new quay is still several years away from alleviating the problem by its completion. I should have spoken out more forcefully at those original meetings and convinced the assembly of the need for prudence,' Nathaniel continued in debate with himself.

'You speak your mind and it is all you could do. Regretfully some men can see no further than their own bulbous noses. That yours is slender and majestic, allowing you to see clearly, can be more of a frustration than a gift,' his friend and mentor Matthieu had often advised and Nathaniel thought on the words now.

Matthieu Alexandre had been Jersey's first master of the printing press, a man of controversial views who was not afraid to voice his vehement opposition to the political Charlot party either verbally or through his many publications. His scathing remarks were known to stir up much ill feeling against some members of the island's parliament, causing them to retort with equal passion, 'Calumny!

Calumny! The man should be prosecuted for the agitator he is!'

But though Matthieu Alexandre had made enemies amongst the local politicians he had earned the admiration and respect of many other men in the island. For he had not only been courageously steadfast in the public airing of his opinions but he had also been a good man, a man who cared for the poorer classes and spoke out against injustices.

Twelve years had passed since Matthieu's death but Nathaniel still missed the man who had befriended him soon after his arrival in the island. The man who had helped him master French, the main language, besides steering him through the perplexing native Jersey tongue which was of Norman French extraction and a dialect all of its own. Who had not only offered useful information of where pieces of land could be had but taught him how to deal with the complex characters doing the selling. Most of all Nathaniel missed the friendly bartering of debate for he had not found another male friend since with the same talent.

There had been a time, he reflected, when Anne his wife of nine years had also been of very strong opinions. When they had first met the trait had led him to wonder, especially with her maiden name also being Alexandre, if she and Matthieu were related but Anne had assured him otherwise. She was aware of the family, she told him, but they were not of the same blood. Matthieu had brought up his family in the parish of St. Brelade, whereas her father was of Trinity and later St. Saviour's.

He had always enjoyed his discussions, sometimes earnest and agitated, with Anne too. But, since she had been beset with melancholia he tended to talk things over silently, as if either she or Matthieu were there alongside him.

'But then, had the meetings taken note of my objections we might not have had even this quay built,' he now considered. 'Oh! Really! I am as contrary as a woman this morning, where is my rightful mind today?'

He gave an involuntary shake of his head, the action aggravating the sheet of pain that had hung at the back of his eyes for the last hour, spreading it forward so that his skull now throbbed in protest. In the hope of relief he gently massaged his closed lids, removing his top hat so that he could also rub at the indentation it left on his forehead.

His hair, which would have fallen around his shoulders had it not been tied back, matched the salt and pepper effect of an early greying beard. This unkempt mass, which all but hid a well-shaped mouth, reached from ear to ear enclosing a ruddy, lined and weather-beaten face. Therefore Nathaniel Westaway could never be described as a handsome man yet there were times, as when his hazel eyes became animated with enthusiasm, that he was considered to be 'goodly looking'.

In character Nathaniel was known to be intelligent, God fearing and generally very patient. However that morning he was feeling a little uneasy, for what reason he was not quite sure, and this in turn was the cause of the nagging pain in his head and his unusual irritability.

The movement of two or three carts coming away from the dock opened up a short narrow path and Nathaniel urged his horse forward to claim it. Nevertheless as he moved closer he realised the futility of trying to drive a way through the rumbustious crowd and decided that he would make better progress leading his men and carts through by foot.

'I will need the boy to go ahead for all that if it is time I mean to save,' Nathaniel muttered, dismounting from his horse and patting its hindquarters gently as he passed on his way to the back of the cart. Once there he slid the nails from their metal eyelets and lowered the tailboard to the ground.

"Bejesus 'tis cold this bitter morning so it is," young Colm O'Reilly muttered as he fell awkwardly to the ground, a freezing lethargy having taken over his limbs. Violently he flapped his arms around his thin body and slapped his thighs in an effort to quicken the blood that felt as if it had stilled in his veins.

"Ye should nah be so contrary about the covering of goose grease, the big sap ye are!" his elder brother Donal chided, leaping to the ground with ease. "I'll be a warrantin' you'm nah wearing the drawers our mam spent the time a knitting for ye either."

Colm glared back, a look in his eyes that sent out a clear warning for the subject to be dropped. It was too late. The remark had been overheard by one of the men who, having lowered themselves out of the two remaining carts in the group, had joined them.

"What's this lad, you'm not wearing your woolly drawers under those woebegone breeches of yourn? 'Tis a shame and them being a good suit for this fancy Protector you'm a showing off!" he jeered, pulling at the knitted hood that covered the boy's head and revealing a thick thatch of dark auburn curls.

Nathaniel looked on warily as, amid the flush that rapidly covered the unusually smooth-skinned face, the boy's green eyes began to flash with imminent rage. Any minute now, he realised, the skeletal balls of tightly clenched fists that were showing from the frayed hems of the ill fitting jacket would be brought up in a challenging gesture and a brawl would follow. For such a thing to happen while in his company, and in a public place, would be to warrant the dismissal of the men involved and their loss would be harmful to the business. He could not afford such a state of affairs to develop because, despite their rough and ready ways, they were all excellent workers.

Quickly he stepped in to diffuse the situation by first sending the boy on ahead, as he had planned, to see what of their cargo had arrived amongst the freight being brought ashore. After that he organised the older O'Reilly and the remaining men as to which of the expected building materials they were to load into which cart and, once loaded, where the materials were to be delivered. A few minutes later he returned to his horse and signalled them to follow.

It was, as Colm had complained, a bitter cold day in the island of Jersey that eighth day of November 1820. There was an icy chill on the brine-impregnated wind that cut sharply into all extremities that any human had either the misfortune, or mismanagement, of leaving uncovered. Gulls circled the air, above the business of the pier, raucously screeching in their search for food. Their noise, along with the shouting of the men all around, was pandemonium to Nathaniel's ears and he wished heartily to be rid of it.

Yet his progress down the quay was frustratingly slow as he inched the horse and cart through the melée. There were so many people he knew that despite his mood his civil nature led him to pause occasionally to greet a fellow tradesman, ask after the health of another, shake the hand of others.

2

"ACHETE UN POISSON MONSIEUR!"

A woman pushed her way to Nathaniel's side and thrust a blood-stained tray under his nose. The large mullet that stared up at him smelt strongly of brine and had the look of one caught within the hour.

He was about to ask the price but changed his mind abruptly when he caught sight of the large bulging stomach beneath the woman's sackcloth skirt. Instead he waved her off with a curt, "Allez vous en!" He clicked his tongue impatiently, not at the woman who was now cursing as she moved away but at his own stupidity as the memory of being at Anne's side, moments before he left the house, suddenly returned to taunt him.

Oh why, he asked himself, had he been content to believe her when, after bending to kiss her cheek and enquiring as to her health, she had assured him all was fine. That she had begun her pains was now obvious, but why had she not told him? Still yet, why had he not noticed? He had after all been waiting for this day to arrive, albeit with feelings that alternated between excitement and trepidation.

Now, with the pain in his head really beginning to nag, Nathaniel considered calling one of the men from the other carts forward to take his place so that he could return to his storage yard, where he would be within calling distance of any news. For the yard was only a few short paces away from his home, in a narrow roadway recently named after the locally renowned General Don, in the centre of town.

How could he have been so callous as to put Anne through another pregnancy so soon? He continued to berate himself. Had he been right to have faith in the view of Doctor Lamont, that a woman's age of 43 years did not necessarily bode ill for childbearing and that the reason their little son did not survive was that it was simply too weak? It was two years on now and she had been low in spirits ever since.

He had tried to be compassionate, reminding himself that Anne had endured the double loss of a husband and a young daughter before they married in 1812, that the pain of those bereavements may have come to the fore again with the death of baby William. So he kept from her the fact that he too had been heartbroken, that unmanly tears had fallen copiously as he carried the small box containing his son's body through the town streets to the cemetery. He also kept silent about his long held wish to father a large brood of children, a wish that by falling in love with her, a woman older by fifteen years, whose child-bearing days were nearing their end, stood little likelihood of being fulfilled.

Instead he tried all kinds of remedies to lift her spirits, buying her new gowns, hiring carriages so that she might make visits to her family members and friends around the island, even discussing a trip to England.

But it was when she began to shrug off the hand he placed lovingly on her waist and turn her face away from his kiss that he became angry. For, despite the fact that he accepted the passion they had once shared must inevitably change it was in his nature to be demonstratively affectionate.

As Eternal God was his witness he was only trying to comfort her, he had shouted in exasperation. How much longer was she going to hold him apart? Did she imagine that he did not understand her pain? Well he had news for her! He understood it only too well. He too had suffered at the loss of his son, and raged against God.

At this he had broken down and seeing his distress Anne was immediately contrite, going to him and clinging to his neck as she cried and begged him not to be so upset. She was sorry, she was truly sorry. She had been selfish, not giving a thought as to how he must have suffered. He had been so kind to her too. Oh! She loved him so much, so much, she repeated between the kisses she planted on his mouth and a few minutes later he picked her up in his arms and carried her into their bedroom.

Their love for each other had always been passionate. On Nathaniel's part especially it was an unexpected and overwhelming emotion that came on him the first time they met, when he had called to see her to offer his condolences on the death of her husband Edward Mourant in October 1811. He found himself making further excuses to visit, taking gifts of wood and coal and when, as a widow, her presence on the Mourant family farm was no longer wanted and she was about to be turned out onto the street, he had offered her the position of housekeeper. By this time Anne too had fallen in love and, living under the same roof, it was inevitable that it would not be long before their passion for each other was consummated. They married on the 19th

April the following year by which time Anne was already expecting their eldest child John Nathaniel.

Now reconciled and ardour spent, the couple talked as they never had before, with Nathaniel confiding that in marrying Anne so soon after her husband's death he had always felt he was walking in the man's shoes. This caused Anne to admit for the first time that she had never loved the dour humourless Edward Mourant, whose parents had pushed him into marrying because of their need of grandsons to continue the farming tradition. Finally they both agreed it had been sinful to rail against God for the loss of one babe when they had already been blessed with three healthy children.

They talked of taking the trip to England that Anne had previously been reluctant to make, deciding to go in the spring when they would visit friends and relations in Warminster, Somerset and Nathaniel's home village of Winkleigh in Devon.

It was after they had returned to the island that Anne had told him that she was again *enceinte*, as she put it, but the knowledge had not cheered her as much as he had hoped it would have done. For gradually she had become convinced that the outcome of this pregnancy would be the same as the last and that this child too would die; neither he nor the doctor could persuade her otherwise.

'Oh! If she was only to bear another healthy child,' Nathaniel thought now as continued his slow journey down the pier, 'a child whose very being would help restore her to her former self, rekindling her full attention to me and our children.'

Anyone watching Nathaniel at that moment would have witnessed a warm glow about his brown eyes as he thought of his three children. Eight year-old John Nathaniel, boarding weekly at St. Mannelier School and growing sturdily at a fast pace; six year-old Harriet, showing unusual promise under the tutorship of her governess Miss Browne, and little Charlotte who, at age four, was proving to have an excellent memory at remembering little ditties. They were all such joy and it was his great delight to see their faces come alive at the sight of him, to hear their earnest, unaffected talk.

He would never understand why Anne had failed to find consolation in their company, especially over the past two years as he had done, and not break herself out of the depression in which she now seemed to be imprisoned. 'Still, she had not appeared well when

I left her side this morning,' he reminded himself now. 'Things may be going wrong as she predicted. I must get a message to Doctor Lamont and urge him to visit immediately!'

A man, head turned in the direction from which he had come, walked straight into Nathaniel, breaking into his thoughts and bringing him back to the moment. In the instant that the man apologised profusely for his inattention the men recognised each other. To his utter astonishment Nathaniel saw it was no other than the doctor in person. 'It is as if I conjured him up by my very thought,' he mused and the absurdity of the notion suddenly filled him with the whimsical need to laugh. He felt his mouth widen to a grin, hysterical mirth begin to fill his being, but in an effort to retain some gravity he bent to pick up the doctor's medical bag that had been knocked to the ground. At the same moment the man also leant forward causing two top hats to touch and fall to either side of the small portmanteau. Nathaniel's chuckle finally escaped.

"Ha! Ha! Ha!... The very man..."

"My dear sir!... I am on my way to..."

"I was just about to... It seems that..."

They spoke together at each turn and laughed heartily as they moved, in unison again, to retrieve the fallen articles.

"After you sir," Nathaniel conceded at last, placing his hat upon his head once more.

"I was about to say that I am on the way to your house. It seems the child you are expecting is finally about to enter this world Westaway," the doctor informed him.

"But by what blessing of God's name did you hear? Anne gave me no sign as I left the house earlier this morning, well, I am afraid no sign that I gave any attention to. I am afraid I..."

Emile Lamont patted him on the upper part of the arm, silently indicating that nothing more needed to be said for him to understand. In all his years of ministering to the sick and dying he had never witnessed a greater devotion than that of this man for his wife, he had once commented to a colleague. Were he to be truthful he would have added that it was a trait he neither admired nor truly understood for he had never known the love of another human being but his habit was to always to appear otherwise. To his true mind this steadfast patience with a woman whose prolonged state of melancholia would have threatened the patience of Job, let alone those like himself who carried out the profession of medicine, showed a character that was either divine or stupid. And he had to own that Nathaniel Westaway could never be described as stupid.

"I had left notice at my rooms," he began now, "that I was attending a dock hand who had met with an unfortunate accident and the girl from your kitchen.... Is she not one of the brood of Jean Fromage of Saint Laurent who came into the town to live just last year?"

Nathaniel nodded impatiently, wanting the man to get to the point, but the doctor prattled on regardless.

"Thought so! 'Tis the way her eyes are set in her head. Well, she came running into the stores...that is where the man had been taken... He will lose his hand of course..."

"The girl?" Nathaniel interrupted curtly. "What about the girl?"

"Well, naturally, having informed me of your wife's condition I sent her back to the house with the message that I would be on my way directly and that the women were to see to your wife's every comfort in the meantime. Do not worry yourself Westaway!" the doctor said, stretching out his hand and placing it on Nathaniel's shoulder. "Your wife may not be well in spirit but she is extremely robust of body. However, as a precaution, I took the responsibility of instructing the girl to go to Madame Le Clair the midwife and tell her to also attend immediately. Mark my words Westaway," he added, removing his hand and making to continue on his way, "by tomorrow you will be the father of four healthy children."

Nathaniel hoped he would be right. For weeks now he had prayed that all would come right. Now he would just have to trust in the Lord.

"Thank you!" he said, grasping the doctor's free hand.

"All in the line of duty my dear sir," the doctor replied. Then remembering that Nathaniel was always the most prompt in settling his account added, "Rest assured your wife will receive the utmost of my care and attention."

When Nathaniel began to thread his way through the crowd once again he noticed that the pain in his head was no longer there.

3

"'Tis the orders from An...Antwerp an' Liverpool sir. The tiles am ashore...an' the lead.... We'm just to await the iron plates to come up from the hold," the voice of young Colm, his sentences broken up by a heavy panting caused by the run up the pier, brought Nathaniel's attention back to the expected cargo.

"Good lad!" he said. The boy did not look so cold now. The eagerness to work had warmed him. It was an unusual streak to find in one so young, the need to prove worthy of hire. As always Nathaniel was impressed with the boy's willingness but habit demanded he add curtly, "Make sure you give a ready hand to the men when it proves you are needed now!"

Master and boy walked a few yards side by side until, having to dodge around three gentlemen conducting a heated conversation in French, Colm darted back to Nathaniel's side with the request, "Sir...I...W'uld it be...c'uld I come to your hou...Aw! Sir! I w'uld na be so bold as to ask meself but Master John said I was to ask if us c'uld play together at t' house one day?"

Nathaniel looked down at him in surprise. He was aware that the boys knew of each other of course, but he had not thought them to be pals. Now as he considered the idea he could see nothing wrong with it though he knew Anne would not be pleased. Perhaps John also realised this and instructed the boy to speak to him knowing that he might be of a more amenable nature. Or perhaps – and as his father it disturbed him to suspect this – John was simply trying to stir up mischief, as he often tried to do against his sisters. Either way John would need reprimanding when he returned from school.

"Tell me, when would either of you have time for play?" he asked, delaying for time enough to think of a kindly way to reject the idea. Nevertheless it was a practical enquiry for John was at school all week from Monday till Saturday dinnertime and the boy never finished work of a day until six, the hour of dark at that time of the year.

"Master John said Sunday after dinner might be...Dats if we played quiet."

Ah! So his son was up to mischief after all! John knew that Sundays were certainly not for play. It was God's given day of rest. A day during which his people might attend divine service and spend the remaining hours in quiet contemplation of the holy word.

"Is that what you do on Sundays, play quietly?"

The boy's family was of the Roman Catholic faith that, for want of a church building, attended a mass that was held in a large hall in New Street on a Sunday morning. Then, as one of a poor widow's fifteen children, living in an old fisherman's shack amongst the wild and windswept sand dunes, the afternoons were generally spent searching for driftwood and logs for the insatiable grate.

"'Tis the evenin's I likes best," he confessed to Nathaniel now. "Dat's when we all sings songs to Donal's fiddling and before we goes to our beds Mam tells us stories about our da and the old country."

Playing a fiddle on a Sunday! And singing songs! Nathaniel was scandalised.

"Well our Sundays are spent as the good Lord intended and John had no right to imply otherwise!"

The artless face flushed red at the rebuke and Nathaniel was unexpectedly filled with regret for having spoken so sharply. The boy could not help his background after all he told himself as, on hearing his name, he turned away to raise his hat in greeting.

"Besides I really cannot see that you have any time left over for play, can you?"

"Uh... Yes sir. No sir... I mean ri...ight you are sir!"

There was such utter dejection in the boy's voice that Nathaniel glanced down quickly. The green eyes that looked back at him were filled with disappointment.

Like most of his workers the boy had every Sabbath, and one half Saturday a month free from labour and, remembering this, Nathaniel found himself asking,

"It is your half-day on Saturday, is it not?"

Colm nodded.

"Well, why not call at the kitchen door about three o'clock. John should be free to play by then."

Now why had he made that suggestion? Nathaniel asked himself testily, as once again he and the boy were separated. Saturday afternoons were times he usually honoured above all to be the hours when he and Anne permitted the children to enjoy various amusements and games before being restrained to the solemnity and sanctity of Sundays. Comfortable times. Times normally spent to the exclusion of others. Why then had he proffered the invitation to the boy?

Nathaniel stared ahead unseeingly as he paused his stride to let bodies busily weave about in front of him and wondered what was it about the boy that made him act so impulsively. It had been less than six months since he had been moved to employ the boy for duties on the building sites – a position which, because of the sheer brawn needed, he usually reserved for one of more mature years.

His inner eye sped to his field at the north of town from where the clay soil was extracted to make the bricks he needed to continue his business. Where, constantly breathing in the heavy mixture of smoke and dust, a small army of men, women and children toiled ceaselessly while extracting the clay from the pits, feeding the kilns or smoothing the finished bricks. It was a place Nathaniel was never keen to visit for the vision of the poorly dressed workers – thickly coated with dust on dry days, mud-sullied on wet – continually coughing and spitting out the mucous from their congested lungs, unsettled him. It was the sight of the children especially that caught at his heart and, even though he knew that by employing them he was helping the families survive, he did not like to witness their frail, listless figures going about their labour. Usually he averted his eyes but that particular day his attention had been inexplicably drawn to the boy in the queue of people seeking work. The lad was trying to catch the overseer's eye by standing straight and square-shouldered, looking earnest against the disinclination of the others, robust against their weakness.

Why he had taken the boy out of the line and set him to work about the building sites Nathaniel could not explain. 'Still that impulse had been a good one. The boy has proved himself well able for the job, even though he remains so puny in size,' he reminded himself now. 'However, I must not let him take advantage.'

So when the boy appeared at his side again fleetingly he added aloud, "That is only provided John has completed his schoolwork mind!"

The boy nodded again, muttering, "Yes, sir," before having to encircle a horse and trap that was making its way between them. When he came back into line he found that Nathaniel had stopped to talk to a captain who was standing at the foot of the gangplank to one of the two cutters tied up at the same bollard, so the boy respectfully kept his distance.

Louis Jean was an old friend and Nathaniel was pleased to see him. He would be returning to Plymouth on the tide he told Nathaniel, but he hoped they could meet up when he was back in the island the following week. Would Friday night suit?

"Suit admirably!" Nathaniel had answered, shaking his friend's hand vigorously.

"We shall welcome the new baby over a whisky or two!" Louis Jean had called after him as he moved away.

"Oui bien sur, mon ami!" Nathaniel had rejoined in the man's own language. The exchange had been short but warm and Nathaniel felt good for it, blithe almost, as he heard the boy ask,

"Mister Westaway sir... Sir, is it hard dis learnin' o' letters an' numbers?... Like Master John does?"

Strange how he liked the sound of the Irish accent, Nathaniel mused. He could almost describe it as melodious to the ear, not like the guttural Jersey tongue. Indulgently he replied, "Not too hard if you have the will."

"Oh! De will sir... I've dat alright, so me mam says... 'Tis just de learnin' I'd a t'inkin' I'd like to try, dat's if you t'ink I's not too dense in t' 'ead, like de beggars say."

Nathaniel had heard the ragged beggars, the unfortunate children who were not gainfully employed and were unable or unwilling to attend school, chanting cruel rhymes against the Irish immigrants. He was about to caution the boy into ignoring the heckling, explain that it was not an abuse against him alone for he had also heard it said against the Jersey peasants but the two were parted yet again, this time with each making their way around a huge mound of limestone. One of the men lifting the limestone into the nearby cart recognised Nathaniel and motioned his mate to stop work until he had passed, a deference that Nathaniel acknowledged with a response to the men's 'Bonjour Monsieur'.

No, he could never describe the boy as being dense, Nathaniel reflected a minute later. On the contrary he thought the child to be rather sharp-witted, considering his age and circumstances. However it would be imprudent to encourage him into thinking he could learn to the extent of his betters. But what if the boy truly aspired to an education? An inner voice nagged. Would it not it be wrong to ignore such aspiration? Yet…a boy from such circumstances? A boy from a home that was nothing more than a hovel, the floors of which were regularly under water when the tides ran high and where cockroaches and rats fought for space amongst the family of, what was it, fifteen? Nathaniel felt himself sneering inwardly before bringing to mind the conclusion to the Reverend Small's sermon the previous Sunday.

'Be ye ever generous of mind and pocket to the poor and judge ye not lest ye be judged,' the Reverend had preached and Nathaniel rebuked himself sharply at the reminder. Who was he to judge those from less fortunate circumstances? Surely, if the boy had the mind to improve himself, he should be given every chance no matter his background?

"I should think you are certainly not too dense to learn Colm," he said kindly, "but unfortunately you are past the age for acceptance to any establishment." A shadow passed across the boy's expressive face. The sight troubled Nathaniel and once again he asked himself why, and why he felt impelled to continue, "but if you have the will and determination for learning the likes of which Master John studies then we will see what we can do." He stopped suddenly and, taking a leather strap from his pocket passed it through the horse's reins. Next he bent to lift the tethering ring that was embedded in the ground and threaded the strap through, gauging the comfortable distance between the horse's nose and ground before finally buckling it. Straightening up again he pointed to a stack of clay tiles.

"Until then, if I am not mistaken, these are the Antwerp tiles meant for my yard so start loading them onto the cart whilst I have a word with the men."

The boy grinned widely, touching his forelock as Nathaniel walked the few paces back to where his men were about to tether the other horses.

"No! No! Have I not told you enough times?" he shouted. "The nags' heads must not be held so close to the ground whilst you are loading the carts. Have any of you thought to bring the straps from the stable? No! I thought not. Well had you done so the extra pair of hands would have lightened your work as it is… Bert?"

A sallow faced man muttered. "Yes Sir?"

"Bert, you hold the reins whilst the others load… "

Nathaniel paused to question a pair of stevedores who were piling sheets of lead on the ground, their faces beaded with sweat under the hessian hoods that covered their heads. "Is this my order? Is there more?" One of them recognised him and said, "Yes, sir, we're just bringing it all up from the hold now."

He turned back to his men and continued, "all of that pile with the addition of what the men have yet to unload is to be placed in this cart while…" His eyes searched the crowded quay and he was gratified to glimpse Donal O'Reilly busily placing the iron into the third cart as he had instructed before they entered the quayside. He never had to repeat his orders to Donal as he did with these men.

Finally satisfied that they had now set about their work he left them to follow the stevedores up the nearby gangplank but whilst they climbed down into the hold made his way along the narrow passageway to where the captain stood on the shore side of the forward deck. It was the first time the two men had met and the master mariner shook Nathaniel's hand vigorously in greeting.

Though Captain Le Roux was new to island waters he had made it his business to get to know his new client's background and was impressed by Nathaniel's reputation for building most of the elegant houses springing up about the town.

"From your yard?" He asked eventually, nodding towards the row of houses that lined the opposite side of the pier. Nathaniel moved to face the shore and looked across at the granite stone buildings, which had been completed before the construction of the quay. "No, not my yard unfortunately for I predict they will be valuable properties when the other pier has been built and the use here is lessened."

"You think the island will build another pier?"

"It is doing so, have you not heard? The foundation stone has already been laid. The arm will project out behind us here." Nathaniel's reply was certain and sure as he turned to face the sea, stretching out his right hand and pointing to the shoreline where the new pier was to begin. There was a hint of pride in his voice too for despite his irritation with the way some political matters were handled he had come to love the island which was now his home. He enjoyed showing it off to newcomers and rarely criticised it in their presence. "The increased anchorage will not only do away with the lying about in the bay but will also provide much needed shelter, I am sure you will agree," he added, sweeping his hand slowly outward until it indicated an area to his right where the projection would end. There, in the shadow of Elizabeth Castle, several small fishing boats randomly trawled the water. The scene was so eminently more peaceful than the hubbub on the pier behind them that both men paused for a few minutes to observe it silently before turning to face the shore again.

"Do those buildings command high rents? I presume they have living quarters?" Captain Le Roux asked, his eyes and thoughts once again on the merchants' houses lining the quay. It would be pleasant to have a home on the island, he was thinking, in this haven of a place where the inhabitants spoke French yet paid none of the impoverishing taxes that were levied by the political masters in his own country.

"Some use only the upstairs as living quarters, though the maisonettes are fine ones for all that. I believe the general plan was to use them for storage," Nathaniel answered thoughtfully as a plan suddenly occurred to him. That was it! Why had the idea not occurred to him before? If he were to buy one of those properties, have his materials transferred directly from the ships, he would not need to spend so much time away from the sites. He could employ an overseer to account for the cargo deposited and then release the goods out again, when necessary, to either yard or site. He could even rent out the maisonette.... Now why had he not thought of that before?

Nathaniel's mind skimmed over the many business opportunities he had foreseen and later profited by over the years. The excitement that had filled his hours as he planned the buildings to go on each successive purchase of land. The selection and direction of the men, the bargaining with suppliers, the feeling of pride in a job successfully completed. All this came back to him with the regret that those sentiments were no longer a part of his life. Where had they gone? He wondered. What had happened to all the...the...fervour? That was it! He reminded himself. There had been a fervency to his days that was no longer there. It had been over a year now since he had enjoyed the inclination for business and he missed it. His worry over Anne had taken precedence, her despondency a dragging thing that pulled at his spirit. He must re-clothe his mind to its former earnestness, for the sake of his children, for the sake of himself, and he would start with buying one of these properties. Nathaniel's thoughts raced ahead excitedly as he made his polite farewells and returned ashore.

Though he always settled his accounts at the shipping office Nathaniel made it his business to talk with the masters of the ships that delivered his materials to the island. He felt it was good for trade to be on pleasant terms with everyone he came into contact with and this was reflected by all who knew him. Indeed he was a well-liked man, someone with whom very few on the island had not made acquaintance and all he met that day stopped to exchange news. Therefore the hour was long past noon when, with Colm straddled atop the tiles in the cart, he eventually arrived back at his storage yard in Don Street.

4

NATHANIEL'S CONTRACTED AND oblong-shaped builder's yard was ideal for business, placed as it was in the heart of town and close to many other traders connected with construction. Behind a large gated entrance, which opened up onto the narrow street, it spanned widthways and was enclosed on three sides by a high wall.

Only one of the sides was Nathaniel's freehold, the other two being party to the official residence of the island's successive Governors, though few occupied it for any length of time during their tenure of office due to their preference for remaining in England. At the time Nathaniel took over the premises in the latter part of 1810 he found the Lieutenant-Governor Sir George Don was living there, the non-resident Governor being the Earl of Chatham.

Along with many others Nathaniel had a great respect and admiration for Sir George Don who, during the three years from 1806 to 1809, had done so much towards the improvement of the island. Besides disciplining the local Militia to reputable standard and fortifying the island against a possible French invasion, he had begun to build roads through what were often impassable lanes. The latter had not been an easy task as to form new roads was not only expensive but also necessitated the intrusion onto private property, which met with vehement opposition. However when the first road, from town by way of Longueville to Grouville, had been successfully completed in the December of '06, it was widely praised, replacing as it did a narrow, sunken and boggy throughway. The next year he built a second road from St. Ouen's Church to Beaumont and twelve months later a third from St. Helier to St. Aubin.

Called away to valiantly embark nearly thirteen thousand sick British soldiers from Walcheren where it had been hoped the army would seize Antwerp, Napoleon's naval base, the island requested Sir George Don's return on the mission's completion. This had come about in the May of 1810 whereupon the General immediately set about the continuation of his work.

So when, on taking over the premises, Nathaniel found the entire wall in a dilapidated and unsafe condition, he asked if he might rebuild it. In doing so, he added, he would like to raise it higher. Permission was granted and the completed work earned him a note of appreciation from the ever industrious Sir George Don for the alterations not only saved him the trouble but gave a degree of privacy to the garden of Government House, which it had not hitherto experienced.

When General Don took up the post of Lieutenant-Governor to Gibraltar in 1814 he left behind a much improved island from the one he had been appointed to eight years before. Applauded with the most glowing of tributes, from both members of Jersey's government and also all classes of the population to whom he had always been the most affable, his departure had been deeply regretted. Nathaniel in particular missed the occasional exchange of conversation, the savouring of the great man's contagious enthusiasm for each new undertaking. His successor was quite a different character. Word had it the man had requested that a more fitting residence be sought at an out of town location. This left Nathaniel wondering what would happen to his neighbouring property if this ever came about.

Within its walls Nathaniel's yard was stacked on either side with various building materials leaving a wide centre pathway running the complete width of the site. On the far right-hand side there was a shed, known as the office, and behind that a large wooden crate supported long planks of timber which rested in turn against the two party walls and the wall that, in bordering the street, continued back to the entrance. Behind this seemingly ordinary stack of wood, discreetly hidden from the eyes of the occasional visitor but openly acknowledged by Nathaniel and all the men who worked for him, was the tiny makeshift hut where Thomas Le Beau, the keeper of the yard, lived. The square lean-to was only large enough to house a narrow cot, a chair and an old rusty trunk, but to Thomas it was home.

Thomas regarded himself very lucky to have come to the notice of Nathaniel Westaway, without whose compassion he considered he would probably have ended up under the auspices of those who administered the Poor Law at the hospital. Worse still, he might have been locked in the ward with the lunatics. The latter was what Thomas, who had a stooped back and one leg shorter than the other which caused him to walk with a grotesque gait, feared most of all. The suggestion that he should be put away from public sight was a fear that had hung over him from the time his parents deserted him as a small boy. It became a threat that clouded the days he lived under the precarious guardianship of his grandfather, whose addiction to gambling finally led them to being destitute. A dread which, when he was forced to beg alongside the old man on the streets, had him avoiding every authoritative figure. For he was terrified that they would incarcerate him on the slightest excuse and by never looking further than his affliction think him to be an imbecile. He was in fact nothing of the sort.

For though Thomas could neither read nor write he spoke well and possessed the ability of being able to work out mathematical equations in his head. His grandfather Charles Le Beau had taught him both these skills for, as heir to the great fortune he later gambled away, he had benefited from an excellent education in his youth.

When he failed to wake that morning in 1806, Thomas could not mourn the man's passing. The latter acrimonious years, when each blamed the other for their desperate situation, had killed the affection they once shared. Thomas was eighteen by the time of his grandfather's death but he looked fifty years more. Both his hair and beard were grey, his skin chapped and ulcerated, his stoop more pronounced.

One day, as he sat begging in his regular place at the road side, his grandfather's battered top hat upturned at his side, he began to recall the early, much happier years when his grandfather would teach him mathematics and reward correct answers with three sous. His mind was so fixed back in time that, when Nathaniel dropped a single coin in passing, Thomas, without thinking, called after him.

"I can count for you sire. Any matriculation you care to call. Two sous more are all it would cost you."

Nathaniel intrigued that such a poorly disposed beggar should speak this way stopped and offered up the coins. He was surprised at the man's accuracy and from then after, whenever he was in that area he would make a point of stopping. He tried to catch him out by setting a more difficult sum each time but Thomas always gave the correct answer.

When Nathaniel opened up his yard he sought Thomas out and asked him if he would be capable of keeping count of the goods stored in a builder's yard, if he was to be so employed.

"No sire, for I cannot use a quill or read the words on any page," Thomas answered truthfully.

"That would not be necessary if you can but tell me by word of mouth, and I believe you can do that," Nathaniel assured him.

So Thomas began working for the only man he was to come to trust and revere, proving his worth time after time by keeping count of each plank of wood, each roof tile, each weight of tacks that left the yard. No worker dared pull a wheeze by helping themselves to goods or demanding them for unspecific jobs. He quickly became alert to all their tricks and organised things, as Nathaniel had intended, so that nothing left the yard unless it had been sanctioned by his own lips.

Throughout all the seasons of the year one of Thomas's tasks was to keep the red-hot coals alive in the circular iron furnace that stood near the yard's entrance and this he deemed to be a particular privilege. For while he would often be seen hovering near it during the cold weather it was at the end of each day, when business had finished and the gates were closed, that he appreciated it most. It was then that he would use the fiery embers to both reheat his mess of vegetable pottage and warm his body before retiring to his bed.

Because of the lean-to's position no consideration could be given in the way of heating but, once warm, Thomas slept well enough, even on the coldest of winter nights, under the pile of old capes and coats that had been passed on to him. Moreover it was dry and, being the area of the yard furthest away from Le Grand Douet, the open stream that crossed Don Street as it meandered its way through the town, it never came under water after heavy rain. The remainder of the yard, along with the flower garden and two rooms of the neighbouring official residence that ran in parallel, did suffer from this vexation. However, whereas the newly sworn-in Governor, Lord Beresford, had added his complaint to that of his predecessors of the official property's tendency to flooding, Nathaniel had the advantage. He had been warned of the problem by Sir George Don, and consequently stored his materials up on platforms, out of the water's path.

Thomas had just finished clearing some room on the platforms in preparation for the expected delivery when he heard the sound of the horse and cart on the street outside. He rushed out, taking the reins that now hung loosely from the nag's neck as Nathaniel dismounted.

"Oh! Sire! I thought you would never come!" he exclaimed. "The girl came across from the house some hours since...."

As he spoke the pleasant smile of greeting slipped from his master's face and the sentence remained unfinished as Nathaniel strode away, barking over his shoulder. "I shall be back later Thomas. Show the boy where to store the tiles and see that he is kept busy until my return!"

Though he had never heard his master speak so sharply Thomas took no offence as he watched the tall figure rush away. Nevertheless he was wishing that he had been given time to finish what he had been about to say, the words he had been rehearsing in his head.

'Ah! Master! If only I could have been the one to tell you,' he muttered before turning and noticing, as if for the first time, the boy who was perched on top of the neat pile of slates stacked on the cart.

"Well, are you going to stay there all day a dreaming or will you deign to begin unloading?" he growled sarcastically.

5

NATHANIEL'S HEART WAS beating so fast that the inside of his chest began to ache. He had not given one thought to Anne or the coming baby since he had spoken to the doctor and now he was filled with dread at what he might be told on reaching the house.

Suddenly engulfed in this wave of guilt and apprehension he stepped carelessly onto one of the large stones placed randomly in the path of the stream, which crossed the street, and lost his footing. The leather soles of his moleskin boots slipped from the wet surfaces and sent him splashing into the shallow water but he failed to notice neither that nor the wet patches that seeped through the uppers, soaking his feet and sending a damp biting chill up and over his ankles. Instead he propelled himself ever forward across the cobbles, cracking the glassy fragments of ice that lay underfoot in the ruts of his path without feeling or hearing anything in the rush to cover the short distance to his home.

His large home in Don Street was quite different to others that Nathaniel generally built but then he had intended it to be. For it was the home he lovingly constructed soon after he had opened up his yard, into which he welcomed Anne after their wedding. It was his comfortable haven, a homestead large enough to house the many children he hoped they would produce, an abode from where he could extend hospitality, a place conveniently situated for most of his work.

The large plot of land on which the granite stone building stood extended back to, and embraced, a small cottage that faced onto a parallel thoroughfare recently widened and given the name of New Street. Nathaniel had the idea of placing his house at the farthest end of the plot, albeit that it was to look directly onto the then un-named throughway, which was now the public road of Don Street. This was in order that the uttermost of land between his house and the cottage would serve as gardens. Mindful too of the proximity of the stream he omitted to include a basement in his plans but left a wide entrance at the side of his house to provide access to the stables and water well, with vegetable and fruit patches behind.

It was a large house, broad in width and three storeys in height.

Nineteen windows faced the front, seven on each of the upper floors and five on the ground with the entrance being slightly to the right of the centre, the entire pattern being repeated at the rear. On each floor four rooms sat aside, and led onto centre corridors, which ran through each level with a grand staircase holding pride of place. The staircase was the first thing one noticed on entering the lower foyer of the house. The main drawing room and library were on the left with Nathaniel's study leading off the latter. On the right the opulent dining room was adjacent to a room Anne had claimed for her own daily use but to where she would guide female guests whenever the men joined Nathaniel for a glass of port and cigar in the library after a pleasant meal. Next to this, but accessed only from the corridor, was a small storeroom. On the opposite side of the corridor a well-equipped kitchen, scullery, larder and cold room faced the courtyard at the rear of the house.

Above all these, on the first floor, the large family parlour flanked by a playroom and nursery overlooked the street whilst across the corridor the main boudoir, a dressing room and washroom looked down on the gardens. Above these again the rooms were all fitted out for sleeping though at that particular time only four were used, with John Nathaniel sleeping in one and the two girls Harriet and Charlotte sharing another. Mrs Kilshaw the housekeeper had the third and the maids, Adèle Fromage and Lizzie Sauvage the fourth, both these rooms being at the very end of the passage and near to a narrow staircase that led back down to the lower corridor.

Over the front door, a magnificent entrance boasting of cut glass panels and shiny brass fittings, Nathaniel inserted a stone shield bearing both his and Anne's initials and the year 1811. He liked his home. He particularly liked the front door, which he copied from the one that had welcomed visitors to his family home in Devon. Even so it was rare for him to pass through that way on a working day. Usually he entered the house by the scullery at the back where in an alcove he would wash himself down at the shallow stone sink and exchange his working boots for house shoes before greeting his wife and children.

However that particular day he burst through the front entrance forgetting, in his haste, to rub his grime-covered boots on the iron scrapers he had installed on either side of the heavy oak door, for the very purpose of cleaning off the worst of the street muck. Indeed, a trail of his muddy footprints would have continued their way up the wide staircase to the upper floor had not the housemaid Adèle, who happened to enter the hall at the same time, brought his traversal to a halt with, "Doctor Lamont is waiting for you in the drawing room Sir."

"Now I shall 'ave to clean the drawing room floor again an' all, and after me doing it so particular this morning," she moaned quietly to Lizzie a few minutes later, keeping her voice low for fear of her complaint being overheard by the housekeeper.

Mrs Kilshaw, whose facial contours never showed any expression other than disapproval, was also free with her hands and complaints were an offence worthy of a clip around the head. "But the master, he didn't look right, not 'appy like what you'd expect him to look after being told that he's got a new little daughter. It's almost as if Thomas forgot to give him my message for the master just strode away without so much as a 'ail or farewell. I didn't even have the chance to take his coat and 'at."

"Westaway, my dear sir!" The doctor hastily moved from his position in front of the fireplace, where he had been warming his rear. "I was hoping you would return before I had to leave to resume my round…"

"How is she?" Nathaniel interrupted.

"She?…Which one?…" The doctor started to tease before, suddenly noticing Nathaniel's worried expression he went on to soothe, "both your wife and daughter are doing very well." He paused again when he saw the worried expression turn to one of puzzlement. "Did you not know you had a most bonny daughter? No? But I expressly asked that someone be sent to your yard to tell you the good news. Really the staff of today!"

"It was nobody's fault but my own," he confided. "But tell me again. Is it another daughter I have? And what of Anne, is all well with her?"

"My, but you look chilled to the bone," the doctor said before answering.

"'Twould be best to divest yourself of that great coat and warm up those bones of yours before you go up to see your wife and greet your new infant. And I suggest you rid yourself of those boots too lest you get a chill that reaches that chest of yours…"

Nathaniel looked down. His boots were wet through and his feet felt like ice. The doctor was right. He could not risk a chill. Crossing to the fireplace he tugged at the bell pull before ripping off his gloves and tucking them inside the top hat he had taken from his head. When Adèle answered the summons he smiled at her as he handed over his outer garments and asked if she would be kind enough to bring him a pair of woollen hose and his house shoes. Only after the door closed behind her did he round on the doctor. "Now, tell me. What of my wife?" he demanded.

"She is well, most well. Resting now, naturally, but she nearly caught us all out with the speed of things," the doctor replied. "I wager you did not expect the child to make such a rapid entrance to the world? But then, how could you when even I was…well…the infant arrived so quickly…. So easily…I…" The doctor was about to add that his presence at the birth had not been necessary and that the midwife could have managed things on her own but thought better of it. Such a statement might suggest that he was not worthy of his fee and that would not do at all.

He was grateful of the interruption when the maid knocked at the door before entering. He watched silently as Nathaniel took off his wet footwear and replaced it with dry before offering, "'Tis a very healthy specimen this time too. Strange how weak the boy infants are in comparison. 'Tis the only reason why you lost the last but you need have no such worries this time. In any case the midwife and I will attend daily until I feel it is no longer necessary. The woman has left now but I thought I would wait and impart the good news myself…." His voice trailed off as he gave a lingering glance in the direction of the large cabinet in the corner of the room.

Nathaniel's mind took a few minutes to catch up with the Doctor's prattle, an unprofessional tendency that at first had deterred him from consulting the man on medical matters. It was Anne who persisted in assuring him that Lamont was the most proficient of doctors. He just had to hope that her trust would prove justified. Looking up he caught the doctor's glance to the corner of the room.

"Would you join me in a cognac before you leave Lamont?" he invited on cue.

As soon as the doctor had left Nathaniel bounded up the stairs and made for the door of the bedroom he shared with his wife, opening it quietly before peering inside.

It was a pleasant room. Large, and elegantly furnished. The two deep-set windows were dressed in peach brocade curtains, flowing drapes that were held back with cream lace which in turn matched the coverlets on the mantle shelf, armoires and bedding chest that were placed about the room. The furniture was made of mahogany, as were the posts of the half-canopied bed, the canopy having been painstakingly embroidered by Anne. Its dark luscious colours of wine and grey sat well beside the pale peach walls and the coverlet of the feather quilt, which was made of the same material as the curtains. On the mantlepiece a pair of porcelain figurines, a shepherd and shepherdess – Nathaniel's gift to Anne during their courtship – flanked the Swiss timepiece which in turn served as a reminder of their honeymoon. On the walls oval-shaped cameos of unknown men and women faced each other. It was a room of Anne's choosing but a room that Nathaniel had come to find very pleasing too.

Anne was resting against several plumped pillows with her eyes closed. Her long hair, usually pinned back neatly in a chignon, tumbled carelessly about her shoulders.

"Oh Anne, my dearest love," he whispered, bending to kiss her flushed cheek. Her skin was smooth as ever and gently he moved his head from side to side enjoying the sensation of her velvety flesh beneath his lips. When she moaned quietly he moved to look in her eyes and saw that they were misted with tears.

6

"I AM SO SORRY I have not given you another son," Anne said sadly.

Nathaniel fell from the bed, bending his knee to the floor beside it so that his face would be on a level with hers.

"My dearest, dearest wife, did you really think I would mind whether you presented me with another son or daughter? I love our children, of that fact I know you have no doubt, but you are the most important person in my life, yes, even above them! You will never know how many times I cursed my weakness for you that caused this...." She put a hand to his mouth silencing him with a smile.

"It was a shared weakness, if that is how you want to describe the love in which we both reciprocate, dear heart, and one that I have missed sorely of late," she said, putting out her arms and drawing him closer.

"Madame Anne Westaway, I am shocked at such wanton talk!" he whispered, planting a kiss on her mouth. It had been so long since he had felt her warm lips beneath his that for a few moments he could not help himself. His beard fluttered seductively as his lips went on to roam her cheek and neck.

"Natty!" she warned, laughing gently, and he moved to sit up on the bed. They grinned at each other, as they had in the long past when their lovemaking had been interrupted by the crying of a child. There would be other times they had told themselves then and, remembering this, Nathaniel was filled with a sudden feeling of joy.

"May I have permission to leave my lady's side to cast an eye over our new little princess?" he asked wittily. "I take it she is in the nursery?"

Anne nodded. "Madame Petit arrived shortly after I had given birth. I know you thought it best that the baby remain in the nursery with her but could I not have it with me at all other times, at least whilst I am confined?"

He had only thought it best for the baby to stay in the nursery with the woman he had employed as a wet nurse because he had been uncertain, as had Doctor Lamont it must be said, as to how Anne would be after the delivery. Now his heart leapt with hope. She had responded to his kisses, called him by his pet name and now she wanted the baby at her side. Surely this meant his beloved was recovering her former self?

There was a knock at the bedroom door and when there was no reply to his call to enter Nathaniel opened it to admit Adèle who was carrying a tray of food. As he stood aside so she could cross the room a delicious aroma wafted his way. The smell came by way of the steam rising from a bowl of cow-heel broth, which was placed alongside a small dish of bright orange isinglass jelly. The appetising sight and smell made him realise that he had not eaten since early morning and he sniffed at the air loudly and appreciatively. He knew his place would be set at the table in the dining room for a much more substantial meal but he felt too elated to eat alone so he told Adèle to bring his meal up on a tray too. He would be visiting the nursery, he added, but she could set it up on a small table beside the bed for his return.

The woman Nathaniel had employed to suckle his new infant was rotund of body with a pleasant face and a mouth that turned upwards at each edge as if the act of smiling came very easily. It was one of the things he had particularly noticed at their primary meeting. The other had been that she seemed to view the circumstances of her life with good humour even though he doubted whether it was so in reality. Her readiness to see the sunny side of things was one of the reasons that he had taken her on against the view of Doctor Lamont who had warned, when his advice was sought, that she was 'of common local stock and may bring more trouble than she was worth'. What trouble that was Nathaniel could only imagine but he was later to base his final judgement on the fact that, and on this point Lamont was forced to agree, she also kept herself clean and wet nurses that kept themselves washed and clean were a rare breed of women.

Germaine Petit put her knitting to one side, rose to her feet and curtsied as Nathaniel entered the nursery. He noticed that she was knitting stockings in the fashion in which, before the factories in England began to produce them in larger and cheaper quantities, most of the islanders had made their living.

"I have come to make the acquaintance of my new little daughter, Madame Petit. Is she asleep?" asked Nathaniel, moving across the room without waiting for a reply. The crib, swathed in frills of sheer white muslin, was rocking slightly on its pivot and when Nathaniel peeped cautiously inside he was surprised to find himself being scrutinised by a pair of the deepest blue eyes.

"Well I never! But you are a knowing one!" he murmured hoarsely, a lump suddenly restricting his throat. He continued to watch closely as perfectly shaped fingers traced the plump little face until they disappeared into an open mouth and were suckled noisily. She was so bonny! He wanted to pick her up but did not trust himself. Instead he just looked and looked, becoming more overwhelmed with love as each moment passed.

Glancing back over his shoulder at last he said, "My wife would like to have the baby with her between feeding after all Madam Petit. I take it that will not inconvenience you too much?" The woman shook her head and he returned her smile through a sudden mist of happy tears.

Later, after he had eaten his meal alongside Anne, he carried the crib across the corridor whilst Madame Petit followed behind with the baby held close to her ample bosom. Setting the crib down at the side of the double bed he left the two women to discuss their necessary arrangements and made his way to the washroom.

On passing the open door to the playroom Nathaniel noticed that a draft from the window was blowing the curtains inward and, shivering in its wake, he threaded his way through the discarded toys to close it. Outside the overcast sky of the morning had opened up to a heaven of palest blue. On the path below a young woman was making her way towards the main street, her wicker basket swaying gently in time with the flowing skirt of her coat. In the long garden that lay directly behind the wall that bordered the opposite side of the street he could see a maid collecting washing from a clothes line to the house and drapery shop he knew to be leased to Louis Batho. Next to that was the fruit garden that backed Luce the Apothecary and beside that again he could see the back doors to the stables of Le Moine the furrier. These buildings fronted the road known locally as 'The New Market Road' though it was now some years since the market was moved from the town square.

The narrow street too had changed since Nathaniel had first built his house. Made public along with the dividing road of Burrard Street three years before, the cobbles and paving had encouraged the building of other houses and businesses in this now popular route to both the Square and market. Thinking of the changes set Nathaniel wool-gathering to such an extent that he quite forgot everything until the sound of a door closing brought him back to the moment. Hurriedly he completed his intended mission and returned to the room a few minutes later. Finding Anne alone he moved back to the bed where he pushed the narrow canopy aside so that he could sit beside her. Together they gazed down onto the face of their new infant daughter now lying contentedly in her mother's arms.

"What are we going to call her dearest?" he asked. They had known what to call the other children from very early days but they had never discussed names for this child.

Anne did not want to admit that she had not dared to think about possible names, to remember the constant fear for the life of the baby growing inside her, the dark days with the even darker thoughts. She had mourned the loss of their baby William, and with that intense grief she had relived the blackness that had overcome her after the death of the beloved daughter by her first husband Edward Mourant. The darling child's ghostly white face, proof of the suffering that no doctor or apothecary's potion was able to ease, would visit her in sleep and stay to haunt her daily hours. When she found herself *enceinte* again she saw those dreams as warnings that she would not produce another healthy child. She knew it had been irrational but she had been powerless to help herself. Now she had been more blessed than she deserved, with such an easy delivery and a chubby, healthy child. It would be hard to fight the devils in her mind but she would try by reminding herself every day of that blessing. Tonight, when she said her prayers, she would ask the Lord God's forgiveness for her foolish ways and thank him for his mercy.

"What about Julia?" she suggested at last.

"Julia? Yes, yes. I think Julia will suit her very well," Nathaniel agreed.

Little Harriet and Charlotte whooped with joy when they returned home from their afternoon walk with the young woman who had been employed as Harriet's governess. Their beloved papa was rarely home of a weekday before they were in their beds, when he would come into their bedroom to hear their prayers and kiss them good night, yet here he was and they had not even had tea! As he listened indulgently they chatted away telling him how they had been taken to visit a farmer and his wife, what they had eaten at their table and how they had helped milk a cow before watching butter being churned. Afterwards he hugged them close, pretending to complain at their cold faces as they snuggled into his neck, laughing with them as he helped the governess peal off their coats and bonnets and rubbing their hands and legs even though muffs and knitted stockings had kept away the cold.

"My little Angels," he said eventually, taking each by a hand and leading them up the stairs. "Come and meet your new baby sister!"

Six year-old Harriet studied the bundle swaddled tightly in a length of flannelette sheeting and now snug under the feather eiderdown in the crib beside her parents' bed. Only part of the baby's forehead and a pair of closed eyes could be seen, the little head being covered in a bonnet of white cotton. To her, there was nothing very exciting about the sight.

"She is not very big," she stated at last.

Four year-old Charlotte was more impressed.

"Pretty baby," she said, leaning over the crib in an effort to kiss the new arrival before being quickly restrained by Nathaniel.

"You must let her sleep Lottie dear. The baby's had rather a long journey....You must remember she has travelled all the way from heaven," he told her.

"Is she going to be another of Papa's little angels then Mama?" Harriet asked, having been brought up to believe that both she and her sister had also been sent from heaven.

"Oh! Most surely!" Anne replied smiling.

"Then that makes one...two...three!" Charlotte cried excitedly. She was immediately hushed but nevertheless determinedly continued to whisper. "Three Papa's angels!"

John Nathaniel was even less enamoured than Harriet and, having ascertained that God had sent them another girl, hardly gave the crib a glance.

"Papa, why did God not let William stay long enough to grow like me?" he asked as he clambered into his narrow cot later that evening. He had just said his prayers, like all good children should, but he wasn't too pleased with God at that moment. In fact he was rather peeved with him for sending Papa another little girl to love. How he wished he had been born a girl, to have his father pet him and call him an angel! Instead he had to bear the burden of being the only boy of the family and sent to school, to be caned when his letters were incorrect or he failed to remember his French verbs or understand Latin. Why could not this baby have been a brother, to grow into a boy who would sleep in his room and share the terrors of the dark?

Nathaniel sensed his small son's unspoken fear and for a minute considered holding him close and reassuring him, as he often did with the girls. But the moment quickly passed as he was reminded of his father's warning that 'Sparing the rod spoilt the boy as does indulgence of childish fancies!' It was hard on the boy but he was a man in the growing and must learn not to be afraid.

"Ours is not to question why but to accept God's will at all times son," he answered abruptly. Then taking the candle he closed the door behind him.

Nathaniel and the children were in the family parlour at three o'clock the following Saturday afternoon when Adèle announced, in a rather contentious tone, that the boy O'Reilly was at the back door declaring that he had been invited to play with Master Westaway. Her young plain face openly showed her disbelief at the idea and she was looking forward to sending the whipper-snapper away with the same vehement flea in his ear that Mrs Kilshaw would have done, had she not been participating in her monthly day of rest. That he should have the audacity to insist she announce his presence and him being the same age as herself. An Irish immigrant, telling her, a Jersey girl of Norman descent, what to do? The very cheek of it! Why, it got her dander up good and proper. Oh! She'd be the messenger to his comeuppance, that she would, and gladly so when the master told her to send him away, as he was sure to do. However to her great astonishment Nathaniel just threw down the copy of the *Les Chroniques* newspaper he had been reading and said, "Oh! I had quite forgotten, bring him up will you?"

And she'd to carry out the master's wishes, hadn't she? The girl reported to Mrs Kilshaw the following morning. She'd had to return to the courtyard where she'd made him wait and lead him up to the drawing room knowing full well that those green eyes of his were sneering at her behind her back. Aw! It went against the grain, really it did, especially after she was told to put another plate and cup on the tea tray to be taken up at four o'clock.

The seemingly established scowl of displeasure on Mrs Kilshaw's face deepened considerably. Adèle, an unschooled girl, had taught herself to study the face of the woman who was free with her hands and tongue should work not come up to her demanding expectations. That Mrs Kilshaw strongly disapproved of what had taken place Adèle was certain, but no one else would have suspected had they heard the woman bark, "What are you stood around a gossiping for? Have you emptied the chamber pots? Washed them in the stream? No? Well, get on with it otherwise I'll warm my hands on your head!"

7

"IT WAS SUCH A PLEASURE to listen to the two boys as they played with John's Noah's Ark," Nathaniel told Anne later. "They got on quite companionably. Furthermore I was impressed at the boy's patient replies to Lottie's constant interruptions to their play with questions as to where he lived, whether he had any sisters or brothers and whether he knew any musical rhymes." He laughed at the memory of the little one's unrestrained curiosity. "The men are apt to stir the boy up into quite a temper with their constant harrying during the working day and I had thought him to be quite a little firebrand, but his composure under the intrusions of our smallest angel was a joy to witness. The example also seems to have a good effect on John who, as you are only too aware, has the habit of becoming easily irritated with his young sisters. I have rarely seen him so genial. I do believe it would be good for John to have such a pal. It would also be good for him to realise that not all boys come from the same fortunate circumstances. Besides I think he misses the fact that he does not have a brother to play with," he added, going on to relate what John had asked the evening his new sister was born.

Had she admitted it, Anne would have confessed to having a deeper affection for her only son than all she felt for the three daughters she had given her husband, but had she done so she could never have explained why it was. For it was not just that he had such a cherubic face with its flawless skin and the inheritance of his father's expressive brown eyes and generous mouth. Charlotte too outshone her older sister in this department for Harriet was quite plain in comparison. It was not even that he could be described as having a loving nature for it broke her heart at times when he held himself stiff in her embrace and would not respond to her kisses.

Yet it had not always been, for John had been a very affectionate little soul before he had begun his education. Loving, good as gold, and trusty as any adult is how she would have described him even from an early age. He was still good and trusty, indeed he exceeded the girls in those virtues for they were inclined to try her patience with their naughtiness at times, but there had been a subtle change in his behaviour of late, as if he was holding himself apart from them all. How long was it since he uttered the words, 'I love you Mama'? She sighed at the thought that perhaps change was inevitable now that her son was growing up. He would, after all was said and done, soon be entering his ninth year.

"In conjunction with a good education he will be prepared for higher schools and universities in England so that he will be well versed to return and take a position in the island," she remembered the Regent of St. Mannelier, Philippe Ahier, stating when both she and Nathaniel attended the primary interview before the boy's acceptance to the college.

'Prepared to take a position in the island!' Anne had presumed, from that remark, that John was being primed for pursuing the likes of a legal vocation. At first she had felt an inner glow at the expectation of what life would hold for the boy. Nathaniel was earning both excellent proceeds and a fine reputation as a builder but, because he ensured that the work was done to his own indomitable satisfaction, his hands were constantly rough and chapped and he was often seen in a begrimed condition. That he had never come to her, or presented himself at table, until he had scrubbed himself down and changed into clean attire was to his credit but it was not a future she saw for her son. No, John would better himself. He would take his place in local society and be a credit to the family name.

However, when the boy began to return from school in such low spirits, refusing to speak of either his lessons or the punishments he received for presenting work that failed to come up to the Regent's expectations, she began to doubt the wisdom of forcing him to continue. She was going to talk to Nathaniel about it but then little William had been taken so suddenly and the intention disappeared from her mind. For from that moment she had been unable to think of anything but the painful crevice that had opened up inside her body where her womb had been. Now, suddenly, with God's gift of this healthy little daughter she must, she would, put matters to right at last.

"Do not you worry your pretty head about John Nathaniel, dearest heart," Nathaniel assured her after she had told him of her concerns. "Our son will be able to follow his own path, we will permit him that choice, but for now we can only provide him with the best means possible to make that preference which I am afraid means enduring a good education." She made to interrupt but he forestalled her protest. "There is not a boy alive who enjoys the harsh rigours of a good educational establishment but 'A strong rod maketh the man' as my father used to quote when I arrived home with wealds across my sit-upon where I had been caned for my laziness or inattention. Establishments today are far less harsh. One can only hope they do not become too lenient when the day comes that education will be compulsory. Oh, whilst we are on the subject of education...." He went on to recount the conversation that had taken place between himself and the boy Colm. "It occurred to me that it might be a Christian act on our part to permit him to attend some of the girls' lessons," he concluded.

Anne had a sudden feeling of unease. She had yet to meet this boy, who might for all she knew act so colourable as to be able to hide his true nature, and here was her dear kind husband suggesting that the boy be invited into their own home for the purpose of educating him! Truly, Nathaniel could be too charitable for his own good. She had never doubted his ability to judge a fellow man's character but this was a boy of penurious background and such boys were known to be wily creatures. He had already been to the house once, and presented himself well by all accounts but it may have been a temporary façade, like the charades played in front of the fire on a winter's evening. No, they must allow time to pass before they commit themselves to taking on such an enterprise besides...

"What would the men think if you suddenly withdrew the boy from a site and brought him here for the purpose of education. The majority of them can neither read nor write and it is to be certain that they would not take too kindly to the boy acquiring more knowledge than they themselves."

"Well considered my dearest," Nathaniel said, taking her hand and slowly kissing each finger. He had missed these discussions, these insights, which had not occurred to him when pondering an idea. It was another of Anne's gifts, this ability of clear thought. How fortunate he was to have found a wife with whom he could converse! So many men of his acquaintance had wives without a single intelligent thought in their heads but then he supposed they had chosen knowing them to be that way, expecting to treat their women as chattels, as the submissive relief to their male needs, whereas he had looked for more.

"Shall we let the subject lie for the moment? See how matters work themselves out?"

Matters began to work their way out when, a month later, Nathaniel was confined to bed with a nasty chill. Snow lay heavily all about and some of the men, seeing the work coming to a standstill, called at the house in the hopes of being allocated other tasks. Christmas was fast approaching and they had mouths to feed and rent to pay and they were desperate to earn their wages.

Anne, being asked to talk to them by a fretting Nathaniel, went into the kitchen where she found Mrs Kilshaw rolling out pastry and Cissy peeling vegetables at a side table.

"Where are the men Mrs Kilshaw?" she asked.

The housekeeper looked surprised. "Why, out there Maam!" the woman replied, inclining her head towards the back door. "I didn't think you'd want them in the 'ouse."

"Well how else am I going to find out what they want? Let them in Cissy for heaven's sake!" Anne ordered impatiently. Really the woman took too much into her own hands!

Anne was not used to dealing with Nathaniel's men and she was apprehensive. Had they spoken either the patois or French, as had the workers on the farm of her first husband's family, she would have had no qualms but these men were Irish, with a way of speaking that was sometimes difficult to understand. However, Nathaniel was worrying about his business and his health would worsen unless she put his mind at rest. She was quite over the birth now, she had assured him, and while she could do little to help with his business affairs she was quite capable of acting as messenger.

A blast of cold followed the three shivering men into the room. None were wearing outer coats she noticed, and their thin jackets were worn and frayed.

"We'm sorry to bother ye maam," one of them said immediately, as he and the others removed their caps. "I'm Donal O'Reilly and this is Sam Murphy and Jack O'Donnell. We've gone about as far as we can go on the big house and was needin' to know if the master had any orders for us and the other men."

That was simple enough to understand! Anne smiled with relief as she asked a few more questions before saying that she would have a word with Nathaniel.

"Whilst I am doing so," she said, "Mrs Kilshaw will pour you each a warming dish of her excellent broth."

For a moment Anne wondered if she had spoken out of turn when she saw the look of astonishment that crossed the housekeeper's forbidding face as she left the room. Throughout the last few years she had gradually left more and more of the responsibility in running the house to the woman, whose overbearing ways she had been too heart-weary to oppose. 'But no more!' she told herself as she climbed the stairs. It was time to reclaim her position.

To her amazement she heard singing as she made her way back down the stairs. On opening the kitchen door she was surprised further still. For there, perched on the knee of the heavily bearded soloist who had been introduced as Sam Murphy were her two eldest children John and Harriet, and being bounced up and down astride the broad shoulders of Donal O'Reilly was little Charlotte.

"Adèle, who had gone back to the kitchen after attending all the fires, was merrily dancing with Cissy in time to the music. I expected to hear Mrs Kilshaw's voice raised angrily above it all any minute but she was… You would not believe it dearest but Mrs Kilshaw was actually smiling! It was a sight I never thought I would live to see!" Anne reported to Nathaniel as she brushed her long mane of hair before her hand mirror later that night. "What charming and happy dispositions the Irish have. There those men were, with hardly any good clothes on their back and living in circumstances that can only be imagined, enjoying the moment in a way that is quite enviable."

"Well, may God bless you my dearest, for being gracious enough to invite them inside and to share some of Mrs Kilshaw's tasty soup. They would have been grateful for the warming of that I have no doubt. To a man they have a hard life and though it has to be admitted their wages are often squandered in the alehouses or gambling dens they serve me well and for that I would like to see them remain in work. The knowledge that the commissions are coming to an end has been worrying me for some time and as soon as I have recovered I must look for some more land to build on." He changed the subject abruptly. "How has John been today?"

John had been the first to succumb to the chill, two weeks past, and though he was no longer to be heard hacking about the house he was listless and lacking in spirit. Anne turned from the mirror and looked towards her husband as she replied with a concerned tone.

"I am fearful for him Natty. I see that he is kept warm, that his chest is covered in goose fat, and watch over him while he ingests a regular dosage of snail linctus, yet he does not seem to be recovering. He just lies about in front of the fire all day. He has no conversation, nor yet any interest in his reading books or playing with his toys."

"I think you are fussing too much my dear, you said yourself that he was lively enough when the men were here," he said, helping himself to a teaspoon of the thick medicine from the nearby gallipot and swallowing it slowly.

Anne replaced her brush and its matching mirror onto the surface of the mahogany cabinet before crossing the short distance to the bed and, taking her lace-edged night bonnet from where it hung on the brass bedpost, pulled it onto her head. Then dropping to her knees she said her prayers aloud, with Nathaniel joining in, before finally circling the room to lower the wicks of the four oil lamps and swill the dishes of heated camphor. "Perhaps it is that he is just in need of company other than that of his mother and sisters," she said sadly. After clambering between the flannelette sheets she snuffed out the candle on the bedside chest.

Nathaniel sought her hand and squeezed it gently. He did not kiss or caress her. To do so would surely have excited him, the passion bringing on a furious coughing that would assuredly cause her to become infected too. As it was he had taken to sleeping with his back to her, grateful that she had insisted on his remaining in their bed and not remove himself to his dressing room as he had done during the late months of her pregnancy.

"Perhaps the company of the boy Colm would cheer him," he suggested. "Why not tell the men to send him to the house? There is little work for even them to do on the site at the moment and he must be getting under their feet. However I think it would be advisable to suggest that there is some task that needs doing here, rather than they think he is merely to act as playmate to John. In point of fact, if the weather is dry, see that John is wrapped up well before setting both boys to clearing the snow from the paths. They can also clean up the stables and see that the horses are fed. The boyish company will lift his spirits and the crisp air will help to clear his lungs and thereby bring a glow to his cheeks!"

He turned away from her as he began to hack and though she made no comment Anne became deeply troubled at the length and intensity of the coughing bout.

"I know I shall feel a lot better for a breath or two of outside air. I do so detest the infernal smell of camphor," he added hoarsely before dropping off into a fitful sleep.

8

COLM CAME TO the house the next day, and the next, and the day after that which was Christmas Eve. Between them, and with amazing good humour, the two boys cleared the snow from the front and back paths and mashed the ice in the water butts each day. They also cleaned out the stables to such a condition as had never been seen before.

"They have done well!" Nathaniel said when Anne told him. "I think they deserve to be liberated for an hour or two this afternoon, do you not?"

The boys were very excited. Whilst cleaning the stables they had come across an old sled and talked of how they would like to try it out. They planned to take it up to the top of the tall mounds near Gallows Hill where there were some long sloping runs to slide down. The girls overheard them making plans.

"Can I come too. Oh! Can I?" Charlotte begged, pulling at the sleeve of Colm's jacket and looking up at him beseechingly. She had decided she liked Colm. He never shushed her when she tried to tell him things like John did, or remind her that she had only just become five and so was still only a baby.

"I want to come!" Harriet demanded imperiously.

"Papa will not let you. It is far too dangerous," John told them both, thinking he was safe in that assumption. Not for one minute did he want his sisters to accompany him, spoiling his fun.

However, once he heard of the boys' plan, Nathaniel, having spent the last two days laying about on the chaise longue in front of the fire in the parlour, had other ideas.

"What a splendid idea!" he said lowering his feet hastily to the ground. "Some bracing air is just what I need and what we would all benefit from. Also the exercise would prepare our appetites for the special feast Mrs Kilshaw is busy preparing at this very moment. So what do you think Anne, will you join us?

Anne looked up from her frame of tapestry.

"Oh! Dearest! Do you think it is wise for either of us to go out of the house so soon? Think of your chest…"

"My chest will be all the better for taking in some of God's clear air my dear and the sooner I can breathe easier, the sooner I shall be back at work. And while it may also be a little soon after the baby's birth for you to consider an outing, neither of us will go far wrong if we prop each other up like two old fogies. Madame Petit is feeding the baby at the moment is she not? Yes? Well, there is no earthly reason why we should not sally forth. Do say you will come and watch the children tobogganing...besides..." He raised his eyebrows at her and she, suddenly understanding, put her needlework to one side saying, "Very well then, but we shall not venture as far as Gallows Hill. There are many more hillocks hereabouts that the boys can slide down."

The boys were perched on top of the oblong chest that stood in the hall, swinging their heels impatiently against its wooden side when Nathaniel, Anne and the girls, dressed for the outside, eventually came down the stairs. The old sled lay at the boys' feet with John monopolising the rope.

"Ah I see you have cleaned it up in readiness," Nathaniel said bending his knees to inspect it, turning it over and tugging at the runners and making sure they had neither warped nor rotted in the intervening years. "My, what fun I had on this toboggan... Do you know I had quite forgotten its existence? How fortunate that you came upon it." He straightened himself up. "Still, 'tis best that you let Colm handle it though John."

"Aw! But Papa! I wanted to..."

"Very well, if you would prefer Colm to ride on the new one that is taking up space in the alcove under the stairs!"

"But...?"

"Butt...butt...Butting, is the habit of nanny goats. Is that not right Colm?"

Colm grinned and nodded. John still looked nonplussed.

"Go and look John," Anne whispered.

His loud hoot of delight sent them all rushing to his side.

"Seeing as you had set your mind on going out on the snow we thought you might like to use your Christmas gift. Happy Christmas John!" Anne said. And with a chorus of "Happy Christmas!" they all admired the brightly coloured sleigh.

With each boy pulling a sled, the girls trying vainly to keep pace and Nathaniel's arm linked securely in Anne's, the small party set off through the narrow thoroughfares and lanes of town. The sky was bright and the air warmer than it had been the past week. Nathaniel, seeing the snow on the ground was beginning to thaw, wondered if the children were to be disappointed in their search for a suitably covered mound because the snow had already turned to a muddy slush beneath their feet. But if the children had noticed they did not say as they rushed excitedly ahead, laughing and chattering, John's delight in his new sleigh overcoming his earlier opposition to sharing the afternoon's fun with his sisters.

"Oh! Dear! I do wish I had not insisted on the girls wearing their better coats. I am afraid I thought only of their warmth and did not think of the dirt they would kick up," Anne said. "Just look at the state of their stockings! I am afraid your little Angels are beginning to look more like dirty rascals!"

Nathaniel moved closer, hugging her arm deeper into his side.

"Ah! But have you noticed something Mama Westaway?" he asked, his breath warming her cheek. "Our little family of rascals, dirty or otherwise, has grown albeit temporarily. Why, watching the four children together now we could be forgiven for imagining that we had a second son, could we not?"

Anne was startled. She had not viewed the scene before her in the same light at all. Would a passer-by assume they were all of one family? Surely not! Surely it would be obvious to anyone that the boy, in his thin, worn coat and patched breeches, with that mop of red curls sprouting out from under that knitted Protector, could not be their child? No no, anyone of consequence would think they were being charitable, which of course they were. But what had caused Nathaniel to have such a fancy? Was he sorry that the baby had been another girl after all, despite his earlier assurances?

"God could still provide us with another son. I may not be too old," she said quietly.

"What...What?" he asked, stopping in his tracks to look into her face, "Oh! Anne my dear! I did not mean.... Why, you must know that I am very happy with our little family and that I love our children second only after you." He began walking on again, his eyes once more on the small group ahead. "It just seemed to me...watching the children with young Colm.... How well they all get on together.... You only have to watch the way his teasing of Harriet, our serious, no nonsense Harriet, is taken without offence...and Aw! Look now how he takes those cuffs from John! Mind you, John should be wary. The boy has got quite a temper on him and would be apt to strike out if John goes too far but then, methinks it would do John no harm to meet his match. 'Tis the very reason I think the boys would be a good influence on one another, become pals. They both have certain rough edges which their friendship could well smooth out."

The feeling of unease returned to worry at Anne's mind as she considered what Nathaniel had just said. What was he about? First he suggested the boy join Harriet and Charlotte in their lessons and now he was talking as if the boy could be a possible pal for John. Oh dear, no! That would not do at all. There were other, far more respectable, indeed influential, local families with sons that John should be encouraged to befriend. No, no. It was one thing for Nathaniel to have his workers call at the house and spend time in the kitchen, even for him to reward the boy with an outing after toiling so well but she must discourage him from envisaging more.

"But they come from such different backgrounds Nathaniel," she protested. "Colm is a working boy of no education while John is still at school and will be for some years yet if he is to succeed in life. John wants for nothing while in truth the O'Reillys are like most of their kind, poorer than the mice that inhabit the churches. Why 'tis a wonder they have not as yet had to go begging to the Constable!"

"And is that not something for which their widowed mother can hold her head high? Fifteen children she was left to care for when her husband was lost overboard during their journey to the island. Fifteen mouths to feed yet never one request for alms!" countered Nathaniel.

"She probably knew that to do so would have placed them all in the workhouse until they were deported back to Ireland! And did they not inherit the luck of the Irish when they found that fisherman's hut when elsewhere there are forty or fifty people known to be living together in a single house?" commented Anne.

"Whee-ee! Papa! Mama! Look at us!"

They had stopped at the foot of a tall, snow-covered mound and watched the children climb to the top as they talked. Now the two sleighs were racing down towards them, Charlotte feeling so secure within Colm's arms that she could wave and shout. Harriet in front of John, though looking a little more wary than her younger sister, was nevertheless bright-eyed with excitement. Nathaniel extracted his arm from Anne's, clapped and cheered and then replaced it, hugging her close again when he did so.

As the children began to climb again he said, "It might be thought that fortune was with that ill-fated family when they came upon that deserted shack amongst the sand hills that they call their home but I would not call it a happy-chance. Not with it being so open to the unpredictability of weather and tides. It must also be a long trek to the nearest water pump yet they keep themselves so clean that well…. All I can say is that it was no surprise to learn the older girls were taken into service as quickly as they were! Five older sisters and two older brothers Colm has and seven more beneath him. Donal, one of his older brothers, you may recall he was one of the men who came to the house, works with me as a mason and the other works as an assistant keeper at Donnelly's Inn at the eastern end of town. With the exception of one girl who is bedridden the four older girls work in what they proudly call 'the big houses'. Donal once told me that every one of them has been brought up to work industriously and to obey God's Law…"

Anne made to interrupt but he stalled her saying, "Yes, yes. They are Catholics and not of our faith but on the other hand they are also far from heathens. Their adherence to their faith would put a few of our sanctimonious knee-bending congregation to shame!"

A horrified look came over Anne's face. "Nathaniel Westaway! How can you say that? Next you will be informing me that you would see no harm in John attending one of their masses!"

Turning her around so that she faced him Nathaniel stared at his wife for a moment before beginning to laugh. Anne's look turned to one of indignation which in turn, when his laughing brought on a fit of coughing, changed again to one of concern.

"Oh! Take care, Natty! Take care!" she beseeched, but when the coughing stopped she cautioned quietly. "There is nothing droll about a son of ours, any one of our children for that matter, attending a Catholic mass!"

"No, my dear Madame Westaway *née* Alexandre, no indeed!" he assured her whilst trying to keep a serious face but failing due to the happy way he was feeling. He had not been mistaken. The discussion they were having definitely became livelier! His wife was indeed back to her former self.

9

ALTHOUGH THE DRIVE through the untamed countryside to the parish of St. Saviour and St. Mannelier School in winter was always made in the dark, John was more fortunate than many of the other pupils. For, besides being a weekly boarder and only having to make the journey once, at the start of each week, he was also taken there in either the cart or trap driven by his father. And, though his father was not particularly forthcoming of an early morning John would not have wished to be one of the day pupils. For he knew that they, being sons of local farmers, had to make fearsome treks across pitch-black fields every morning, often alone and with only a small lantern to help light the way. Their fears of the darkness, the sounds of wild animals, the taunting movement of bushes and trees, were terrors he also shared but, in this instance at least, he did not have to face them alone.

Nevertheless the dread of the thrashing, which awaited boys who were late, dogged them all equally. John had been late twice, once when the time on the hall clock had been misread, and another when the horse cast a shoe. His father, anxious as always to attend to his work, had not thought to stop and explain to the Regent on either occasion, so John too knew what it was to begin the school day wincing in agony from the punishment.

Still, that first Monday of the new year and the day he was being returned to school after several weeks' absence, he consoled himself that they had not only left the house a little earlier but were travelling at a swift pace. Furthermore, his father was to talk with the Regent so he only had to keep his wits and do his work correctly and he would get through the day without punishment.

Nathaniel had not questioned John as to why he feigned illness rather than return to school and, though he had pooh-poohed Anne's suggestion of the boy's unhappiness, he had been prompted to think more about the boy and his future. So during the previous weeks, after talking with Anne and much further contemplation on his part, Nathaniel had made up his mind to take the boy away from the school. Nevertheless he was not looking forward to the interview that lay ahead.

Nathaniel would never have admitted to anyone as to how he always experienced a bout of nervous apprehension at the thought of talking to Regents or Masters of educational establishments but it was a fact. Though he was now a man and considered himself strong in every other manner, their very stance, the combined smell of chalk and manly odour, the sight of the high desk and the ever-ready cane lying in wait, reduced him to the no account, quivering boy he once was.

It was cold. The sun had not yet risen fully and the prevailing night air had a bitter feel to it. Nathaniel felt his son shiver but made no comment. He did not mind the cold. In fact he embraced it knowing that it sharpened his brain. And that morning he needed to be sharp. The Regent of St. Mannelier was a man to whom slights came easily and Nathaniel did not want to antagonise the man by his words.

'At the end of the term the boy will be leaving for a school in England,' he began rehearsing in his mind. 'And as his father I am abiding by my duty to give notice in person.'

The Regent would be sure to remark that he hoped the decision was not taken due to any dissatisfaction, he told himself, in which case he would just state that he thought it was time the boy had a thorough knowledge of the English language. This was a true concern for the Regent refused to teach any other than the French and Latin languages and though this might be enough for local boys who attended the school Nathaniel had worried that John might be at a disadvantage in the future. A large group of settlers were lobbying for English to be used more widely in the island, even for the British Sterling to become common currency. And while both he and Anne worried that the very character of Jersey might change, should this latest agitation come about they wanted John, indeed all their children, to be fully prepared. Because of their parents' different nationalities they had all been weaned to understand both English and French and were able to converse in either but it was the reading and writing of the two languages in which Nathaniel was most anxious they be proficient. For it was his unspoken intention that one day they would all be land and property owners and as such would need to be ever on their guard for dealing with notaries working on the necessary legal work. However, the lack of English lessons was not the main reason for taking John away from the school.

'Yet I should not have to make further explanations,' he reminded himself as he reined the horse back a little. 'I do not have to go so far as to challenge the man about the allegations of his petty foibles or peccadilloes. The rumours that have recently reached my ears may not have been true, for surely if they had, the clergy, under which cloak the school is run, would have stepped in? No, it is enough that I am no longer content to leave my son under the educational guide of that establishment.'

So deep in thought was he that without realising it Nathaniel had spurred the horse on until once more they were going at a lick of a pace. But this time they were travelling so fast that the lanterns swung crazily against each side of the trap and John was forced to cling to the narrow plank of a seat. Suddenly the cart jolted perilously over an unexpected rise in the path, bouncing the boy into the air and compelling Nathaniel to reach out and yank him back into the safe circle of his strong right arm as he reined the horse to a slower pace.

"Oh! Papa!" John cried suddenly. "Do you recall the time you took me for a drive, sitting on your lap? You taught me how to hold the reins and Mama was…Mama was sitting in the carriage behind with Hattie in her arms!"

"Upon my word John Nathaniel! You have certainly been hiding your light under a bushel to remember something that occurred when you were only two years of age and still in gowns!" Nathaniel said, shaking his head in amazement. "'Tis a good clear memory you have in that brain of yours after all. Here…," without slackening the reins he nudged at the boy with the inside of his elbow until the little body was wedged securely between his knees, "let us see how much of that early lesson you remember."

For the first time since he had begun school at St. Mannelier John arrived with eyes that were alight with anticipation. Forgotten was his fear of the cane, of his inability to be able to recall all that he had been taught during the difficult and tedious lessons. According to his papa he had steered the horse through the narrow country lanes with 'the dexterity of an adult' and he meant to relay this snippet of praise to the other boys at the earliest opportunity. Furthermore, having once captured their attention with his version of the event he would continue to do so by describing his future journeys in great imaginative detail whether he had held the reins or not. It was a pity that he was leaving.

Perhaps the school might not be so bad after all.

The late spring of 1821 saw John enrolled as a day pupil at an academy for young gentlemen in Exeter. Nathaniel, having travelled across some weeks previous to make the initial arrangements, accompanied him. The sea was so rough that the captain warned them to keep to their airless cabin below deck throughout the channel crossing. Yet neither father nor son succumbed to *mal de mer*, as did most of the other passengers for on Anne's advice they nibbled at small bits of ginger, a root that burned the mouth and throat but settled the weakest of stomachs.

"Nevertheless I do believe John has inherited my sea-legs," Nathaniel told Anne on his return. "He was bright and breezy within only minutes of being ashore and, with the colour back in his cheeks, was soon hanging out of the carriage window excitedly pointing to each and everything he saw as we made our way out through the port and along the roads to Exeter."

"Was he so cheerful then Natty?" Anne asked surprised, having been plagued with imaginings of the child's utter dejection. The thought of John being so far away tore at her heart, as it had done from the time the decision to send him to England had been taken. Yet, paradoxically, she had been the one to encourage the plan in the first place, quietly reasoning with Nathaniel that it was for the best. Now she must convince herself once again that there was no other choice. Her aspirations for John were high and to that end she must hold fast to the thought that the boy needed a better education than that offered in local establishments.

"That he was!" Nathaniel began to reply cheerily before hearing her give a deep sigh. "Oh! But then I exaggerate a little for he quietened considerably as it came for the time for me to leave, which in itself is a natural thing for he has been left in a strange place, without a single person that he knows. 'I shall miss you and Mama sorely,' he said as we parted. 'Please tell Mama that I love her and will work hard at my lessons so that you might both be proud of me.' "

"Ah! The dear child!" Anne said brokenly.

Nathaniel reached out and, taking her in his arms, held her to his chest so that she could not see his eyes suddenly blur with tears as the true memory of John's piteous appearance on being left in the care of the school's Regent returned to haunt him. For, remaining silent throughout their last moments of parting, the boy had displayed a look so wretched that Nathaniel had to restrain a sudden urge to hug him close. Instead he had forced himself to shake the hand of the Regent yet again, pat the boy on the shoulder with the words 'work diligently son' and walk quickly away to the waiting carriage. And since those painful moments he had been filled with regret, berating himself for not having spoken to the boy earlier, nor coming to some easy understanding during their long journey from the island. That was when he should have assured John that he would soon settle down, that the weeks would quickly pass to Whitsuntide when, by special arrangement, he would be permitted to join them all for three days holiday. Instead their last hours together had been wasted in small talk and diversions such as identifying landmarks and now he would have to live with the regret and disturbance to his peace of mind. And it was with certainty that Nathaniel knew the memory of his small son's disconsolate face at their parting would continue to fill his mind with unease for some while, as would his lies to Anne. For he also knew that though he had lied to help ease her pain it would be no defence in the eyes of God. Rubbing his lips against the crisp starched cotton of the white bonnet on her head he vowed to silently plead for the Almighty's mercy, when he knelt to say his prayers that night.

John was away from the island for seven years during which time his parents and sisters saw very little of him. They could only be sure of his company for three of the six days' annual holiday, those that fell at Whitsuntide, when Nathaniel collected him from the school and took him to Winkleigh in Devon where the family had begun to make an annual visit to relations.

His short Christmas visits, though eagerly anticipated, were always fraught with trepidation after two disappointing times when first a heavy snowstorm confined masters and boys to the school and secondly when there were gales of such terrible ferocity blowing up the English Channel that ships had not sailed. And even when it was possible for John to reach the island in subsequent years the long and often perilous journey meant that he was too weary to enjoy the two evenings and one day of amusement thoughtfully and joyfully prepared for him.

Though, at first, John suffered terribly from homesickness he soon learnt to both suppress his nightly tears and put on a brave show in the daytime. To do otherwise was to invite an even worse humiliation meted out by the older boys who delighted in discovering such weaknesses. As the months went by he gradually began to settle down and this was mostly due to his knowledge of French, which made him a favourite of the Regent who called upon him to teach the other pupils. This in itself might have led to his unpopularity amongst the boys had it not been for his new found gift of mimicry, a fortunate talent that, acted out of sight of the tutors, earned him many admirers and friends.

Unfortunately, as life at the school enveloped him more and more so John became progressively estranged from his family. Between times of the occasional letter and the even less frequent reunions he taught himself to dismiss thoughts of them from his mind as soon as they appeared, for to let them linger only encouraged the painful feelings of homesickness to return.

On the other hand his parents and sisters began to revere him, overlooking his terse letters in the excitement of their arrival and acceding to his every wish during his scant visits. 'Dear John Nathaniel is working hard at his studies in England but when his education is complete he will return to work and live in the island, a time we eagerly anticipate', they were heard to tell people.

It came as a great disappointment to them all therefore when, during the Christmas visit before his final term at the school, he announced that he would like to remain in England.

"But what will you do for a living John?" his mother asked aghast. She had long since accepted the fact that he would not excel educationally and therefore would never obtain a position of note and instead had come to imagine him learning his father's business so that he might eventually work alongside him. She was sure now that was Nathaniel's wish too.

"I have not as yet decided but I hoped Papa would grant me an allowance until I do."

"What? That I will not!" Nathaniel vehemently declared, mortified at both his son's wish to remain away from the island and blatant expectation to be kept further at his parent's expense. "You have had seven years of excellent and expensive schooling in which to prepare yourself for a worthy position. However, since you have shown neither an inclination to study or discover a pursuit of your own choosing, I expect you to return to the island and join me in the trade. You will learn everything you need to know so that one day the words, 'and son' will be alongside mine on the yard's sign."

"Do you mean work alongside the likes of Colm O'Reilly, as a ten-a-penny labourer?" There was a hint of a sneer in John's tone as his eyes met those of his father's.

"Not alongside Colm for he has proved himself beyond all expectations in the years that you have been away. No, you will learn from him, because apart from myself I feel you would have no better teacher."

"But Papa, you cannot be serious! Why he's... He is nothing but an illiterate navvy!"

"You have become ignorant on both counts for Colm is now a self-educated craftsman whom I am proud to have working for me," his father replied sharply.

"'Tis true John!" Anne cried, hoping to calm the situation. "You will find you have so much more in common now than when you were boys together."

"The likes of Colm O'Riley, glorified navvy or educated craftsman, could never have as much in common with myself as the young sons of gentlemen with whom I have come to make friends," John muttered.

"Did I hear right?" Nathaniel demanded.

"I do not know what you heard but Papa, look at me. Do I look as if I would be suited for work on a building site?"

Nathaniel looked at his only son and took in the lean, handsome face, the slim breadth of body beneath the smart clothes before noticing, as if for the first time, the tapered smooth hands that were now refolding a Christmas gift of a silk cravat. Did I ever look as young and as perfect as that, he asked himself, suddenly clasping his swollen and calloused hands behind his back.

"I will give you this John, should you find a suitable position, one worthy of the education you have received, then I will give my blessing to your staying in England. However, my financial responsibility for you will cease one year's quarter from the end of your school term."

"I understand Papa, thank you," John said.

John might not have been the most industrious of pupils but he certainly had become one of the well favoured of the academy. However, this popularity with both pupils and teachers had given him a false sense of security with which he felt that the fellowship would continue beyond the school's perimeter. Firmly believing that he would find a suitable position either within one of the family concerns of his friends or on a letter of recommendation from the Regent, he returned to school and confidently set about making enquiries. Unfortunately John found that his lack of attention to his education made him quite unsuitable for the few positions he aspired to. And he was not prepared to settle for anything less for to do so, to his mind, would reduce him to the same level as working on one of his father's building sites.

Yet, as matters worked out, that was precisely what he finally had to accept. After three months of being unable to find any other occupation in England he was forced to return to the island and obey his father's ultimatum to join the family trade. It was a humbling experience and one that was made all the worse by his growing resentment towards Colm O'Reilly.

It came as a disagreeable shock to find that the esteem with which his parents spoke of the once waif-like ragamuffin was augmented by fact. Colm had indeed educated himself to a good standard and become so well versed in all needing to be done on a building site that he was respected by many both inside and outside the trade. But John also resented that, finding it increasingly difficult to be genial himself, Colm's character was always so jovial the family seemed to revel in his company, inviting him to join them all on family outings and picnics. It seemed he could never get away from the fellow, which caused John to brood all the more on the possibility that Colm was usurping his place in his father's affections.

He begrudged the fact that his father adored his sisters, dressing them well and seeing that their every need was catered for, whereas now he was expected to earn every penny he needed to both clothe and amuse himself. He was also incensed that he was kept short of money while the list of his father's property grew longer by the year.

But, whilst harbouring these feelings of pique, John said not a word to his parents, indeed he became so uncommunicative at times that Anne declared it was unnatural, that with everyone else in the family being free to voice opinions he should too. She began to draw him into arguments by bringing up subjects she sensed he might have ideas on and was gradually rewarded by his well thought out replies even though the agitated, sometimes angry discussions that sometimes ensued, especially between him and Harriet, disturbed her.

Still, as the years passed Anne was gratified to see him grow from a well-built, slightly podgy youth into a lean, handsome man. With his hair brushed back the centre point, known as the 'widow's peak', was well defined as were his full lips and dimpled but firm chin. However it was his eyes which drew immediate attention to the clear-skinned, side-whiskered face for they were a rich brown in colour and their depth unfathomable.

Nathaniel however, in slowly relinquishing the hope of adding the words, 'and Son' to the sign that now advertised his business from the gate at the entrance to his yard, had to reluctantly admit that John did not take well to manual work, or indeed to taking orders. So, after gradually realising that he would be more suited to the giving out of the latter, Nathaniel set him up as a coal merchant.

Though it was not what he might have chosen for himself, John worked hard in building up the business. His intention was to succeed to such an extent that he could not fail in winning his father's praise. Indeed he succeeded so well trading in coal that he branched out, leasing a larger store and taking on extra staff to supply general goods as well. But, though Nathaniel would offer him advice from time to time, he never added the words of either praise or encouragement that John longed for.

10

*Several years later
in the autumn of 1832*

"AND I SAY THAT you will scratch that name from the guest list Mama!"

Anne watched the sheet of vellum leave her son's hand and flutter down onto the open top of the escritoire before turning to face him in surprise. The look on his handsome face was taking on a truculent appearance as the well-shaped lips drew to a fine line, the beguiling brown eyes darkened to the colour of ebony.

"But he was your boyhood pal John…"

"An early friendship that was foisted on me, with little choice of my own. 'Twas you and Papa who persisted in placing us together. We had nothing in common then nor have we now but then 'tis to be expected, our backgrounds being so utterly different."

"Oh John! Differences in your backgrounds there might have been but I thought even you would have acknowledged how well he has overcome his poor beginnings, how hard he has worked to better himself. Why, I can hardly believe that you should think this way after all the hours you two spent together, after all that your dear Papa and I have tried to instil in you? By making your father's workers welcome we hoped…"

"By making the labourers welcome," he interrupted again, this time the imperious tone on his voice becoming more emphatic, "you not only gave them ideas above their station but made a rod for your own backs at the same time."

"Now what do you mean by that remark?" she countered sharply.

"Do not tell me you remain in ignorance Mama?"

A malicious gleam lit up the almost hypnotic eyes, accentuating a smile that was beginning to play at the corners of the boyish lips. It was not a pleasant look. It was not the agreeable face she had noticed him don as soon as he walked into a crowded room, with the beaming greeting that caused people to declare, 'That young Mister Westaway, so charming…. Much like his father but more so, do you not think?' Neither was it the seductive twinkle that held the reputation of sending every young maiden blushing behind her quivering fan. It was the smile she had come to recognise as pre-empting one of his cruel goads.

He was challenging her to what she likened to be a verbal duel. It was a game they had begun on his return to the island after his schooling. A game she had once unwittingly encouraged in the mistaken view that the innocent bantering would teach him the art of debate but, whereas she had long since tired of the sport, he had not. Instead he had perpetuated the play, proceeding, as in these moments during which they were alone together, to demonstrate a ruthless desire to break her spirit. She knew she should refuse to take part, deny him the confrontation that would inevitably lead to distress, but pride would not let her.

"Remain in ignorance of what?" she demanded.

The malicious gleam faded as he studied her face.

"Well?"

"Well you may ask Mama dear…"

"I am asking. Explain that remark!" Anne demanded.

He sighed, an exaggerated sigh.

"I mean to say Mama that, unwise as it undoubtedly was to invite local gossip by welcoming that uncouth upstart into our home, any delusion in imagining that he will convert to our religion on marriage is even more harebrained."

He let the remark sink in before adding, " 'Tis a pity that you did not consider the possible consequences earlier, or think on the quotations of the Bible which states in Galations, chapter 6, verse 7, 'Whatsoever a man soweth, that shall he also reap.'"

The partly quoted verse from the Bible, the large, heavy tome that always lay open on the handcrafted wooden lectern in the family parlour from which her beloved Nathaniel read out a passage every day, was said in such a sacrilegious tone that she felt deeply offended. The remark had been aimed to sting and it had reached its mark.

Though inwardly outraged she held his eyes until her sight became misted with tears. She knew it was the response he was looking for, the reaction he had learnt to create over latter years and she cursed the weakness that invariably brought her to this. She watched helplessly as with a triumphant lift of his shoulders he spun round on his heel and strode quickly from the room.

Anne heard rather than saw the door close behind her son as she sank back into the chair that stood alongside the desk and placed her elbows on the open top. She covered her face with her hands. She wanted to submit to a bout of copious weeping but steeled against such an action, knowing that within the hour ladies from the chapel would be arriving to discuss their latest plans for the distribution of food and clothes to the poor. The family regularly attended the Wesleyan Chapel where Nathaniel's generous donations were often commended and where his wife Anne had a certain position to hold.

'I must regain my composure,' she told herself. 'It would not do to set them prattling.' Even so the tears trickled unbidden down her cheeks, dripping into her cupped palms.

When or at what stage John had turned the once harmless game into a cruel sport Anne could never remember but the utterances had become so vitriolic that, for a matter of an hour or so afterwards, her peace of mind would be quite disturbed. Then later, while she was still simmering from the onslaught, he would behave so pleasantly, agreeably approving the colour of her dress, making her laugh at some humorous detail or hugging her impulsively that she would soon dismiss the memory of his earlier baiting from her mind. She was always quick to forgive him in any case, loving him as she did with a passion she did not ever feel for the girls, so the incidents were never reported to Nathaniel. Besides, none of the upsetting scenes were ever witnessed by any other member of the family so the affectionate acts that followed would have contradicted any complaint she might have made. It had been some time since he had caused the last upset, an incident that she had later quite forgiven in the intervening pleasure of witnessing his happiness with Anne Guillet and the acceptance of her proffered help in furnishing the house in Bond Street to which he had moved. For a few months all had been pleasant between them but now he had opened up the old wounds and disturbed her happiness once again.

The tiny rivulets of tears were entering the sleeves of her gown and she moved to retrieve a lace-edged handkerchief from the little drawstring bag that hung from her waist. As she did so her gaze fell on the sheet of vellum, the catalyst of this recent agitation, lying face up on the open top of the desk. It was a list of guests that the matronly gardienne of Anne Guillet had kindly requested; names and addresses of family members, friends and acquaintances that she and Nathaniel might like to be included in the celebrations for John's forthcoming betrothal to the orphaned girl. They had spent a pleasant hour or so the previous evening discussing who should be invited and that morning she had retired to her room on the ground floor to write the list in a clear hand.

Before starting on the writing of the embossed invitation cards she had invited John to read through the list, thinking that he might be pleased that she had sought his approval to the selection of guests, a role officially undertaken by parents. Instead, to her chagrin, he had studied the sheet of paper carefully, as if it were a legal document set out by some unscrupulous lawyer and not the harmless register it was. He had read it slowly, deliberately now she concluded, for he must have been looking for a name he could object to and he had found it at the very bottom of the list.

Though the addition of Colm O'Reilly's name might have been an afterthought, forgotten altogether had it not been for Nathaniel's prompting, it had been a favourable one nevertheless. For since the day that Nathaniel had taken the boy out of the line of people seeking work in his brickfield and set him to labouring on the building sites, Colm had proved to be an extraordinary young man. By observing, learning and toiling at all the aspects of construction over the years he had become an artisan whose diligence and natural gifts had earned him respect throughout the island. He had worked his way from the lowly position of site boy to eventually becoming what Nathaniel claimed to be his 'right hand man' yet he had learnt the various crafts without a single apprenticeship, the tenets of which his early penurious circumstances could never have underwritten. And, as if these achievements were not sufficient to satisfy the unspoken hunger that seemed to drive him, Colm had also attended to his own education at the same time.

A brief smile creased the corners of Anne's eyes as she thought back to those early days when the boy, thin and waif-like in his ill-fitting clothes, had eagerly taken his place beside the girls to be taught his letters and numbers. He learnt quickly, soon surpassing her simple lessons and taking to words and sums with more ease than she could ever have imagined. Also his accent for the French, the main language of the island, became as natural as if it were his native tongue and she was quite sorry when eventually he came to ask her if she could recommend a private tutor.

'I'm a t'inkin I w'uld like to learn as much as Master John. Dat's if you t'ink I cud,' he had said hesitantly. She had known of course that he was referring as to whether he could afford to pay. Nathaniel had told her that most of the boy's wages went towards feeding and clothing his ailing widowed mother and the remainder of his sisters and brothers who were, at the time, still living in the tiny shack among the sand dunes at the lower end of town. She promised to make enquiries but instead had talked to Nathaniel. In turn they decided to speak with the venerable Monsieur Regnault with whom they privately arranged to contribute towards the fees so that the boy be charged a relative pittance. The arrangement had not lasted long before the tutor waived his fee instructing the boy to 'consider it a bursary' and telling Nathaniel privately that, 'Tis the greatest of pleasures to discover such an appetite for learning!'

Colm continued to be a visitor to the house during the following years, rapaciously borrowing books from their steadily growing library and always surprising Anne by returning them in the same clean condition as they had been taken, almost as if the pages had not been turned. That each tome had indeed been studied was proved in the earnest discussions that could be heard between him and Harriet, another avid reader. The two had become great friends, Anne reminded herself now. Had the friendship deepened without her knowing? Was that what John was referring to when he said, '...unwise as it undoubtedly was to invite local gossip by welcoming that uncouth upstart into our home, any delusion in imagining that he will convert to our religion on marriage is even more harebrained.'? Their union, of two opposing religions? No, no, no! It would never come about. Harriet, the most devout of them all, would never wish to marry outside of the faith. John must be greatly mistaken.

11

"Mama! Mama!"

Anne jumped nervously at the sound of Julia's voice. Deep in thought she had not heard the child enter the room.

"Julia! What are the family rules concerning creeping about the house and startling people?"

"But Mama, I truly did not creep."

No, Anne grudgingly admitted to herself, Julia would not have crept. At 11 year-old the girl had still to lose the exuberance of childhood and with it the need to tear through the house or continually raise her voice in excitement. She must simply have been too absorbed in her own misery to hear.

'Mercy! How time has flown!' she thought, suddenly glancing across at the clock on the mantelpiece. 'The ladies will be here shortly and I am quite unprepared.' She picked up the sheet of paper and, putting it into one of the open sections in front of her, closed the lid of the desk saying aloud. "Well, nevertheless you have interrupted your poor Mama," before murmuring, "however thankful your mama is for that interruption."

Replacing the now crumpled handkerchief into the little drawstring bag at her waist she slowly turned to look at her daughter. "So, speak up, what is the excuse for interrupting your industrious Mama pray?"

The girl was swaying from side to side, her soft leather slippers brushing the wooden floor in the spirited rhythm of excitement, her starched petticoats rustling in accompaniment from under the gathered folds of her skirt. Deep brown curls burst out from under the white embroidered cap that enclosed the well-shaped head, rippling their way down to the narrow waist in an infusion of movement. Violet eyes shone vividly from the smooth-skinned but mostly pale face that held just a hint of colour on the well defined cheek bones and lips.

"Oh! Mama, I am sorry to have interrupted you, I truly am but..." Julia skipped across the room to her mother's side and twined an arm around the familiar neck. "My new gown has just been delivered from the dressmakers and...I thought perhaps...you would wish me to put it on that you might approve it."

Though two of the latest porcelain figured dolls, one from Bonn and one from Paris still sat at the child's bedside, they had been replaced in her affections by fashionable clothes, many of which would have been quite unsuitable for one so young had she been permitted to chose. And had her fancy to change her dresses frequently throughout the day also been permitted there is no doubt she would have but on this Anne had been firm. Still the wish to pose in this new gown, even for a short time, was so apparent that Anne wanted to give an indulgent laugh. However she kept a straight face as she replied, "But I have seen your new gown. Have you forgotten so soon? I saw it during the final fitting yesterday."

"But Mama... Do you not think I should try it on before it is hung in the armoire? It might not suit. I...I might have eaten too much pudding at supper last night...or perhaps too little."

"Oh! I do not think we need worry on that score," Anne replied, unable to keep from laughing any longer. Wanting to tease she hesitated before adding. "However I do feel your Papa's judgement should be sought. I suggest that you...you display it tonight after our meal and before you and your new gown retire to your room for the night!"

The girl squealed with delight as she snuggled her head into her mother's neck and, after a few minutes during which she was held close whilst she in turn stroked her mother's face, she remarked. "Your face is wet mama. Have you been weeping?"

Anne disentangled herself. "Now what would I have to weep about with three beautiful daughters and a handsome son, who is soon to celebrate his betrothal to yet another beautiful young lady?" She walked across to look in the mirror that hung above the mantelpiece. "Why! That is just my silly old eyes! Have you not noticed how they have begun to water lately whenever I read or write?" she lied, wiping her face with her hands. "My, but I shall have to minister them with a cold, wet cloth otherwise the good ladies of the church will think the same as you. Come, we will make our way upstairs."

"May I go and see if Papa has returned to the yard instead Mama?"

"Have you nothing else with which to occupy yourself? I would not like the devil to find work for those hands of yours should he find them idle. What about the schoolwork Miss Browne set for you, have you completed it all?"

The child nodded. The governess had returned to her home to care for a dying parent but before leaving had issued very strict instructions, so strict that the child had not played a single game, nor spent one minute daydreaming, until all her schoolwork had been completed.

"Then you may go to the yard but remember you are not to misbehave or get in the way of either Thomas or your Papa, should he be there. And...." She held the girl by the arms, looking directly into the violet eyes so that she could emphasise the point she was about to make, "you are not to linger about the street should they be too busy to attend to you. You are to return to your home immediately."

"Yes Mama," Julia promised.

Though Julia was not aware of it the town had grown and changed greatly in the intervening years since she had been born. Most of the open fields and meadows where her mother had gathered herbs and wild flowers as a child had been lost forever under the foundations for churches, shops, schools and terraces or crescents of houses. Tracks had been widened and surfaced with cobblestones before being made public thoroughfares and named after famous people, places or historical events. The stream, which once flowed openly through the town was now, mostly, covered over and part of the sand dunes to the right of the harbour was gradually vanishing under the construction of an esplanade.

The official residence of the island's Governor had moved from what was now known as Halkett Place to Belmont, a more suitable house standing in large grounds near the church of St. Saviour, and the party walls of her father's yard were now shared with various people. This occurred because Matthieu Amiraux, the man who had originally bought the old Government house, had sold the land off in plots for the building of shops and businesses.

There was a Post Office at the corner of Minden Place and Bath Street, with a Public Baths a few yards away from it, and a glorious theatre had been built in the centre of a fashionable crescent in Don Road. Julia knew that her parents had viewed a play at this theatre, the Theatre Royal, for afterwards they had marvelled at the talent of the performers. They had also admired the painted backdrop to the stage which, they related, was a view of the town harbour and St. Aubin's Bay from La Collette.

Thomas Edge, as recently as the previous year, had introduced a supply of gas to the island and some of the shops in King Street, a few yards away from the family home, were the first to be connected. Though the weather was inclement Nathaniel had taken his family to view this wonder and together, amongst a large crowd of others, they had excitedly pushed their way into Saunders the Chemist to watch as a taper was placed to the mantles. There were thirteen small burners shaped in a semi-circle and with a single burner giving more light than that of ten candles the resulting brightness was greeted with a roar of astonishment and delight from the audience. Mr Abraham De Gruchy had lit up his shop windows with dual burners encased in globes of frosted crystal as had Misters Guiton, Perchard and Labalestier. Then later, on the first evening of November when the gas lamps that lined the harbour were ceremoniously lit, the family had taken an evening stroll along its length, bathing in each glow of light and stopping to listen to the lamplighter whose job it was to attend them.

' 'Tis a bit different than tending me pigs' he had japed, 'though sometimes methinks them can snort just as loud!' And they had laughed along with everyone else.

The South Pier had been completed for some time and, as had happened after the construction of Le Quai des Marchands, the congestion eased for a while. That was until a company of steam ships began to provide a regular service between the island and Weymouth, bringing in thousands of moneyed English people who were fleeing the high taxation still levied on them to pay for the long Napoleonic Wars.

Nathaniel was happy that he and his men were kept in the work needed to provide the residences the invasion demanded. However, once again he and his business friends became frustrated by the cramped facilities now that steamships joined the schooners, ketches and brigs in vying for space at the St. Helier piers.

He had bought Number 24 on Le Quai Des Marchands, using it for storage as he intended when the idea first occurred to him. It was proving to be very beneficial but there were still times when his goods could not be brought ashore either because of tidal movements or lack of berths. When this happened his normally genial nature was sorely tried. He was down at the harbour, enquiring about an overdue delivery of cargo, as Julia made her way to the yard.

The August sun was already high in the sky and its heat soon seeped through her bonnet and the shoulders of the brocaded bodice of her dress but the child hardly noticed as she skipped along in happy reverie. She was also so deep in her childish imaginings that she was oblivious to the fact that most of the adults were holding handkerchiefs to their noses against the strong stench pervading the town.

One of her father's horses and carts – he had three of each which were used to transport goods and men to the various sites around the island – was standing outside the entrance to her father's yard. She stopped to stroke the nag, letting the animal nibble her fingers as she stared through the open gateway, her eyes searching for the familiar figures of either Thomas or her beloved papa but they were nowhere in sight.

She walked quietly through the aisles of building materials expecting to come across them both preoccupied with business of some kind. She planned to surprise them, knowing they would participate in the game they sometimes played. In her imagination she saw Thomas bowing his head towards her and touching his cap with the habitual respect that always made her feel grown up. She heard her father's mock alarm at being surprised, then the laughter as she clung to the comforting smell of wood and dried clay while he held her close.

The undertone of a man's voice drifted out from behind a large metal drum and she tiptoed slowly forward in its direction envisaging the fun to come. Instead she found to her astonishment, not her father or Thomas, but a man and woman embracing.

Instinctively the child knew that she should leave and began to inch her way backwards. As she did so the couple moved slightly and a gasp of shock escaped her lips as she recognised both her sister Charlotte and Colm O'Reilly. Alerted to her presence the pair sprang apart and Julia could not help but notice the flush that crept over her older sister's face. It was the mark of shame their mother said always visited them whenever they were doing wrong.

"Julia! Must you always creep about! What have you been told!"

It was the second time that morning that the child had been accused of creeping about but this time the charge was correct. She had indeed been tiptoeing through the yard but she had done so for the sole purpose of playing a game with her dear Papa. Still she wanted to retaliate, to deny that she had been doing anything other than walking through the yard in a normal manner, argue with her sister as she was wont at times to do, but what she had just seen confused and muddled her will.

"You t-two were... " she spluttered eventually.

"Julia!... What are you suggesting?" Charlotte demanded, looking appalled.

"He had his arms about you Lottie!"

"Well o' course I did!" Colm said quickly. "W'uld you not expect me to save a young maiden from fallin' over?" He kicked at a piece of timber lying on the ground. "That's the culprit. Tripped your sister up it did. 'Twas a good thing I was here to catch her afore she fell else she'd have hurt 'erself." He squared his shoulders before adding, with an air of importance. "A builder's yard is not the place for the likes o' young ladies. I've said so afore and I says so agin."

There was a tone of authority on his voice that made Lottie's hackles rise.

"This is our Papa's yard and we can come here any time!" she argued, staring defiantly up into the roguish face that was now glaring imperiously back at her. Their eyes locked in confrontation for some minutes before Julia finally looked across at her sister for support. However Charlotte was busily shaking dust from the hem of her voluminous skirts and seemed not to have heard the exchange.

It was the first time Colm had ever crossed Julia. Up to that moment she had rather liked him, enjoying his frequent visits to the house. He always showed an interest in her toys and games and sometimes let her brush his dark, wavy auburn hair. She had enjoyed listening to his lilting voice when he retold stories he had heard as a boy and watching his green eyes light up with laughter when he spoke of mischievous little leprechauns. But now, now she was not so sure she liked anything about him any more.

It was obvious that her father could not be in the yard but Thomas was bound to be. She would talk to him instead. He was much more amusing than Colm anyway. Thomas's stories were different. His stories always included praise of her papa and sometimes the retelling of the time she was born. 'A gift from heaven itself' he often said she was. Yes! She would find Thomas and talk with him.

She began to walk away, calling as she went, "Thomas? Where are you Thomas? Are you hiding?"

12

"THOMAS IS NOT here today Julia," Charlotte called after her.
Julia turned back quickly.

"Why not? Thomas is always here."

It was true. Her father once told her that it was Thomas's place to look after the yard and he had never missed a day in all the time he had worked for him. Even after he moved from the lean-to in the yard to live in the one-roomed cottage at the bottom of Pier Road, he was always at work from the break of each day until the dark closed in the night.

"Thomas is sick in his bed. Papa found the yard closed earlier this morning, with not a sign of Thomas, so when Colm arrived a few minutes later he was sent to see what had become of him…"

"'Tis I that found him sick," Colm interrupted again. "He was sitting to his table, all dressed up as if he was about to leave for work but with a face on him as pale as a ghost. 'Twas plain as a pikestaff that he was too sickly to even leave his cottage so I helped him undress again and put him back to bed. When I told the master he said I'd done right and that he w'uld get the doctor to look in on him later today. In the meanwhile I'd to watch the yard."

"Will he be better tomorrow?"

Seeing the concern that was now etched on the young face Charlotte answered gently, "I do not think so Julia dear, Colm fears, no… He believes… Do you not Colm? That Thomas has a high fever and ought to stay a bed until it passes."

"Can we go to visit him?"

"No, not yet a while. He's too sick to receive visitors," Charlotte told her.

"But Lottie, he is all alone!" the child protested.

When she had been ill the previous winter her mother had stayed with her throughout the days and both her parents had slept with her during the nights comforting her whenever she woke. But poor Thomas had no mama or papa, or even a sister or brother, to comfort him. She ran to her sister's side.

"We must go to him!" she begged, unbidden tears trickling down her cheeks. She looked directly up at Charlotte as she added, "he will have no one to comfort him. No one to coddle him or soothe his brow."

Charlotte took her young sister's head between her hands and drawing it to her chest, gently poked a wayward curl back under the white cap from where it had escaped.

"We cannot Julia. We must wait until we learn what his fever is about. Papa will see that he is well cared for. Why, it is to be certain that he would have already contacted Doctor Lamont and asked him to call."

But such a thought only set to alarm the child, who immediately wailed, "Oh! No! How terrible! Doctor Lamont will be sure to apply leeches, and they will suck at his blood, just as they did when I was sick." Julia shuddered at the memory of the way the slimy worms clung at her flesh and grew fat on her blood. The look and feel of them appalled and horrified her so that, weak and pained as she was at the time, she could not help but cry out in terror. Her parents had tried to hush her, assuring her that the leeches were friendly creatures that were going to make her well again but for once she could not believe them. The dread had stayed with her, returning in her dreams occasionally and when they did so she woke up screaming in fear.

Colm's mind was in turmoil as he watched the two sisters embrace. Had he been successful in convincing Julia that he had caught Charlotte as she was about to fall, he wondered anxiously. For the moment the child's thoughts were of Thomas and not of the incident she had just witnessed, a happening that had been truly quite accidental but one that if repeated to another's ear, even with innocent undertaking, would have a catastrophic outcome for both Charlotte and himself. Julia was still very much a child, kept that way by the petting and spoiling by all who were entranced by her violet eyes, but there was a wiliness about her, a trait of character that would make her both a fine friend and a bad enemy.

There would be ructions if the child mentioned the incident to either of her parents and they would have every right to take umbrage against him. For though the action had been quite innocent he could not swear before God that he had not relished the moment of pulling Charlotte close, an action he had secretly rehearsed in his mind many times. Yet whatever the outcome he would never regret, or indeed forget, the moment he held her in his arms and gave into the temptation of laying his lips against her cheek. The sensations of having his darling so close, inhaling the smell of her, feeling the softness of her skin under his lips, hearing her heart quicken its beat, was still with him etching its way through his very pores and causing his whole body to tingle with heady desire.

He knew now that he had always loved Charlotte. He had loved her when as a four year-old she had demanded his attention by plying him with questions and loved her for not scoffing later, as the others did, when he was slow to learn under her mother's tuition. As she grew he came to love her ability to play as robustly as any boy one minute, yet act in the most ladylike way the next. He loved the way she laughed, the way she moved and the kindness she showed in visiting his ailing and elderly mother. However, nurturing an unspoken love was one thing, taking advantage of an unguarded moment quite another. No gentleman would have laid himself open to such a crime. And that, in plain speaking terms, was where the difference between them lay. For though the master insisted that all his children consider themselves to be the offspring of a tradesman, they had enjoyed the education and company of the gentry, whereas he had been born a peasant and would always be considered such. 'Only an ignorant peasant would think a silk purse could be made from a sow's ear!' John had once jeered. And he had been ignorant, hadn't he, thinking he could better himself enough to be worthy of acceptance into the family.

"Please do not get yourself in such a state Julia," Charlotte was pleading now. "If any doctor has the ability to cure it is Dr Lamont. Has not mama always said that he is the best physician in the island? Come, let us go home and ask Mrs Kilshaw to make up a jug of her special broth for Thomas."

Julia disentangled herself from her sister's arms to ask. "Then can we take it to him Lottie?"

"No Julia, I have already told you we cannot. Until Doctor Lamont has attended Thomas and we are told from what he is suffering, father would not want us to visit."

The child began to cry again.

"But there'd be nuttin' stoppin' me from tekkin' the broth to Thomas," Colm offered.

Julia looked at him, her weeping temporarily suspended. "He would need it feeding to him...and his brow cooled with soothing lavender oil and his sheets and coverlets straightened," she said authoritatively.

"I c'uld do all that," Colm promised, though he was not too sure of the last two orders. Thomas might not take too kindly at being wiped with lavender oil or indeed have sheets or fancy coverlets on his bed to straighten. Still the child was not to know Thomas's true circumstances. "And p'r'aps Mrs Kilshaw c'uld be a coaxed to make up a basket with some junket and a bottle of her famous sloe gin that Thomas is a partial to. I c'uld tek it all to him. What d'you think?"

"Oh! Thank you! Thank you Colm!" Julia enthused as Charlotte wiped the tears from her cheeks. All memory of the earlier incident and antagonism the child felt towards Colm was now put aside and she could not wait to return to her home and talk to Mrs Kilshaw. The housekeeper frowned a lot and was often heard shouting at the girls who worked about the house, berating either their carelessness or idle ways, but Julia had come to learn that her bark was worse than her bite. She also knew the old woman liked Thomas and would be upset to learn he was unwell. She would be sure to be quite generous in making up a basket and might even let her help.

"Then what do you say to the notion that you and I should visit Mr Cory the apothecary and purchase a phial of lavender oil to add to the basket?" Charlotte said leading her by the hand out into the street. They left the yard without uttering farewells to the young man who stood watching them depart for both were distracted. Julia, her thoughts on the pleasant shopping trip ahead, had already dismissed him from her mind but, though she nodded and murmured the occasional response to her young sister's constant chatter, Charlotte had not. For a long time now she had fancied how it would feel to be enveloped in Colm O'Reilly's arms and now she knew.

She closed her eyes momentarily as the memory returned bringing with it a slight attack of giddiness. Had he really kissed her cheek or had she dreamt it, she asked herself. 'Why question?' An inner voice taunted. 'Nothing matters but that you have a fancy which will raise low spirits and help you to sleep through the long nights.'

Oh! What was she about? How could she think such things! Her parents would be quite appalled were they to find out. Especially her dear papa, who still called her one of his angels. What would he say if he learnt that the devil found her such easy prey, filling her head with such unbecoming, evil thoughts.

Yet how could thoughts of Colm be evil? She argued with herself. Colm who alone out of all his large family still looked to his ageing mother and the crippled sister who shared the small home he had bought in Hue Street; who remained upright and sober though his elder brother Donal had succumbed to the demon drink and was no longer capable of work? Colm, who had thrown off ridicule to educate himself so that he could read and write; who without an apprenticeship had learnt both the trades of carpentry and masonry to such a goodly standard that her father's clients asked for him in particular to undertake certain works? A truly worthy man, whose only crime was that he was of a humble background?

No, that was not the only matter, Charlotte reminded herself sharply. He was also a Roman Catholic and that was the true divider.

Charlotte's head ached unpleasantly by the time she reached her home several hours later, time during which Julia had chatted non-stop while they not only purchased the lavender oil but strolled through Abraham De Gruchy's store to seek out hair ribbons to match her new gown. So it was with blessed relief that the excited young voice quietened as they both entered the front door.

Anne, having hosted a successful meeting with the women from the church and seen them on their way just minutes before her daughters arrived, was about to climb the staircase and make her way to the family sitting room. However, on hearing Julia's animated voice on the street outside, she had turned about, wondering who the child was talking to. On seeing it was Charlotte she smiled warmly, holding her arms wide to welcome them both and Julia ran swiftly into them.

"Mama, Thomas is ill and all alone but Lottie says I cannot go to see him. Please say I can Mama, please!" she pleaded immediately.

Anne looked at Charlotte over the child's head, noting the flushed cheeks and bright eyes of her middle daughter. 'I do hope you are not sickening for something too Lottie dear,' she worried silently before asking the child,

"It is very unusual for Thomas to be ill. From what does your papa think he is ailing?"

"Papa has not yet returned to the yard but Colm says Thomas has a fever," Julia replied, still clinging to her mother's waist.

"Then you cannot possibly visit him until the fever has passed."

"But Mama, can we ask Mrs Kilshaw to make up a basket of food to help him get better? Colm said he would deliver it."

"Now that would be a much better idea. Why not run along to the kitchen and ask her?"

As Julia sped away Anne stretched out her hand and laid it against Charlotte's forehead. It was cool to her touch. There was no need to worry. The girl must simply have been hurrying against the cold wind that blew outside.

"I am just going up to the drawing room Lottie, let us go up and join Hattie who was in there reading when last I saw her. The fire should still be ablaze and we can sit by it until John and your papa return. Then we can all dine together."

13

THERE WERE FIVE tiny cottages surrounding the yard at the bottom of Pier Road, four of which consisted of two rooms whilst the fifth, once nothing more than an outhouse, had been converted by Nathaniel's men into a cosy one-roomed home for Thomas. Having spent 16 years living in the lean-to amongst the building materials and half a lifetime before then wherever he could lay his head, it was understandably Thomas's pride and joy. Unlike the overcrowded and sometimes putrid interiors of other houses in the area he kept it neat and tidy and usually sweet smelling with bunches of lavender hanging from the ceiling. However, that day, the stench emanating from where he lay on his bed was almost overwhelming.

It was not only the smell of the vomit and dysentery that caused Dr. Emile Lamont to suddenly cover his nose and mouth with a large white handkerchief but a feeling of dread as he neared Thomas's side and recognised the deadly symptoms. Having fought an earlier epidemic of cholera, in which he lost both his parents and a brother and sister, he had dreaded that it might take him on its return and because of this had worked alongside another physician, a Doctor Hooper, towards lessening the toll of a further wave. Aware that poor sanitation was one of the main causes of this virulent disease he had joined Dr Hooper in complaining vociferously about the overcrowded, unsanitary streets of St. Helier where foul sewage not only flowed openly but wells had either become polluted or dried up. Unfortunately, while they had fought for a better sewage system to be introduced in the town, very little had been done apart from the installation of additional water pumps here and there.

However, they had successfully encouraged the island's leaders to set up a health office and to their proud boast also organised that a house be furnished to serve as a hospital in every parish. And it was to the town's 'Fever House' that Thomas, thrown carelessly onto a handcart and trundled roughly and hastily through the streets, was unceremoniously dispatched.

After informing Dr Hooper, who in turn told the health office and town officials of the case, Lamont set out on horseback to tell as many

others as he could. It would be impossible to predict how fast the
scourge would accelerate or how many lives it would claim, he warned,
but, if the list of safeguards previously drawn up by Dr Hooper and
himself was adhered to, the number would be greatly lessened. He
saw it as his duty to visit everyone he knew, especially those holding
important positions within the island. Though the news of the outbreak
was grave many expressed their praise and gratitude for his vigilance.

As he rode towards the large site where Nathaniel and his men
were building a terrace of houses it occurred to Lamont that he was on
the brink of the public recognition he had long sought and the thought
cheered him greatly. He was therefore feeling quite full of his own
importance by the time he drew his nag to a halt.

"Your man has cholera!" he announced without any preamble and
in a tone that, to the men within earshot, sounded suspiciously like an
accusation.

Nathaniel was too shocked to note the tone. His concern for Thomas
blinded him to the lack of polite greeting, the absence of a proffered
hand to be shaken.

"Are you certain Lamont? Is there any chance that you could be
mistaken?"

The doctor's eyes flashed with anger.

"I would not presume to question your ability to erect buildings
Westaway, kindly award me the same courtesy by leaving the medicinal
diagnosis in the hands of those who have been fully educated in that
profession," he snorted.

Nathaniel was immediately contrite but Lamont ignored his apology
by adding curtly, "You say young O'Reilly found him. Where is he
now? He must be ordered to scrub himself down and burn the clothes
he is wearing. I take it he still lives in...?" He was about to add 'that
vermin infested hole amongst the dunes' but stopped himself just in
time. The men around Nathaniel had downed tools and moved to their
master's side, and though Lamont permitted neither time nor sympathy
for their likes he would not wish them to know it. His show of arrogance
gradually waned and he began to play nervously with the horse's reins.

"Back to work men. Remember we only have a half hour or so of
daylight left," Nathaniel said, moving away and signalling for the
doctor to follow. When they were on the road and no longer in danger
of being overheard Nathaniel asked, "Pray tell me, in all true honesty,

how you found Thomas."

"In a very bad way, Westaway. I have had him removed to the fever hospital but I fear he will not live to venture out. He is an old and frail man. You say that this is the first day he had not arrived at the yard yet he must have been unwell for a week or more. Did you not notice?"

Nathaniel shook his head slowly as he thought back in time. Thomas had not shown any change in his demeanour, no sign that he had felt unwell. He had looked pale, yes, but then he had never been ruddy of face.

"Had I enquired Thomas would never have owned an ailment," he answered regretfully. "He was afraid of doctors and hospitals, especially hospitals...."

"Well, I warrant he will be too ill to feel any fear now," the doctor interrupted. "Did he live alone?"

Nathaniel nodded. "His deformity caused him to keep his own company and counsel. Those who did not know him thought him to be an imbecile but he was far from it. Incredible though it may seem he had an astute head on his shoulders and because of this he was... is... greatly esteemed both by myself and all my men. As it will be impossible for any of us to visit him we can only trust that you will see that he is afforded equal respect and well treated. I will of course be responsible for any expenses incurred.

"Well, I ask again, what of O'Reilly? Does he still live amongst the dunes? If so he might likely be the source..."

Nathaniel shook his head, realising that the doctor referred to the tiny hovel at the lower end of town where the large brood of O'Reillys once lived. He told him that for some time now Colm, along with his two remaining dependants, his widowed mother and a sister who had never been able to work after being crippled from rickets when young, had lived in a house that fronted onto Hue Street. "However," he added "I am sure you will be equally surprised to hear that he will shortly be moving once again but this time into a house he has crafted to his own liking, a fine building at Town Mills with room at its side for a dower wing."

Lamont was indeed surprised to hear this piece of information and to note the odd sense of pride with which Nathaniel relayed it but he was tired and the flesh beneath his breeches sore from the hours of sitting above his nag.

"Well he is not there yet!" he snorted nastily. "Nor will he ever be if he gets taken. He must be spoken to and quickly."

"You have no need to worry on Colm's account. I will see that he takes all possible care," he assured Lamont.

"I presume you and yours will be carrying out all the precautions set by the authorities?" Nathaniel nodded though he bristled at the man's imperious tone. They had three girls working in the house now and under Mrs Kilshaw's excellent guidance every surface was scrubbed and disinfected daily as a routine. "Yes of course, I should not have doubted it," the doctor went on, "still if you could try to instil a little basic cleanliness into the heads of your men it should only help matters."

How could he lecture his men on the need for cleanliness when foul drains overflowed through the yards where their crowded homes lay, when there was only one water-pump to serve several streets? Nathaniel wondered. Yet it was a task he could not afford to shirk. Cholera was a disease most feared, a plague that was not particular of who it chose as it swept through the populace. What would he do if it took any of his dear girls? How would he survive if God took them from him?

Nathaniel was fretting over these thoughts as he entered the drawing room on his return home and saw Anne and their three daughters, their heads close together as they looked at something lying on the Georgian table. They moved towards him as he entered and he felt his heart lift with love and pride as he returned their smiles of welcome. Anne, his dearest sweetheart who, despite their being wed for twenty years, still shared his bed with a youthful passion that had failed to pall. Harriet, their serious, intelligent, eldest daughter who at 18 puzzled them both by refusing to entertain the attentions of the equally serious Charles Le Touche. Then there was 17 year-old Charlotte, whose beauty and bright sunny personality had already won the hearts of several young suitors but for whom he and Anne were hoping for a match with the son of one of the island's most respectable newcomers, and finally their youngest, dearest Julia. He loved them all so much. How was he to protect them from the cholera scourge? But for all of his worries he would not have mentioned the subject immediately had not Julia cried, "Oh! Papa! How is Thomas? Can I go to see him?"

He shook his head in reply.

"Well, will you and Mama visit and tell him I am thinking of him?"

"We will not be able to do so for poor Thomas has been taken to the Fever House and cannot receive visitors," he replied, his eyes looking directly into those of Anne who gasped aloud, as did both Harriet and Charlotte. They all knew the precautions each parish had made and why.

"Then it is…?"

Anne could not say the word. Nathaniel went to her side and drew her close.

"Yes, my dearest, but we should not need to fret if we are vigilant in looking to our states of cleanliness and remember to adhere to the list of precautions the authorities have set down," he said looking across at Harriet and Charlotte with more confidence than he felt. Harriet's face had paled but Charlotte's had reddened and her eyes had suddenly filled with tears.

"Now, there is nothing with which you need immediately distress yourself, Lottie dear. Thomas is in good hands. He will receive the best of care and with God's Grace will be back amongst us in a short while" he said.

But though Charlotte was upset for Thomas her distress was for Colm as the memory of how he had described his tender care of the old man now haunted her. He had tended Thomas and Thomas had cholera. Surely Colm too would become infected?

Her deep concern gradually turned to relief as he continued to appear for work each day especially as during the next ten weeks alone the count of those with the disease rose to nearly eight hundred. Half of those victims, including Thomas and two other of her father's workers, died. As the weeks turned into months it seemed that very few of the families with whom they were acquainted were left unaffected. It was a sad and extremely worrying time.

14

OVER THE YEARS Charlotte had become a frequent caller at the O'Reilly home in Hue Street and, although several of the residents in the closely built up throughway had been taken with cholera, it did not occur to her to stop visiting. Indeed she could never have done so for, even though she had felt relief at finding that Colm had not become infected, she had taken on an obsession where she could not bear to go through a day without either the reassuring sight or sound of him. Besides, spending time with his mother and sister was always pleasant because to her eyes they, like Colm, were the most endearing and amiable pair.

The cottage at 12a Hue Street with its two rooms upstairs and two rooms downstairs was 'just a start for the lad,' his mother boasted to anyone within earshot. 'The new house 'e was building at the top of town? Why wasn't that with 'is glorious future in mind, with 'im being in such demand as a craftsman? But no, she wouldn't be moving into that fancy cottage alongside that 'e called the dower wing, much as 'e might beg. She was happy where she was, thank you, stinking cesspit an' all!'

The cesspit that Mary O'Reilly was referring to was the covered trench in the middle of the communal yard into which both she and the occupants of surrounding cottages emptied all of their human and household waste. It was similar to that in yards throughout the poor and overcrowded neighbourhood and their combined stench the subject of everyday conversation among all who either lived or passed through the area.

The smell was never as bad in the winter however so Charlotte hardly noticed it as she hurried towards the house that early December morning. Her mind was going over the events of the previous evening which she had spent lacing narrow satin ribbons through the lavender dollies she was planning to give her two special friends for the coming Christmas. In her mind's eye she could see the delighted looks on the faces of Colm's mother and sister. Absorbed in the daydream she walked blindly into a man who was deliberately barring her way.

"I do beg your pardon…" She began before looking up into a bloated and blurry eyed face. "Oh! It is you Donal!"

"Ye cannot go near!" he said gruffly, holding out his arms wide to prevent her passing and rocking from side to side as if playing a game. His breath stank of ale and his clothes were badly in need of a clean but she forced away the rising feeling of disgust in accepting that this was one of Colm's older brothers. He had not always been like this, she reminded herself, in fact her father had often described him as having been one of his most trusted workers, as well as the most fun loving, but that was before the tragic death of his lovely young wife.

Charlotte could never forget the wedding of Donal and Rosie and the revelling afterwards to which all her family had been invited. She had danced the jig with Colm to the sound of the fiddle and she had felt gayer than she had ever felt in her life before. What happened later, after she, Harriet and her parents had left she never learnt despite her enquiries as to how John came to have grazed knuckles. However, the following morning, before little Julia had claimed her attention, she had overheard part of the dressing down he received from their father who had upbraided him for not walking away when the fight started. "I might expect it of Colm, he has always been fiery," he had said, "but not of any son of mine."

Yes, Colm was known to be fiery but he had never been so with her, she argued silently, with her he was always kind and cheerful. Donal too had been kind and cheerful until the day that runaway horse had trampled down his lovely Rosie, killing her instantly. He had never been cheerful since, even with the drink in him.

"Please do not jest Donal," she said, "your mama is expecting me."

"Me ma-am," he replied exaggerating the difference in speech, "will not be at 'ome for anyone today."

"Oh! Pray stop teasing Donal, let me pass do," she pleaded.

"I'm not teasin'," he insisted. "Ye can't go no nearer. Colm 'as said."

"Colm would never say such a thing," she said, suddenly darting onto the cobbled roadway to go around him.

"No! I says!" Donal turned quickly and lunged at her, catching her around the waist as together they stared down the length of the street to where Colm was gently placing his mother onto a mattress-covered handcart. Charlotte gasped aloud. The sight could only mean one thing, the dear woman had cholera and Colm was taking her to the Fever House. Charlotte called out but he did not hear.

"Go 'ome Miss Charlotte," Donal said quietly. " 'Tis no place for you, never 'as been."

"Oh! Donal, Donal," she cried, "what ever can I do?"

"Nuttin' but go back to your 'ome and stay there. Go quickly afore our Colm knows and starts getting at me for letting you see."

"I will, though reluctantly, but before I do please will you promise to tell your ma....mam that I love her and will be praying for her recovery?"

"Aye, I'll do dat," he promised softly, and impulsively she reached up and kissed the unshaven cheek before dashing away.

Sobbing quietly she ran back through Union Street to her home, thankful that there was no one about as she hastily made her way to the room she shared with Harriet. Once there she threw herself upon the bed where she continued to weep until she fell into an exhausted sleep.

"You are not to return to that house, do you hear Lottie? You have already put yourself to great risk as it is," her mother ordered later that day.

"But Mama, his sister will be there all alone," Charlotte begged.

"No, she will not. Your caring papa has told Colm that he need not return to work until he is able to arrange his family affairs."

"But Mama..."

"You have been told Charlotte!" Anne said sternly. "Furthermore you are not to leave the house until the cholera is completely over, is that clear?"

Charlotte was aghast.

"Is that clear?" her mother repeated, to which Charlotte had no choice other than to reply, "Yes, Mama."

"And Hattie dear," Anne said, turning to Harriet who was sitting by the window embroidering a sampler with a quote from the Bible, "It would be best not to encourage Colm to visit for a while and should he return any books he may have borrowed they should be burnt. You do understand why, my dear?"

"Yes, of course Mama," came the reply in a tone that surprised Anne with its coolness. She was about to comment further but was surprised again as Charlotte upped and rushed from the room causing her thoughts to move to reflecting on the difference in character between her three eldest children. Here was the serious Hattie, calmly putting her mind to her needlework after being told that she must not see the young man with whom John had hinted there was a matrimonial interest. Then there was the normally loving and obedient Lottie throwing a temper at being ordered to stay in the house and lastly the obstreperous John who did not seem the least disappointed at postponing his betrothal party because of the outbreak. Really! Would she ever understand the present generation?

Mary O'Reilly had never been separated from her invalid daughter except for the week she spent in the Fever House before the younger woman was also admitted. Yet even in death they were not divided as, dying within days of each other, they were interred in the same communal pit at the foot of Gallows Hill, the area that had been selected for the burial of all victims of the plague.

News of the deaths upset Charlotte greatly. She began to fret for Colm realising that if she was feeling so sad then he, who had made his mother and sister his whole concern, must be more so. She had heard that he had returned to work and longed to ask her father for more news but held her tongue, suspecting that, should her face give away her feelings for Colm, he might not be too pleased. Her parents had been encouraging the attentions of Edward Rowley, the son of a prominent silk merchant. Though she cared nothing for the man she knew that if he made an offer of marriage they would expect her to accept.

The next two weeks were the longest she had ever spent, with the days being particularly devoid of interest without a daily outing. It had also been some time now since, heeding the official advice against unnecessary gatherings, they had either entertained or received visits from family or friends. Neither had they seen much of John who was now spending all of his free time overlooking work on his new home. They had also missed the company of Anne Guillet who, after being warmly welcomed into the family as a new daughter and sister, had not been to visit since the very onset of the outbreak. According to Nathaniel, who had spoken to her once in the town, she had regretfully explained that her lack of visits had not been for fear of the infection. She had been kept busy caring for her *guardienne* who was suffering the discomforts of old age, she said, an act of devotion which they all agreed was admirable.

'Even beloved Papa lacks his usual conversation,' Charlotte bemoaned silently to herself. 'With three more of his workers having become ill he arrives home so late in the day and carrying such weariness about him that he often falls asleep wherever he sits and has to be woken to have his meal.'

But for Charlotte the worst of it all was hearing so little of Colm. He had not come near to the house since the day his mother had become ill and though she positioned herself at the window of the family drawing room at various times throughout the day she had not even caught sight of him on the street below. Christmas was now four days away and she had so wanted to search the shops for a suitable gift for him but, though the epidemic was believed to be on the decline, her father had insisted they still be confined to the house. He would only worry about them otherwise, he said.

'We must abide by your papa's wishes and still remain vigilant,' Anne had told her three daughters the previous week. 'So this year I suggest there is no need to present your papa and myself with seasonal gifts but occupy yourselves in stitching a little something for each other instead by using materials from the coffe.'

The coffe was a small mahogany chest that stood against the far wall of the family drawing room. Its four drawers were filled with various remnants of material, the hinged lid opening up to exhibit a selection of sewing necessities such as threads, ribbons, scissors and thimbles.

Charlotte, having decided to give Julia the lavender dollies she had originally planned to give the dear friends for whom her heart still mourned, had worked industriously but without enthusiasm on a richly embroidered bookmark for Harriet. However now it was finished and, though in finding her idle once more her mother had set her to learning passages from the Bible by heart, she was finding the time particularly oppressive.

When Donal called at the house to say that Colm would not be in to work that day she thought she would lose her mind.

" 'E don't think it's grave, just 'is own punishment of making a pig of 'imself with the unripe apples 'e ate yesterday,' she overheard Donal report to her father, "but if it's alright with ye sir, Colm says, 'e'd wait for the runs to settle before getting back to work."

She hardly heard her father's assurance that 'of course Colm must stay at home until he feels fit and would Donal wait for a basket of refreshments to be made up and deliver it to him with their good wishes?' as she sped upstairs to the privacy of the bedroom.

Standing with her back to the door she shook her head from side to side in an effort to escape the words that screeched round and around in her head but it was no use. 'Colm had the runs! Colm had the runs! That can only mean one thing,' they mocked. Her heart and mind were filled with dread. She must find a way to go to him! She could not, she would not permit Colm to be sick with no one to comfort him. Oh! But how, how could she escape the house without being missed?

As fate would have it the opportunity presented itself that very afternoon when, feigning a headache so that she could remain in her bedroom to work out a plan, her mother decided that she, Harriet and Julia would attend a Christmas Carol Service at the Chapel without her. Charlotte waited patiently until they had left, then again afterwards until she heard the elderly Mrs Kilshaw make her way along the corridor for her regular afternoon rest, before quietly creeping down the stairs. She did not want to risk being seen in the streets so, correctly suspecting that the maids would still be in the kitchen, went swiftly out of the front door and through the archway that led back through to the stables and gardens onto New Street. Once there she looked from side to side before crossing the street and taking the long narrow pathway that wound its way past the rear gardens of properties in Union Street before ending up in one of the communal yards that backed Hue Street. From there it was only a few yards to number 12a and having run all the way unseen it was some relief that she finally let herself into the house.

With the curtains drawn against the daylight the room was so gloomy that Charlotte had difficulty in finding her bearings at first. When she did it was to see Colm lying under the feather quilt of the bed in the far corner of the room, his sister's bed, which had always been empty and respectably covered whenever she had previously visited. She pulled back the curtains and the light that flooded the room caused Colm to sit up. On seeing her he rubbed his eyes before sinking down again muttering, " 'Tis dreaming, the sad fool that I am."

"Oh! Colm! Colm! I have been so worried at not seeing you," she cried rushing to his side.

"Go away Lottie, me darlin' girl. 'Tis only a dream you are and this time I don't have the strength to fight for you."

"Open your eyes Colm, I am really here and not a dream so whatever your dream was about you will not have to fight for me."

"Oh! Me darlin' darlin' Lottie, leave me in peace there's a good girl" he said, pulling the quilt over his head.

There was a terrible smell nearby and having glanced down into the half-filled pail at the side of the bed she resolutely undid the ribbons of her bonnet, pulling it off before removing her cape and placing them both on the back of the armchair that stood alongside the fireplace. Noticing the embers in the grate were growing dim she took some faggots from the nearby box and threw them on top before adding a shovel of coal from the scuttle. Then returning to the bed she gently tugged at the quilt.

"Colm," she insisted softly, "please talk to me and tell me how I may help you to feel better."

Suddenly he sat bolt upright and put out his hand to stroke her face.

" 'Tis you, 'tis really you! I thought I was dreamin'. Oh! But you must go Lottie darlin', 'tis the fever I've got and 'twould break your family's hearts if you were to be taken."

"What about my heart should you not recover? Do you think I fail to return the love you have for me?" She asked boldly. "You do love me Colm, do you not? Oh! Please say that you do!"

"Me darlin' darlin' girl I've loved you for always...always. Why do you t'ink I took up all that schoolin' and started buildin' that grand house at Town Mills? But it can't ever be, me darlin'. John's right, that's why he set about me at our Donal's weddin' when I boasted of my intentions. Your father has other plans and why not, doesn't his beautiful daughter deserve better than a man who comes from this?" He said this wearily, pointing around the room before adding sadly, "and before this a place only fit for swine."

Her eyes did not follow the direction of his hand but stayed on his face. She had never entered the hovel on the dunes where the family had lived when they first arrived in the island but she was familiar with the cluttered interior of this room and did not need to look around. Besides she was unexpectedly filled with the overwhelming need to study every inch of his dear face and confine it to memory. This was the man she loved, had loved for as long as she could remember, but he would soon be lost to her. How she knew this for certain she could not fathom but the knowledge settled her. She would not leave him.

Instead she would care for him and savour the time they had left together.

"The boy who came from that hovel in the dunes won my heart from the first time I set eyes on him. Since that day he has filled my life with so much friendship and fun that I could not help but love him."

"Ah! Me darlin' Lottie, how I've dreamt of hearing you say those words but..."

"Butt! Butt! Butting is the habit of nanny goats, is that not what Papa has always claimed?" she chided, laughing as she bent to kiss him on the forehead. He lifted his face and their lips met in a lingering kiss.

Leaning back at last she said with mock severity, "Now you must be a good patient and not demand too much of your nurse's time. Tell me have you fresh water from the pump?"

"Aye, Donal filled that large ewer in the corner, as he did the scuttle afore he left. He's been good so he has and not single drop passed his lips for weeks now. He said he'd call on your father to tell him, but not as I had the fever 'cause we didna want to worry him..."

"Or me!" she finished. "Oh! Colm. Did you not know how worried I would be when I heard you were ill, especially after...?"

She was going to add, 'losing your dear mother and sister,' but he had put his finger over her mouth and asked, "D'you t'ink I could have a drink o' water please Nurse?"

When Donal returned later that day he was surprised to find Charlotte bending over the fire stirring a pan of steaming broth, her face glistening with sweat under the untidy tendrils of hair that had escaped from the starched cap on her head. He could not fail to notice that the sleeves of her brocade dress were rolled up to the elbows as she turned and, putting her finger to her lips whispered, "Colm's sleeping!"

"No, I'm not me darlin', the patient murmured. "Come here will you?" and when she went to his side he took her hand and said, "now that Donal is back I want you to go home..."

Her protests were drowned under an insistent rap at the door and both she and Colm turned to watch as Donal opened it to reveal Doctor Lamont.

"Ye have come to the wrong house, we dinna' ask for ye to call!"

Donal said rudely, his dislike for the arrogant man obvious. For this was the man who had refused to let a loving family visit their mother and sister in the fever house, walking hurriedly passed as they waited outside in the cold and sleet and ignoring their pleas for news.

"This is 12a, the house of Colm O'Reilly?" the doctor persisted, then taking the silence as agreement continued. "Well I come under the benevolent instructions of his employer so either you let me in to tend the patient or I will have report back that not having seen him I can only assume that he is skiving."

Donal still did not step aside until Charlotte said, "Oh! Please let the doctor in Donal, he will have all the potions to make Colm better. He is certainly not skiving, Doctor Lamont, as you will see."

The look on the doctor's face changed from one of disdain to shock as he recognised the untidy young woman who motioned him inward. It changed again to one of great concern as he glanced down at the ghostly white pallor of the young man in the bed.

"I do not know what misplaced goodness of heart has led you here Charlotte but I must insist that you leave. This is not the place for you."

"I am staying," she said defiantly. "He needs someone to care for him."

"Donal will do that," Colm said gently. "And now that the doctor's here and sets about dosin' me with one or two of his magic potions, I'll be back at work a'fore you know it, won't I doctor?" His expressive green eyes, set in dark grey sockets, earnestly pleaded agreement as he stared up at the doctor. Moreover, and this was something the doctor was often to recall later, they appeared to be silently asking him to take part in a conspiracy. That he felt compelled to submit to such wishes was to puzzle him until the end of his days.

'It was obvious that the young man wanted the girl to leave,' he was to relate later, 'and quite rightly too! Inheriting her father's misguided paternal care of his workers had placed her in grave danger, though it was doubtful that the visit had been made with her parents' permission.' And he would go on to give an account of how he found himself playing out a short charade beginning, "I was told you had a bad attack of the gripes. If this is so, which I will certainly ascertain after a short examination, you should be back at work within a week or two."

Then, after a great display of looking in the pail, taking Colm's pulse and feeling his neck, all the while a-hemming and a-humming he asked, "Have you been eating unripe fruit?" When Colm nodded in reply he grumbled, "Well, 'tis only to be expected then. Normally I would let the upset take its course but as your employer is too benevolent for his own good I shall get the apothecary to make up a potion which will see you returning to some hard work in gratitude. And you," he added, turning to face Charlotte, "should get back to your home before your absence is noted.... I take it neither your Mama nor your Papa are aware of your visit here today?"

'I felt I could take this position with her for I had not only delivered her into the world but nursed her through many childish ailments. And to her eternal credit she hung her pretty head in shame,' he would say.

Charlotte was in a quandary. One part of her wanted to query the diagnosis that it was only an attack of the gripes with another part wanting so desperately to believe that her dearest Colm would live. If only she knew the truth! She looked up into the face of the doctor and, finding it inscrutable, looked down at her beloved. His eyes also lacked any sign of emotion as he looked back at her and said, in the tone of a polite stranger, "I cannot thank you enough for your kind ministrations Miss Charlotte but you must worry about me no further. As the doctor says 'tis only an attack of the gripes and I'll soon be back on my feet again. Please return to your home and in passing on my thanks to your father for arranging for the doctor to call, give him an account of the outcome."

His words were so cold, so unlike the soft words and endearments he had uttered a short while before, and though she knew they had been said for the benefit of the other two men in the room, they stabbed at her heart. Looking away she grabbed at her cloak and bonnet which were still on the back of the armchair and hurriedly put them on.

Returning to his side she said, "I leave you in good hands then Colm, see that you rest easy," to which he respectfully replied, "I will Miss Charlotte, that I will."

Nodding to both the doctor and Donal in turn she made her way to the door.

"May God bless you Miss Charlotte," she heard Colm say as, with tears choking her throat, she ran into the street.

15

WITH THE KNOWLEDGE that Colm's mother and sister had died of the cholera, Nathaniel feared that the reported 'gripes' had been a fabrication to ease his mind, and dreaded learning otherwise. For over the years since the boy had come into his life he had become favourably inclined towards him, in business treating him as his right hand man and, within his heart, looking on him as a son he would like to have sired. So when Lamont came to him at the yard with the diagnosis that it was indeed cholera he had to turn away lest the doctor saw the tears that filled his eyes. But the doctor did not notice as he felt a sharp ache in his stomach. 'Hunger pains,' he thought.

"And we had thought the outbreak over!" he grumbled, taking his top hat off and wiping the beads of sweat that had broken out on his brow.

"Has he been taken to the Fever House?" Nathaniel asked, his voice hoarse.

"Yes, the brother took him. Mind you neither of them wanted it. I had to agree that the older one could stay at the hospital to look after his brother which, between you and me will help for two reasons. One, we have very few women left to see to the remaining patients we have and two, in keeping the elder brother confined also, we may help to contain the infection. One just hopes that young Charlotte has not contracted it."

Nathaniel swung around. "Charlotte? Why do you mention Charlotte in particular?"

The doctor hesitated before replying, half mesmerised in watching a single tear escape from the corner of one of his patient's eyes, eyes that were now glistening with what he took to be a look of agitated concern. For a moment he wished he had not said anything before common sense prevailed and he realised that it was his place to forewarn the man.

"You were aware that she was a visitor to the O'Reilly house?"

"Yes, the two women were her dear friends, but I believe she had not visited them for a time before they became ill and never after. How could that have placed her in danger?"

"I fear you may have been misled in that quarter but perhaps those visits in themselves might not have placed her in danger, However, setting herself up as an administering angel to the young man may well have."

"She visited Colm? At his home?" Nathaniel's tone was sharp.

The doctor nodded before replying, "I wondered if you were aware of the fact. No doubt she meant well but nevertheless the visit was ill-advised from all aspects, the very least being that by visiting him unaccompanied she was providing food for gossiping tongues. Quickly realising all this – and I hope you do not see it as usurping my authority in any way – I took it into my hands to send her home immediately I met her there," he said. He decided not to mention the strange events that followed his arrival at the house. 'Mesmerised' was the word that came to mind as he walked away from Hue Street earlier, 'I never thought it possible but I was mesmerised into acting out a charade by a pair of green eyes.'

"You behaved only as I would have done," Nathaniel muttered. He was shocked, shocked that one of his daughters should behave in such a way. In not only disobeying his strict orders she had risked both her reputation and very life in visiting Colm. Yet how could he blame her when he himself had dearly wanted to visit the boy and in doing so cursed the demands of work that kept him away? But then his visit would not have encouraged gossip, gossip which in surrounding Charlotte would place the promising liaison with Edward Rowley in jeopardy. "I trust we can keep this matter between ourselves," he added quickly.

"Of course my dear Westaway, you can rely on my discretion."

Nathaniel did not entirely trust the doctor to keep his word, especially after his tongue was known to loosen after a glass of brandy or two, but he pushed the doubt to the back of his mind as he went on to discuss Colm's condition.

For the first time since she had been born Charlotte's actions had evoked her father to great anger and he meant to reprimand her sternly on his return home but his intention was quickly forgotten with the news that Anne had taken to her bed.

"She has spent most of the afternoon in the wash room Papa," Harriet told him almost as soon as he entered the front door, "and she is not at all herself."

"Send one of the maids for the doctor," he said, fear causing his voice to rise an octave higher than usual. "No, on second thoughts, go yourself Hattie for seeing you he will know it is urgent and come immediately. Go straight to his place of residence in Val Plaisant, for he said he was about to return there after we met earlier."

Without another word he dashed up the stairs. He found Anne in their bedroom. She was sitting on a chair at the side of the bed, rocking backwards and forwards as if in pain, a flannelette wrap covering her underclothes. He ran forward and put a hand to her cheek, it was cool to the touch yet he could not help but notice that the tendrils of hair escaping from the cap on her head hung lank and damp about her neck.

"Oh! Nattie, I feel so ill," she groaned, "and Julia is also afflicted." He moved slightly as if he intended to leave so she put out a hand to stop him. "No, do not worry about Julia for the moment, Lottie is with her. She is trying to calm the child who is overwrought with fear and keeps begging for reassurance that the sickness is not cholera. But oh! Nattie, let us pray that it is not. I do not want Julia to die. I do not want any of you to die, neither do I want to leave you all yet. There is so much I want to live for, so many more happy hours with you, partaking in that travelling we are always promising ourselves we would do as soon as you could take time away from work, seeing John happily married and then the girls and…"

"Stop talking this way dearest. We cannot know that it is cholera, or if it is that you will not survive it as others have. Yes! people have," he insisted as she shook her head. "We must have faith. You must hold fast to our faith that you will be all right and Julia also. I have sent Hattie for Lamont so let me help you into bed in the meantime."

"Then will you pray with me Nattie for I really am afraid."

He too was afraid, so afraid that his stomach felt as if it were filled with ice but he did not let her suspect as he said calmly, "Yes, as soon as you are settled we will offer up a prayer that God will be merciful towards you and Julia."

Harriet was away a long time and when she returned a stranger accompanied her into the house. After giving their outer clothes to the waiting maid she led the man up the stairs.

"I am sorry to have been so long," she began to explain to her anxious looking father who met them on the hall landing, "but Doctor Lamont was indisposed. His housekeeper recommended Dr Pierce and gave me his address. He insisted on accompanying me back here immediately though it must have meant leaving his meal before he had finished eating it."

Nathaniel shook hands with the tall gaunt looking man. "Please accept my apology if that is so," he said. "I cannot think what could have suddenly indisposed Lamont as I saw him only a short while earlier but I thank you for coming so readily in his place. It is my dear wife and daughter, I am afraid they are very ill."

The doctor made no comment as he followed Nathaniel and simply nodded curtly when the older man stood aside for him to enter the room first. He walked across to the bed where Anne, on seeing the stranger, drew the bedclothes high into her neck.

"This is Doctor Pierce," Nathaniel began.

"Where is Doctor Lamont?" she demanded querulously, frowning under the long stare with which she was being regarded.

"He is indisposed," Nathaniel explained. "Doctor Pierce has kindly come in his place."

"He looks too young to be a doctor," Anne said. "I do not want him near me."

"In that case you will not wish to be cured Madam so I shall leave you to your sick bed." The doctor made to move away.

"I am afraid it is cholera," she said.

"Ah! So you too have endured the long years of medical school and are fully qualified to diagnose your own complaints?" He turned and grinned at her unexpectedly. "In which case Madam you will be under the same delusion as many a doctor for even our minds are apt to play tricks at times, especially where our own health is concerned!"

The smile played on her mouth but did not reach the worried look in her eyes as she lowered the bedclothes.

"Well, it is my considered opinion you are not suffering from cholera but gastric fever. There is a lot of it about the town at the moment," he said at last. Turning to Nathaniel he added, "now, I believe one of your daughter's is also unwell?"

To her family's relief Julia was also found to be suffering from gastric fever and not the dreaded cholera but the relief was only temporary as one by one every member of the household, with the exception of

Charlotte, fell victim.

"But how will you manage without me and the girls Miss Charlotte?" the very sickly Mrs Kilshaw, who had been ordered to stay in her room, worried. "Let me at least set them back to work. I'm sure they are not as ill as they say. Girls today would skive forever if you wasn't at them all the time."

"Nevertheless having visited them in their room I have no doubt that they are feeling as bad as they look, as you must be at this moment. Now get yourself off to your bed and do not worry about me. I will be able to cope with whatever is necessary. It is not as if I would have to prepare much in the kitchen for no one has much of an appetite. I surely do not wish to eat anything at present." In fact she was feeling a little queasy herself but was certainly not going to let anyone see. They were all far from well and there needed to be one person in the house able to tend to them. Besides it kept her mind occupied.

For over a week Charlotte was kept extremely busy caring for the eight patients: her father, mother, two sisters, Mrs Kilshaw and the two young maids who all needed constant attention. Doctor Pierce, having informed Anne and Nathaniel that he had subsequently learnt that Lamont was suffering from the same complaint and would not be attending to his patients for a while was requested to call, which he did several times. Worried at how pale and ill Charlotte looked despite her protestations that she was just tired, he suggested that a nurse be employed to help her but she would have nothing of it. With Colm never far from her mind she was glad of the constant demands that kept her too occupied to worry. It was only at the end of each exhausting day that the thoughts and memories came flooding back, setting her tossing and turning and keeping her from sleep.

Christmas passed by without the usual attending of church services or family celebrations for the Westaways that year of 1832. Instead of huge repasts from a table laden with meats of guinea fowl, mutton and pork with equal amounts of potatoes and vegetables, Charlotte was serving up tiny dishes of quince, steamed fish and egg custard and then only to those who were rallying. Nathaniel and Harriet, the two members of the family who were the last to succumb, took the longest to recover but by the first week in the New Year even they were up and about again. By this time Charlotte, who had driven herself relentlessly throughout, was now a shadow of her former self.

"You are in need of a holiday, we are all in need of a holiday and I declare that we should take one in the spring!" Nathaniel said as he left to go about his work. "But in the meantime you must rest and recover from your nursing duties. So off to your room Lottie dear and let your mama and sisters care for you for a change." He had forgotten that he had been angry at her for risking her life and reputation by visiting Colm, so relieved was he that the sickness had not been cholera. Not only had his prayers been answered but there had not been any new cases of cholera for weeks. Anne and his darling girls were safe. The Good Lord be Praised.

It was as she was wearily making her way up the stairs and heard the regular rapping on the front door that Charlotte knew, even before it was opened, that it was the news she had been expecting. Colm her love was dead. She had known two hours earlier when she had been sprinkling the over dry laundry and rolling it up ready for the girls to iron later. It was then that she clearly heard him say, "May God bless you Miss Charlotte." Her heart had leapt as she turned around, expecting to see him standing behind her, but the scullery was empty. That was when she knew.

Without waiting for confirmation she continued up to her room where she took off her clothes and got into bed. When Harriet came to tell her she did not cry, neither did she give any outward sign that she cared about his loss, unlike her parents who wept unashamedly. But unknown to them Charlotte had always cared. She had cared so deeply for Colm O'Reilly that her loving, blithe young heart felt broken beyond repair.

Wrapped up in what everyone agreed was the sad loss of a young life in which Colm achieved so much, it took some time for the family to notice that Charlotte was not responding to the medicine prescribed by Doctor Pierce. When they asked him to visit her again a second time he stared at her for a few moments before assuring her gently that she would feel a lot better if only she would eat and drink a little something. She nodded and smiled in response so a subdued Mrs Kilshaw sent up fresh food several times a day – delicious morsels that were recommended to tempt the weakest of invalids – but every spoonful was met with a shake of the head.

With the exception of Julia, who was considered to be too young, they took it in turns to sit with her and attend to all her needs but soon, to their great distress, they found she hardly acknowledged their presence.

Charlotte died on the 23rd January 1833. Just before dusk the following day, two men, one of them a sober and darkly dressed Donal, slowly drove the cart carrying her simple wooden coffin to the cemetery on the south-east of town. Leading the small procession of men, most of whom had known Charlotte through her family's commitment to the Wesleyan Chapel, was the Reverend Minister, Nathaniel and John.

A short while later, as Donal stood alongside them at the open grave with eyes closed as the minister offered up a prayer for Charlotte's eternal soul, his thoughts were naturally drawn to the recent burials of his mother, sister and brother. Their graves would remain forever unidentifiable from the other hundreds of poor souls who had been taken with the cholera, for even the simplest crosses had not been permitted to mark their resting-places, but it pleased him to think that Charlotte's would not be. Her grave was soon to be identified by a hewn headstone. He opened his eyes and let them drift across the graveyard to where a simple wooden cross marked his darling Rosie's last resting place and wondered if it would cheer the two grieving men to be reminded that their lovely Charlotte would not be lying alone and friendless.

Donal had left his Rosie to lie alone. 'The first to lie in this newly consecrated ground' the Constable and dignitaries had said at the cemetery's opening ceremony. They had said it as if by way of consolation but he had not been comforted to think that she, who had been so full of joy so as to be always found amongst the company of friends, was lying alone, albeit for a short time. Yet even as the graves surrounding her were soon taken his irrational grieving mind was haunted by the fact that they had been strangers to her. The thought had been one of many that had driven him to drink.

However, the night that his mother had died he had a dream where she had told him she had not gone to hell for not taking the time to listen to the scriptures, as one of the women visitors from the Protestant Bible Society had once predicted, but was living in God's glorious heaven. His Da was with her, his Rosie too, and it would not be long before his sister joined them. 'Look to our Colm, he will need you,' he heard her say just before he awoke.

He had thought it was another drunken imagining until his

mother's prophecy of his sister's death came true. From that moment he had not touched another drop of drink for suddenly he knew that the immortal life the Priest talked about was true. Rosie was no longer alone. Four members of his family were there with her in heaven and soon they would all hold their arms out to welcome Charlotte who was surely destined to spend eternity at Colm's side. He wondered whether he should voice his comforting belief to her father and brother but decided against it.

Within days of Charlotte's funeral Nathaniel fell ill with a severe chill which, with Doctor Lamont having departed for a holiday in Brittany where he had been born and brought up, necessitated in further visits from the 'not so fierce, Doctor Pierce' as Julia came to call him. She much preferred him to Doctor Lamont, she confided to her mother as they both sat by the fire in the family drawing room, because he told her he did not believe in using leeches. And besides he talked to her as if she was a grown up and she liked that. When he had found her alone and crying after being told that Lottie had died he had explained that God would not have taken her from her loving family without a lot of thought. But his need of Angels to welcome souls into heaven was as great as his need to have some people and especially good little girls on the earth below. So it was quite a problem for God to decide who to leave and who to take. 'But I will miss her so!' she had cried. 'But you can wave to your sister every starry night, did you not know?' He had asked. She had shaken her head and he had gone on to tell her that stars were the heavenly windows through which the angels looked down on their loved ones on earth. So whenever she saw a star in the night sky she could suppose that Lottie was looking down on her and give her a wave.

"I must admit I had not thought to remind you of that," Anne said, grateful to the doctor whilst at the same time feeling guilty that she had not given a thought to how much the child had been grieving.

He liked to talk to Harriet too she could tell, the child went on, but then with them being both grown up she supposed they had lots to talk about anyway. Her mother agreed before telling her to get back to quietly reading the book lying neglected in her lap whilst she went to see her poor papa.

16

Anne was very worried about Nathaniel. The men had begun calling at the house asking for further orders but Anne could not rouse him into giving them his attention. "On the morrow," is all he would say at her gentle probing but on the morrow his reply was always the same. Even when the gastric fever had laid him low he had given Charlotte instructions for the men to carry out, had told her where he kept the key to the money draw and how much wages were to be paid to each man. But this malaise was completely new and was worrying enough for Anne to forget her grief in concern for him and how the work was going without either him or Colm in attendance.

Eventually she took it into her own head to seek out Donal. Nathaniel had often spoken of how reliable Colm's older brother had been before he had taken to drink but he had been sober for some months now. Besides she had no one else to ask. Knowing he would understand she told him of Nathaniel's malaise and asked him if he was capable of taking on the position of overseer until Nathaniel was better.

Donal's eyes lit up with gratitude. Doubting his intention to stay sober other employers had turned him away time and time again. The only occasional work he had been able to get was helping out Grimes the undertaker, and that had only been when the man's other assistant had been too drunk to turn up for work.

Donal was in fact rich, or would be if he could raise enough money to pay the lawyer who was dealing with the will Colm had written after he had bought the land at Town Mills on which he had been building his grand house. For after first mentioning his wish to leave the property to his mother he asked that, should she precede him it go to Donal. Donal loathed the idea of having further dealings with the supercilious lawyer dealing with the official sounding probate but he had no choice. Now, with this chance of permanent work, he was sure that he would be able to prove his worth again to Mr Westaway; he would be able to save some money, and money had the habit of changing the look on lawyers' faces.

Colm had told him of the works involved, he informed Anne, and though he didn't have the craftsmanship of his younger brother he was once known as a reliable grafter and would prove so again with this chance to work. The two sites being developed on at the moment were undermanned, she told him, and with no one to look after the yard she suspected it would not be long before the wheezes began. Donal said he would need the plans of both sites but would employ the workers where the job was still within his capabilities to oversee. Then he would go to the yard and take a note of the stock before returning to her with a list of what might need ordering.

"There will be no need to do that Donal," she said and, trusting in Nathaniel's earlier good opinion of the man went on, "If you consider goods need ordering you just make a list and take it down to Jem at the warehouse on the quay and if he has not got the items there then just tell him to order them on my word."

For Anne to be involved in Nathaniel's business was an extra-ordinary change of events but one into which Anne threw herself with great intent. Indeed she was grateful to find something that would occupy her mind and keep her from falling into the same abyss of depression as Nathaniel. He was no longer crying openly, an act which was apt to set them all off, and she put this down to her decision to rid the house of all that would remind him, and them all, of their beautiful Lottie. However, whereas this had helped ease the grief of the girls and herself to some extent Nathaniel had become heavily despondent. She knew how he felt, recognised it as the same blackness that had claimed her after baby William's death and up to the time of Julia's birth, but she was afraid to talk to him about it. In doing so she might have joined him on that road to despair and it was a murky journey that she never wanted to travel again.

Donal used one of the horses and carts to reach the sites for the two under Nathaniel's construction at the time were as far in distance as in style from each other. One large site, on the hill above Town Mills, was to hold two very elegant detached houses over which Colm had had sole responsibility. More and more rich English families were arriving to settle in the island and demanding houses that gave them a status they had hitherto only aspired to. In realising this Nathaniel had given the talented Colm the opportunity of designing and overlooking this new project. However only one of the planned two houses had been started by the time of his death, and then only with the foundations and three rows of bricks to the outer walls laid. Donal found the men at the far end of the site playing 'Toss the Shoe' and, after informing them of his new position, he helped them to load all the tools on the cart before driving men and equipment down into town.

The second site was in the heart of town in a street, which was yet to be officially named but known locally as 'La Petit Rue Derrière'. There Nathaniel was building a long row of two-storey cottages in the frontage to three of which he had installed large windows so that they might be leased or bought as shops. Here again he found the men idling so he set all but two of the men to work, taking the duo back to the yard for supplies. He felt unable to spare any of them to look after the yard however.

"Besides ma-am," he began to confide to Anne when, later that evening, he called at the house to inform her of his progress. "None of us had the likin' for learnin' as our Colm did, or the quickness with numbers that old Thomas had, so we wouldn't be too good with the countin' and such."

"Can you just make sure that the wheezes are kept down Donal, at least for the time being?"

"Yes I can do that Ma-am. If I keeps the yard locked and only open up meself when we needs goods then nothing should go astray."

Still Donal could not be in two places at once. He was needed on the site for the best part of each day, both overseeing the work and passing on his knowledge as the most experienced mason.

Anne tried to talk to Nathaniel about it but all she ever heard from him was the now familiar phrase, 'on the morrow.' In desperation she had taken to talking to Harriet and it was Harriet who came up with the solution that she should look after the yard.

"Oh! Hattie! Your Papa would not be at all happy with the notion that one of his daughter's is working!" Anne said immediately.

"If he was in his right mind he would not be at all happy with the notion that you are, to all intents and purposes, running the business Mama! So, less said, soonest mended," Harriet retorted. "Now as to the workings of the yard I may not be able to lift and carry. We would need to employ a boy for that, but I am quite capable of keeping a ledger and I would defy any of the men to try and pull a wheeze on me!"

Yes, Anne had to admit. None of the men would dare to try and pull a wheeze over Harriet, any who did would get very short shrift.

However the task of looking after her father's building yard was more difficult than the studious Harriet had ever imagined. Everything was so alien to her that the loss of pride in having to consult Donal on so many things caused her to be even more abrasive that ever. Still, to her credit she was quick to learn and never needed to be told anything more than once and for all her no-nonsense attitude every man she dealt with had to grudgingly admit that, for a woman, 'there's no flies on 'er!'

Anne was beginning to lose patience with Nathaniel for try as she might she could not lift him from his depression. Even the medicinal drafts prescribed by Doctor Pierce were not having the effect of raising his spirits. 'Have I not lost the same as you?' she wanted to rail at him when he was at his most trying. 'Do you not think I fail to suffer also?' But she did not, for deep inside, her own crevice of loss was still raw and she was loath to disturb the invisible scab, which was beginning to heal the painful wound of grief. Besides, he was still continually hacking.

Doctor William Pierce was not exactly losing patience with Nathaniel but he was spending a lot of time thinking about him. He had been helpless to prevent the death of the man's beloved daughter, who he was sure had simply lost the will to live, and now he was in danger of losing him to the same cause and that of unreleased grief. Knowing his fellow physicians would pooh-pooh the idea he would never voice his earlier suspicions that the girl had not wanted to recover, that she had died of a broken heart. However, after talking to Lamont soon after her death he was certain of it.

After commenting derisively on the family's Christian attitude towards the peasant classes Lamont had gone on to relate the events of the afternoon he had come upon the girl at the house in Hue Street. He added slyly that he suspected that there was more to the girl being there than her excuse to tend the sick bed. Yet his lips were sealed, he assured the younger man. Aw! But what talk there would have been had certain people become aware of what was going on between that upstart of a peasant and Miss Charlotte Westaway! Not that she had been brought up as anything more than a daughter of a tradesman but there were tradesmen and tradesmen and Westaway was one of the most respected and a devout Protestant to boot whereas the O'Reillys were… Ah! but we physicians must keep our observances to ourselves, must we not, he had said before turning away, by which action he failed to notice the look of contempt that flashed across the face of his listener.

William Pierce did not like Lamont, nor did he share his views on the Westaways' generosity of heart. In fact he considered Lamont to be as pretentious a vulgarian as he had ever met whereas the more he saw and heard of the Westaway family the more he admired and respected them. His good and dear Amelia would like them too of that he was sure. She had been away in Africa these last three months, visiting with her parents who were missionaries, and he missed her sorely. It would be another half year before she returned and they could be married to which end he counted the hours.

"Your husband is still not eating?" he asked Anne after making a visit to see his patient two days later.

"So little it hardly counts against the hearty appetite he once had, but then he has very little rest from the hacking, despite the new linctus you prescribed."

He thought for a minute before asking, "Tell me, do you keep the fire going all day and night?" She said yes of course. "Then I would suggest that you see that it is bedded down during the day and that, when the weather is dry, you see that a window in the sickroom is opened a little at the top to let in the fresh air."

She said she would but added, "I am so worried about him Doctor, he hardly speaks. I am worried that he is acting the same way as our…our darling Lottie before…," a sob suddenly stopping her ability to continue.

"There now, don't distress yourself. Tell me, has your husband spoken of your daughter's loss?"

"Not since he became ill, but then we have not wanted to encourage it for fear of making him worse."

"Well, once he begins to recover I would advise you to let him mourn openly. I am a great believer that grief should be expelled from the body and that weeping for the dead should not be the sole prerogative of females. In the meantime I shall get the apothecary to mix up a new compound of herbs which I trust will help. "

Whether it was the new compound of herbs or whether it was the improvement in his chest Anne was never sure but she was pleased to find Nathaniel standing up and gazing out of the window when she returned to their room one morning a week or so later.

He turned and stretched out his hand. "It has been snowing Anne. Come, see how beautiful the garden looks dressed in white."

"Yes, dearest, it is, " she agreed, slipping a rug around his shoulders.

"It reminds me of the last time I was recovering from a chill on the chest, it was a Christmas time. We bought John a new sled and took the children out so they could use it, do you remember dearest?"

"Yes, I remember Natty, it was the Christmas after Julia was born."

"I confess I had momentarily forgotten that fact. It was with her being too young to be taken out I suppose. Oh! But I could never forget how crisp the air was that day! Colm was with us, do you remember? He used my old sled. What a joy it was to see our little family having so much fun. Our little family..."

He began to sob then and she held him as gradually her tears too fell and mingled with his.

17

THE FOLLOWING WEEKS were very difficult ones for all the family, but particularly Nathaniel who, in coming to accept the loss of one of his beloved daughters, also had to adjust to being without two of his most loyal hands at work. Thomas's death had caused him to feel empty enough but, without Colm's dependability and willing spirit to lighten his working day, he began to see all the effort he put in as meaningless.

At the same time, whilst he had been both surprised and grateful for both Anne and Harriet's intervention during his illness, he saw it as interference once he was back at the helm. He took an unfair dislike to the 12 year-old boy Jonas Browne that Harriet had employed to help her in the yard, comparing what he saw as laziness to Colm's eagerness at that age. Harriet championed the boy however and standing up to her father stated that if he had been at the yard throughout the working day as she had he would have arrived at a better opinion. Nathaniel was shocked at her outburst and retaliated by telling her that she was getting above herself and that he would not have his authority usurped in this way. It was time her work at the yard was terminated, he went on to declare, in which case the boy was too young to run the yard alone so would be sacked. Harriet said she was sorry that her help had not been appreciated but she could not consider the subject closed. Whilst she had to agree the boy was too young to run the yard alone he nevertheless had the making of a sturdy hod carrier and sacking him, as he was suggesting, would be a grave mistake. Nathaniel said grave mistake or nay he would only give the lad one month to prove his worth as a hod carrier and duly put him to work with Donal.

It was some months before Nathaniel admitted the employing of Donal again had been a good move on Anne's part but when he did so it was with good grace. Donal was an excellent mason and, now certainly off the drink, was proving to be a reliable hand once more. Jonas Browne was turning out to be a hard worker too but Nathaniel was never to reveal this admission to Harriet though he grudgingly admitted that she had done a good job as keeper of the yard. He was adamant however that she should not continue and, unable to find suitable man to take her place, decided to carry on as he had done after Thomas was taken ill by opening the yard himself as and when necessary. This of course would have been far from satisfactory if it had not been for Donal being able to oversee the site in his absence.

The work on the row of cottages in La Petit Rue Derrière was progressing well but even so Nathaniel's mood did not improve. When he continued to be testy with his family Anne took the unusual step of insisting they took a holiday and in the late spring of that year, 1833, they, along with Harriet and Julia, endured a rough sea passage to Weymouth at the start of a ten-day holiday. At first Anne had spoken of a possible visit to London but friends who had recently returned told of a city shrouded in fog, a fog so thick that a person could not see their hand in front of their face. 'That sort of air would not be good for Nathaniel's chest surely?' they intimated. 'And though it might be clear at the time of their visit the air was just as likely to thicken again because it didn't have the sea winds that continually swept the island coast to clear it. Besides hadn't they heard of the outbreak of cholera there? Aw! But then, what place could ever escape that scourge once it was set free?' Eventually the family decided to travel about the South of England, staying at various small hotels and inns and of course calling in on Nathaniel's relatives in Devon.

It was on their return to the island that the aged and weary Mrs Kilshaw asked to be relieved of her post so that she could go and live quietly with her younger and widowed sister in Saint Laurent. Her temperament had mellowed considerably over the years and the family had become quite fond of her. But her legs were badly swollen from years of continual standing on the stone kitchen floor and though she had not complained they felt it was a kindness to let her go. They would visit her, they promised, and this one or other of them did with unfailing regularity, with laden baskets, until she died peacefully twelve months later.

A dour woman, of Scottish birth and Presbyterian religion, replaced her. She was only with them six months before she gave notice to leave and they employed a very pleasant widow who had been recommended by the minister of the Wesleyan Chapel.

Bertha Dutot had been just sixteen when she married Samuel and by the time she was twenty-two she had given birth to five children. She, with the children at close hand, had been a familiar sight around the streets of the town, and at the tradesmen's entrances of the large houses as she plied the fresh fish caught earlier each morning by Samuel. They were a happy, hard working family who, for some years, regularly attended chapel together until the eldest boy Jack enlisted in the Militia and one by one the four girls were taken into service.

Just a month after the youngest had started work Samuel was drowned when his fishing boat floundered off Les Ecréhous and, despite her knowledge of the industry and known capacity for hard work, Bertha was unable to find a fishmonger either willing or able to employ her. And being uneducated and unskilled for any other work she soon found herself without the means to pay the rent on the little cottage the family had occupied behind the boat-building yard on the shore at La Collette. She confided her plight to the minister when he happened to visit, saying she feared that there was nothing left for her but the workhouse. He told her to have faith and led her in a prayer of deliverance from her troubles before paying a very fortuitous visit to Anne to discuss the setting up of a fund for a new church organ.

Bertha could hardly believe her ears at being offered the post of housekeeper to the Westaways. She had never had much to do with them but in attending the same church had learnt they were a good, Christian family whose head was not only a tireless builder of houses but as generous to the needy with his money as his womenfolk were with their time.

"But I've never done work like that, Madam," she admitted honestly.

"Neither had I," Anne began to admit. Then, realising that she was about to reveal a part of her past that she preferred to keep hidden, continued quickly with, "You have managed a home and brought up a family of five children whilst you went about your husband's business of selling fish, have you not?" And when Bertha nodded said, "Well then, once you have acquainted yourself with the running of the house, and what is expected of the two girls, the kitchen maid and the house maid, you should have little difficulty."

Well, she knew what the girls' duties should be, she told Anne, for her four girls were in service in the big houses and never stopped talking about what they had to do when they came home on their monthly day of rest. Then suddenly she looked very sad and Anne, who had been watching her, asked if she was all right.

"Oh! Yes, Madam, it's just, well I was just thinking when I live in 'ere, as is expected, the children won't be able to visit me on their monthly free day like they does. Aw! But I mustn't be so ungrateful eh? After all they wouldn't be visiting me down the workhouse now, would they?"

Anne was at first puzzled at the mention of a workhouse until she realised that Bertha was referring to the part of the hospital which housed the vagrants and people with no home or money. The inmates that were able were encouraged to work each day for their keep and in England such places were referred to as workhouses so she supposed the description held firm to what was known locally as the 'Poor Ward'. Still, the family had obviously been close and it would be a great shame if they were unable to call on their mother during their free day.

"I would not look too favourably at them walking through the house to your room Mrs Dutot but I would have no objection to them visiting you in the kitchen," she offered generously.

"Oh no! 'Course not Maam, I mean to say I wouldn't let them come up to my room, no I wouldn't. 'Tis grateful I am that you'll let them visit me in the kitchen. They won't be a nuisance, you've my word on that."

"No, I am sure they will not be, Mrs Dutot," Anne replied.

And they never were. In fact the occasional presence of one or more of the Dutot offspring helped to lift the despondent atmosphere of the house and yet, whilst during that time it often seemed as if a second, albeit subservient, family had joined the household, it was never intrusive. Though they might hear soft laughter and talk coming up the passage during those hours the Westaways never felt excluded in the naturally warm but respectful welcome that would follow should they happen to enter the kitchen. Jack and his sisters seemed inordinately happy to help out with outstanding chores during their visits too, as Nathaniel realised when he found the young man cleaning out the stables one day. But then she would not be surprised to find one or other of the girls peeling the vegetables or hanging out the washing either, Anne commented when he told her. The Dutots were an extraordinary family.

The two maids, Liza and Mary, very different characters to Adèle and Lizzie whom they had replaced some years before, had not particularly enjoyed working under Mrs Kilshaw's keen and critical eyes. But workshy as they were they swore they would have trebled their efforts and so gained her hard-earned approval had she returned to oust the dour, parsimonious Scot that replaced her. Yet, though Mrs Dutot turned out to be a real blessing compared to those first two housekeepers the maids soon learnt that the woman was an exacting taskmaster nevertheless. She was however fair and good-humoured and these two virtues ensured that they soon became willing workers under her regime.

Within this pleasant setting the Westaways gradually picked up the threads of their former lives once more. Much to Anne's relief, Nathaniel, his interest in buildings reawakened during the family's visit to Bath, where he had seen the most impressive crescents under construction, had returned to the island with renewed enthusiasm. However, unable to face working on the site above Town Mills for which he had given Colm full responsibility, he sold it to another thriving builder, before immediately looking around the open spaces of town for those large enough to hold long terraces or crescents. Nathaniel was gratified to find there was still plenty of land to choose from, land that was ripe for development into houses and businesses demanded by his fellow Englishmen and he was as keen as ever to satisfy their needs.

Anne and Harriet, on the other hand, having experienced the busy days of being involved with the firm during Nathaniel's indisposition, would have become bored with their reclaimed but mundane existence had it not been for the chapel's new undertaking of feeding the poor. They would be following in the footsteps of Jesus, the minister informed the small group of women volunteers at the initial meeting. Each Sunday they would be given a Bible text, then on the allotted day of the following week they were to visit the named family at the address he would also give them. The dish should not be rich but either a plain stew or thick broth, he went on to instruct them, and should not be served until the Bible text had been read out aloud followed by the Lord's Prayer.

It was with great fervour that mother and daughter, Anne laden with a steaming tureen of vegetable potage and Harriet carrying a Bible and basket of bread, made their way across the town on that first day. They were heading for the narrow lanes behind the Wesleyan Chapel where, having asked the way several times, they were finally directed to a tumbledown shack. Two small, grubby looking urchins, so neglected in appearance that it was impossible to say whether they were boy or girl, stared at them from the open doorway as they approached.

"Is your mama...?" Anne began.

But before she could finish a woman pushed the children out of the way and thrusting herself forward demanded, "Wot you want 'ere then?"

'I was disappointed and shocked at her attitude,' she told Nathaniel later that evening. 'But I was quite unprepared for the belligerence of her rough looking husband who we met when we followed her into the shack where we came upon three more little mites. I introduced myself and Harriet as the minister had told us to do and the man was looking forward to his meal I could tell, but when I said we must give thanks to the Lord first, he demanded to know what for? What had the good Lord done for him but seen him without hope of work, or a decent home, with five ever hungry and ailing children and a wife who was good for nothing? Then he said, he said...Oh! It really does not matter...'

Nathaniel, who on hearing this was becoming increasingly indignant on behalf of both his wife and daughter, insisted she continue.

'He said...he said...who did we English think we were anyway? Treating the likes of him like ignorant peasants, bringing over our own workers or giving preference to the Irish.... Oh! He ranted on and on about all the ills of the island and I regret to say I found myself getting angry in return. I do not know what came over me but I found myself shouting back at him in patois and telling him that I could very well have been in the same position only I had been very fortunate. I had married a good man who, though he was English, showed me more kindness in the first week that we met than all my relatives throughout my life and to this date. I had only wanted to share my good fortune, I went on, but if that was the way he felt I would take the soup where it would be better received!

I do not know who was more surprised at my outburst, Harriet, the woman and children, the man or me, but it seemed to take the wind completely out of his sails. He was most repentant from that moment on, listening attentively to the lesson, which was the first book of Chronicles, chapter 16 and verses 8 to 36, by the way.

But oh! Natty taking a tureen of potage, into such poor homes, was too pretentious of us! I was telling Harriet that we must carry the stew in a jug in future and take some small pewter tankards with us too, for others might be like that poor family who had no utensils and had to sip from the ladle in turn.

Did she really want to continue to make these visits after such a baptism of fire, he asked. What if she met such ingratitude from others?

Oh! But she was sure she would not she replied, with more of an outward show of confidence than she actually felt inside. Yet though such a beginning might well have deterred less intrepid women from continuing with charitable works, Anne and Harriet were to carry out these kind and evangelical acts not once but twice a week for the next five years or so.

John was happier than he had ever been in his life, he told Anne Guillet on their wedding day at the end of October 1833. It was a lovely wedding. Anne Guillet had worn a white dress with a shawl of gossamer lace across her shoulders and gathered at her breast with a small nosegay. A second identical nosegay, tied to the wrist of her left hand as if to draw attention to the bright gold band on her third finger, fuelled the delight of Julia who thought it was a very pretty idea and one that she would certainly copy on her wedding day. John had looked even more handsome than usual in a new black outfit, a shining gold watch chain proudly draped across his grey waistcoat.

The gift of the watch and chain from his parents had been his mother's idea, a gift to both signify the importance of the day and to hopefully soften the memory of the harsh words uttered when John insisted on going ahead with the wedding. For Nathaniel had adamantly argued that he should not do so as it was too soon after his sister's death but, though she had not done so in front of John, Anne had stood up for their son. She reminded Nathaniel that the betrothal party had been cancelled because of the cholera outbreak and that the house in Bond Street had been ready, waiting for the young couple to move in, for some months past.

'Besides it is well time,' she had told him gently. 'John needs something that we as a family have failed to provide. I fear he has never been very happy...'

'What nonsense!' Nathaniel retorted, still brooding over what he saw was the precipitation of the wedding date. 'Really Anne, where is your sense on the matter? John has had more provided in his short life than ever I or my parents and grandparents before me so how could you make such a claim!'

And although she said no more on the subject Anne knew she was right. John had not been content for some time and she felt guilty that she had not realised it earlier. For things had not been right with him, she knew that now, but the knowledge had been slow, so slow, in coming.

It was the upset over the betrothal invitations and the later puzzling why John had not wanted Colm to attend that first made her question the reasoning behind it. Afterwards, on going over and over the incident in her mind, she became convinced that John was suffering from jealousy. Yet how could that be? How could a young man who has everything be envious of one whose life began so piteously? Then she suddenly thought of the many times she and Nathaniel had often boasted of Colm's achievements, all quite innocent remarks but obviously disturbing to John who on hearing them must have thought he took second place in their pride, when of course that was never so in reality. For John was their son who, though he had not achieved all that they would have hoped, was still a precious part of their family. Whilst they all held a great affection for Colm he could never be anything more to them than one of Nathaniel's workers. John had been correct when he told Charlotte so, during another incident which left an indelible memory on her mind but for quite a different reason.

'Colm is dead and you are alive Lottie dear,' she had overheard him say during one of his visits to his sick sister. 'Any union between the two of you would have been doomed even if he had lived. For you know in your heart that neither Papa nor Mama would have sanctioned it, with him being a Catholic. Forget about him and live for us, please Lottie. We love you dearly, I love you dearly, we all do.'

She had been outside in the corridor at the time and his words had made her rush into the empty drawing room nearby. Yet it was not the revelation that it had been Charlotte and not Harriet that he had been referring to when suggesting the romance with Colm which made her suddenly want to weep, but that she had never heard him speak so endearingly to any of his sisters before. 'Live for us, please Lottie, he had begged softly. 'We love you dearly, I love you dearly, we all do...'

A large party of relatives and friends joined John and his bride for the wedding breakfast and much singing and jollity filled the air. Anne was so happy for him and as she looked around the familiar faces she counted many parents amongst them who had once looked on John favourably, many hopeful daughters too but she could not fault his choice in the orphan Anne Guillet.

Anne Guillet could not remember much about her parents. Her father had died a year before her mother, leaving Anne and her nine assorted brothers and sisters to be separated and brought up by different guardians with Anne and three of her sisters being cared for by a loving, though strict, aunt. The sisters had been well trained in all aspects of household management and this quality, added to the fact that Anne Guillet was a very caring, intelligent and affectionate young woman with a docile nature, made her the perfect match for John Nathaniel. His mother caught up with them both as they made to leave the wedding party and head for the horse and trap, which was to take them down to the quay where they would board the steamer for France, and hugged them both.

"Please be happy my son," she had whispered in his ear.

"I will Mama," he promised, returning her hug with unexpected warmth.

"Take care of him daughter," she said to Anne but her words were lost as both Julia and Harriet rushed between them to hug their new sister.

"Bon voyage, notre belle soeur!" Julia cried.

"Oui, bon voyage notre belle soeur," Harriet echoed.

Then Nathaniel came forward to kiss his new daughter-in-law on each cheek and shake his son's hand.

"May God bless you both, " he said stiffly.

"Thank you Papa," John said quickly before grabbing his young bride's hand and rushing away. And everyone waved until the horse and trap turned the corner and was lost from view.

John Nathaniel Junior arrived in the world two years later, a chubby infant with a lusty pair of lungs which, when used, defied all attempts to be ignored. Julia, rushing around to her brother's home in Bond Street at every opportunity, was found to be a great distraction at those times as she was also in helping her sister-in-law to either dress him in his day gowns or take him for walks in his perambulator. He was two years old and beginning to teeter precariously about when Annie was born so Julia spent longer hours tending to him and even changing his swaddling rags.

It was after Annie was born that Nathaniel, who was building houses in the throughway that would be eventually named Belmont Road, decided to give John a house with an adjacent plot which was ideal for use as a coal yard. The young couple were delighted and named the detached house Surrey Lodge. In the eleven years that followed another eight children arrived to fill the rooms, two sets of twins Henrietta and Charles and Maria and Nathaniel then James, Alexander, Charlotte and Susan.

At first Nathaniel could not help but be envious of his son's good fortune in producing such a large family but as the years passed he found that he did not have the patience to cope with them all together. Because of this visits from the young family, which had begun in quite a frequent manner, gradually became less as both his and Anne's demand that the children 'should be seen but never heard unless spoken to' was strictly enforced. Perversely this saddened both grandparents.

The decision to move from the home in Don Street was not an easy one. Nathaniel had built it to celebrate his marriage to his beloved Anne and they had gone on to spend nearly forty years under its stout roof. Of their five children born there only Harriet and Julia remained to share it. Neither had married so neither had experience of any other home, nor could they envisage another that would enfold them with such a cocoon of familiarity, where memories echoed from every creaking floorboard or chip in the furniture. They were happy there but yet they had to agree with their father. The area outside the house had changed, and not for the better.

When Nathaniel originally built the house it had been the only one in the street but over the latter years others had been erected in the back gardens of the businesses and shops in Halkett Place. This change might not have unsettled the family had the houses laid back with the gardens fronting them but to their disquiet the row of terraced houses not only lined the street but were built with windows looking directly across onto them.

This all coincided with the added construction at the lower end of Don Street, which included some very imposing buildings and shops upon the gardens of what was once Government House. This left

Nathaniel's untidy storage yard, wooden planks and rods of steel overhanging the walls, to stand out unattractively against them. The sight of the rot nibbling its destructive way across the bottom of the old wide gate at the entrance also displeased him.

'Replacing the gate would be a simple task but the whole thing looks such an eyesore amongst the rest of the street,' he complained to Anne. 'Yet I am not really sure how I can disguise it or even if I want to keep the yard going.'

It was the first time he had voiced the possibility of finally dissolving the works and though she worried how he might fill his days if he was to be without the business, Anne did not discourage him. This relinquishing of his life's work had taken him a long time in any case with the sale of the brickyard being the beginning. He had not been sorry to sell it. Ready formed bricks had become cheaper to buy but also, it must be said, the giving up of responsibility for those wretched workers had been more of a relief to Nathaniel than regret.

Then, when the completed New Harbour claimed most of the cargo shipping, he found it just as convenient to have his goods taken directly to the yard as to the store on Le Quai des Marchands, so he sold that building too. The merchant who bought it was so keen to turn it into a home that he surprised Nathaniel by not haggling over the price, as was the custom.

But to give up the yard, which had become not only the storing place of all the equipment but also the morning and evening assembly point for Nathaniel and his men, was to give up the heart of the business itself. And therein lay the crux of a matter that consumed Nathaniel for many years before he finally made up his mind to retire. Building houses had been his life's work, he had been responsible for so many about the town and country he had lost count. What would he do without work to fill his hours? he frequently asked himself. How would his men manage? Would they find it easy to find other employers?

However his concern for the welfare of his workers lessened somewhat after the disturbing 'bread riots'. That event, where his own men had left the site, land that he had bought so that they might be kept in work when others were unemployed, to join the mutinous rampaging through town as a protest against the States putting up the price of bread, grieved him. He took it as a personal sleight especially as he had been one of the employers who had spoken up on their behalf, arguing vehemently against the State's discontinuance of the reduced rate of one shilling for a four pound loaf, the mainstay of diet for the poor.

As fate often will, it presented a series of events that combined to make both the thoughts of retirement and moving away from Don Street more appealing. The family's sleep began to be occasionally disturbed by youths devilishly rapping on the lower wooden shutters of the house, an aggravation that increased as time went on. This was compounded later by a spate of marauding thievery that caused him to protect his property by topping the walls of his garden and works yard with fragments of glass and metal spikes. The town was becoming a far too unpleasant place in which to live, he told Anne. It was time they moved away.

Still he delayed, fascinated by Constable Pierre Le Sueur's introduction of sewers and drains throughout the town until, to the family's great shock and distress, the sudden and brutal death of Centenier George Le Cronier. When this friend and honorary policeman was stabbed in the course of his duties the talk of a change in residence became more urgent.

In the first instance of Nathaniel suggesting the idea Anne would have chosen to have him build a house apart, a grand house amid its own grounds, but he refused. Though a man of considerable wealth he did not approve of ostentation. He had a fancy he told her, to occupy one of the new houses in the terrace he was building near Le Coie, at the foot of the hill to St. Saviours.

For some years now Harriet and Julia had shown a great interest in their father's business and had, with his full participation and agreement, bought the land on which the terrace was being built and had also been invited to come up with certain suggestions as to the inner design.

On completion, united by porches on the ground floor, each house was of Georgian tradition and built with three stories over a basement. With his penchant for light and air Nathaniel had designed them all to have twenty-six windows apiece and while each basement had two unsheltered casements back and front, all the upper windows boasted shutters of dark Venetian wood, which contrasted agreeably against the light stuccoed finish of each house.

The windows at the rear overlooked the Spring Fields, a large field known for its abundance of wild flora during the first season of each year and also the spring that wound its way past whilst journeying across from the nearby valley through town to the sea. From the front however, the main road out of town into the Parish of St. Saviours might have dominated the view had not Nathaniel given the original site plan a great deal of thought.

Placing the houses in a straight line he designed the pavement at their front to be flagged into an arc of an outer third to a large circle, so that the hogged carriage drive curved at each end as it ran to meet the road. Then finally, at the centre of this arc, enclosed by a two-foot high granite wall topped with iron railings, he provided a small communal garden for the occupants to enjoy.

Yet though he explained this to Anne, all the while abiding excited interjections from either Harriet or Julia, she was not pleased with the idea of moving there.

'A teraced house?' she had repeated appalled. 'Do not even consider the thought, I beg you. Why it would be as if we had neighbours living permanently in the next room!'

But the idea began to appeal to them more and more. As a consideration to Anne however Nathaniel redesigned the placing of the houses so that numbers One, which he planned they should inhabit, and number Six, were to be detached whilst numbers Two and Three were to be joined as were Four and Five. Anne was at once placated, even more so once she had seen his plans for the carriage drive and garden and the move went ahead without any problems. Indeed they had all settled in very happily.

18

Friday 23rd January 1852

NATHANIEL REMAINED on the doorstep until the maid closed the front door behind him. The biting east wind of the previous morning, which had then greeted him viciously with sharp icy nips to the exposed flesh of his face, had finally lost its teeth. The new day had replaced it with air that was pleasantly invigorating and Nathaniel drew this freshness into his lungs, filling them to capacity before slowly exhaling.

'What a pleasant constitutional I shall have today,' he thought contentedly as, gripping his silver-topped cane between his knees, he used his leather gloves to flick some dust from the top hat he held in his hand. 'Why, I might even walk as far as Mount Pleasant and cast an eye over the building of the new college.'

Placing his hat on his head he patted it down firmly and fastened the lower button of his voluminous cape before slowly pulling on his gloves, all the while listening to the melodious voice of one of the housemaids coming from the basement kitchen.

' 'Tis indeed such a day to sing one's favourite hymn, young Miss, and for two stout pins I would join you,' he muttered quietly, 'if my earlier attempts to praise God melodiously had not been renowned for being the cause of many a Sunday earache.' He smiled as he remembered the discreet way Anne put her hand to her ears, pretending to push stray hair under her bonnet; the crease that began to furrow Julia's brow; the gradual turning of heads in his direction. Only Harriet, amongst the whole congregation, seemed unmoved throughout his heartfelt renderings, but then Harriet too was deaf to the true tones of music.

Crossing the driveway he opened a small gate that was one of two entrances to the communal garden and made his way to a nearby stone seat. Odd droplets of dew glistened on the top of the long narrow slab so, reaching down, Nathaniel drew out a square of wood from its hiding place underneath and, placing it on the bench, promptly sat on it.

Visiting the garden before his morning stroll into town had become almost a daily ritual in Nathaniel's now leisurely life. He had disposed of the business some two years past and, though there were times in the latter part of each day when he found time hung about making him feel like a lost soul, these moments were different. These moments were his time of quiet reflection, of observing nature, of listening to the bird song. Things he had rarely had time for during his working life.

Most of the shrubs were sorry looking now but soon new shoots and buds would be making their appearance, with the promise of their individual and radiantly coloured blooms to come. In the spring the birds would begin building their nests and he determined that this year he would watch their comings and goings so that he would know where the nests were. If they returned to the mulberry bush, where he had found an empty nest one day last summer, he would be able to keep a discreet eye on the chicks as they grew. He was looking forward to that, and seeing the garden come into bloom. That was something he took for granted when they lived in Don Street. Throughout all the years they had lived there he had hardly acknowledged the garden's existence.

The clanging sound of a pail being placed on the ground, followed by the gentle scrubbing of bristle on cement told Nathaniel that one of his neighbour's maids had begun the cleaning of the outside steps and it was time for him to begin his walk. So he stood up and replaced the wooden cushion beneath the bench before retracing his steps back through the gate.

The young girl, who was scrubbing the front step of Number 3, suddenly left her brush skidding in the suds whilst she brought herself to her feet to bob a curtsey before sweeping away the errant ripples that flowed across Nathaniel's path. Finding the sight amusing, he grinned widely as he bid her 'good day' and was rewarded with a shy smile in return.

'She looks so young,' he thought strolling slowly passed, 'just a child who could not be much more in years than young James who will soon be celebrating his eighth birthday. Yet 'tis difficult to tell the age for the poor make short and frail statures. Dear, dear! With little or no education, what will become of her?'

'You cannot be a worrying for all the world's children!' Anne reminded him more than once, especially after she had overheard his instruction that books be delivered anonymously to the Ragged School, and she was right of course. 'Perhaps John's generation will somehow bring about an end to poverty where parents have no choice but to ignore the law on compulsory education in sending their children to work,' she had suggested hopefully but they both knew it was wishful thinking. Very few able men of John's generation seemed to consider anyone but their own selves.

"John!" Nathaniel was not aware that he had actually uttered his only son's name aloud until, from the corner of his eye he saw the maid start up suddenly. Embarrassed, he quickened his pace a little. He had been talking to himself! Perhaps John was right after all, perhaps he was becoming senile.

'You becoming senile my dearest?' Anne had scoffed gently after he had once asked if she had noticed any slowing of his mind since his retirement from daily work. 'Why there are few brains yet that can match yours when it comes to business! Whatever or whoever put that notion into your head?' But he had not told her. To do so would have led to his admission that John's constant need to dominate every decision he had made of late was gradually undermining his confidence. Whether it be about where to take a holiday, the services of which tailor to use or even which tenant to take in to any of his properties John had an opinion to exhort on the subject. It was as if his son considered that retirement had softened his brain somewhat and taken away his ability to make decisions.

"Whoa there!"

Nathaniel jumped visibly, his heart beginning to thud erratically, as a horse was reined to a stop at his side.

The Very Reverend William Corbet Le Breton, Dean of Jersey and Rector of St. Saviour's, was most apologetic. "Pardon me for startling you sir, but in truth I thought you had heard my approach. I have often said that these carriages should have a bell as do the fire carts so that we could warn pedestrians."

" 'Tis I at fault Dean," Nathaniel replied politely. "I had heard your carriage but took it that you were visiting one of the houses. I did not want to turn around for fear of appearing over-inquisitive. Still no harm done. You were not, after all, driving on the pavement!"

William Le Breton laughed. "No, I am not that inconsiderate a driver though I fear I did quicken the horse's pace when I saw you leaving as I entered the crescent."

Though his hair was prematurely white and receding from the brow, the Dean was still a very handsome man for his 37 years. 'It is no wonder that the number of females amongst your congregation is increasing,' Nathaniel thought as he looked directly into the blue eyes that smiled down into his.

"You were about to call on me?" he asked, wondering suspiciously as to what the man was after. Already that week he had made donations to several worthy causes. He must watch his generosity, he told himself, or otherwise he would indeed become what Anne described as easy pickings.

"Yes, my dear Sir. I was just about to call at your house with this..." He handed over a white envelope. "It is an invitation for you and your wife and daughters to come to tea at the vicarage on Thursday of next week. My dear wife insisted that I drop the invitation in on my way through to the town and I, ever obedient both to the will of God...and my wife...!" He laughed again. It was a nice laugh. It made Nathaniel grin companionably. "Mind, I would be failing in my duty were I not to warn you that if the weather is inclement our youngest sons may be heard romping about the place that afternoon. I am afraid their noise can be a little disconcerting to visitors who are not used to the natural exuberance of children."

Dean Le Breton and his wife had five small sons. Nathaniel had seen them about as a family and looked forward to getting to know them better, the small boys especially. He looked back with great fondness to the time when his own children had been small and regretted the fact that John had not encouraged his children to be more generous with their visits.

"That would be very pleasant," he said, reaching inside his cape and tucking the envelope into the pocket of his coat. "And you have no need to worry that the noise of children would disturb us. We have a large brood of grandchildren whose racket *en masse* has been known to miraculously restore the hearing to those unfortunately deaf to lesser noise. However naturally I shall make enquiries of my wife and daughters first but I foresee that they should be only too delighted."

"Good! Good! We shall look forward to seeing you," the Dean said. "My wife has never forgotten the note of warm concern she received after her accident last month and looks forward to thanking you all again in person."

Nathaniel was puzzled at first by this last remark until he

remembered that in early December Madame Le Breton's carriage had collided with a van carrying furniture in Halkett Place. He had not known of the note but writing it would have been a natural response on Anne's part.

"I believe one of your young sons was also in the carriage at the time. I hope they have both fully recovered from the shock. 'Tis with thanks to Almighty God that the outcome was not much worse. Some of these van drivers should be curbed the way they race about the town and country!"

"Ah! 'Tis difficult to lay the blame when a woman holds the reins," the Dean said laughing, then becoming serious again he added, "but yes, we immediately gave thanks to Almighty God that it was no more serious."

Taking up the reins that had lain slack across his lap during the meeting, he said, "Well I must away. I am off to see how they are getting on with the new college. Several members of my congregation have already enrolled their sons for when it opens in the autumn and with five sons of my own to educate I too must look into all the new establishment offers."

'And as Dean of Jersey and head of the Clergy under which the poorly attended grammar schools are run you might well be wise to observe your rivals at first hand,' Nathaniel mused cynically before commenting aloud. "Then I may see you again for I too am making my way there this morning."

"Are you really my dear sir? Then you must let me offer you a ride."

"That is very kind of you," Nathaniel said, walking around the back of the carriage so that he could climb aboard. When he was seated alongside the Dean he asked, "Surely your eldest is already receiving education?"

"Both he and William our second. They are at St. Mannelier. Fine old establishment and a good starting post."

"Indeed," agreed Nathaniel quietly. "My son John attended there when he was a small boy." But he had profited more in England, he held himself back from adding.

There was no need to antagonise the man. Being part of the clergy under which cloak the school was run probably obliged him to send his sons there.

"Yes, I believe he was one of the older boys whilst I was there, though I'm afraid I was only there a short time before I too was sent away to further my education," the Dean said. "Does he live in the town?"

Nathaniel nodded.

"I wondered if you were related when I met him. Though the circumstances under which we were introduced were far from auspicious, it was whilst I was officiating at a funeral last week, I could see he was a very personable man and much admired judging by the way people referred to him. Tell me, what does he do for a living? Did he follow you into the building trade?"

'John following in my footsteps?' Nathaniel thought. 'Nathaniel Westaway and Son'. Oh! If only that wish of mine could have been granted! But alas it was not to be. John tried. Give him his due he did try to work at that apprenticeship I secured for him but it was as plain as a pikestaff that his heart was not in it. Then when I took him onto the sites, hoping he would take to one or other of the trades by his own volition, he took badly to taking orders and being told what to do, especially from Colm. Ah! Colm...Colm!'

"Did he take to the building trade?" the Dean repeated.

"As like a fish to water, or a babe to its mother's breast. And what workmanship! I was on the point of offering him a partnership, young as he was, just before he died. What terrible afflictions they were, first losing him and then my dearest daughter Charlotte following so soon after. It was almost more than I felt I could bear at the time, but....But God must have had his reasons and we must learn to accept his will."

The Dean turned towards him, a look of deep consternation on his face. "My dear sir, I am most sorry. I seem to have made the most terrible of mistakes. I thought the man I met, John Westaway, was your son. It must be the fact that he bears the same surname. I did not know your son was dead."

"No...Oh! no...He is not dead." Nathaniel blustered. "I must have ...given you the wrong impression...John...John is alive and well... Thanks be to God."

'Now whatever did I say to make him believe otherwise?' he asked himself. 'Oh! Dear, dear! I really must keep my wits about me.'

It was at that moment that they reached the junction where St. Saviour's Road crossed with Simon Place and he pointed down its length. "And you were correct in thinking he lives in town. I built most of the houses down there and beyond the bend, in Belmont Road, and gave him the house Surrey Lodge as a wedding present. John is now the proud father of ten most bonny children, including two sets of twins. His five sons will no doubt be joining your boys at the new college for I believe even my eldest grandson John will be coming back to the island to finish off his education there once the building is complete. He has the makings of a lawyer that one."

'Oh! Dear God! There I have done it again,' he berated himself. 'Rattling on and boasting outrageously too. Really I am not myself today!'

The Dean guided his horse into Plaisance Road where suddenly he called it to a stop. "Do you mind if we go up the steps here? I would rather not set too much of a burden on the horse by insisting it pull us up the steep path. Besides I rather wanted to take a closer look at the Temple on our way," he said, jumping down with the envious agility of a youth and attaching the horse's reins to the steel ring embedded in the wall.

The steps to the hillside at Mount Pleasant were very steep yet once at the top the Dean, seemingly unaffected by the arduous climb, continued to walk around the outside of the peculiar, pillared, belvedere. Nathaniel on the other hand, puffing from the exertion, was gratified to see a pair of chairs within its dim interior. He sank down on the nearest one and, taking his top hat from his head, withdrew a large handkerchief from its inner pocket to mop at the beads of sweat that were running down his face. 'My but I am getting feeble!' he said to himself. 'There was a time when I too would have sprinted up those steps without any ill effects.' He had been foolish to consider the visit, he went on to admonish himself. He should have remembered that the approach from any direction necessitated a steep climb. Now he had tired himself out and he had yet to cross the grounds to look at the construction, after which there would inevitably be the slow trudge around the site before making the descent and long walk home.

" 'Tis rather a handsome resting place but an odd requisition, don't you think?" The Dean said, suddenly appearing in the open doorway. "Heaven knows what the hordes of boys will make of it."

Nathaniel did not comment as the younger man entered to inspect the interior. He was trying to slow his breathing and consequently calm the racing beat of his heart. His legs too felt very heavy and he was suddenly overcome with a great weariness. 'Oh! Dear!' he thought. 'Here I am with all my energy spent and the Dean no doubt eager to step onward. What excuse could I use to send him on alone so that I might sit a little longer without drawing attention to my need to rest?'

But Nathaniel need not have worried for the Dean appeared to be in no particular hurry to venture further into the grounds. Indeed he began to give such an illuminating soliloquy on what he had learnt of the Greeks, including some entertaining quotes from Virgil and the Greek Testament, that by the time he suggested they move on Nathaniel felt quite rested.

"May I ask your opinion of it?" the Dean asked as they regarded the impressive Gothic frontage of the college that was going to bear the Queen's name.

"Noble, a truly noble design," he said. "The clever use of local granite is admirable but I fear those dressings of Caen stone will not weather. It would be interesting to look about inside once it is completed."

"Yes, yes indeed," the Dean agreed. "But what a setting, such vast grounds, such views of the town...."

It was some time later that Nathaniel made his way back to St. Saviour's Road. He was alone and enjoying a pleasant reverie, having politely taken his leave of the Dean who had been caught up in conversation with a group of fellow politicians. He imagined telling Anne about it expecting her to suggest that, as it was such an admirable establishment for their younger grandsons in which to be educated, that they offer to pay the fees. In the meantime he determined to book a carriage to take her to the opening ceremony in the autumn, which promised to be equally as grand as the first.

They had missed the laying of the Foundation Stone which had taken place on the Queen's birthday two years before because Anne had been laid low with fever. That splendid event had been attended by thousands of islanders, with bands of musicians accompanying the States members as they walked in procession through the flag-adorned streets all the way from their Chamber. It was bound to be an even grander occasion this time and in his mind Nathaniel saw the happy smile on Anne's face turn to an expression of wonder as he walked her through the beautiful grounds, pointing out the different landmarks in the town below. He sighed with contentment at the prospect. There were so many outings and pleasures they could share now that he no longer had to think of the business. And the visit they had made to London's Great Crystal Palace Exhibition the previous year had been just the beginning of the travelling experiences they planned to enjoy together. Life was good, yes indeed.

So deep in reverie had Nathaniel been that he was nearing the entrance to the crescent before he suddenly remembered that he had intended to call in on John that morning. He shook his head in vexation at his forgetfulness. 'Yet John did not know of my intentions' he assured himself, 'so I can make the journey tomorrow and he will be none the wiser as to my wool gathering. I really must talk to him about certain matters dictated in my will and my reasons for setting it out the way I have. He must not have command over the affairs of his mother or sisters, as I fear he would be wont to do unless I otherwise request it. However I shall have to be tactful for it is not a subject about which I would wish to become embroiled in petty bickering.'

Of late it seemed he could do nothing right in his son's eyes and little incidents where they had exchanged fiery words came back to haunt him. He felt himself getting vexed and, not wishing to present himself to Anne in a temper, crossed to the small park fronting the crescent. Being in the garden always seemed to calm him. A bevy of foliage belonging to a camellia bush was poking its way through the railings and he leant to stroke the shiny leaves.

'This is what I retired for,' he murmured gently, fingering a ripening bud. 'To watch as buds such as these open and brazenly show off their blooms and to have time to appreciate God's handiwork in their making. I took so much for granted in my working days....'

He opened the narrow gate and walked across the grass noting the different shrubs, bushes and newly planted trees as he made his way to the farthest end and the second gateway that faced his home. 'This really is quite a pleasant little garden,' he told himself, sitting down on the familiar stone bench and glancing around appreciatively. Suddenly he noticed some patches of white amongst the green of the lawn a few feet away and frowned in puzzlement.

'Now what on God's good earth can that be?' he wondered, peering through a mist that had suddenly blurred his sight. He bent forward, stretching out his hand as far as he could reach with his rear end leaving the seat and toppled forward to fall face down amongst a group of snowdrops.

When he came to later, in the comfort of the large double bed he shared with Anne, he had no recollection of leaving the house, of his ride with the Dean or of his subsequent fall.

"He has suffered an apoplexy, a cerebral stroke," he heard Doctor Pierce inform Anne. 'Tis is a good thing that you were watching from the window and witnessed his fall else he may have lain out in the cold for some time before being found. Don't worry. He is a fit man. Just see that he remains quiet and untroubled and with God's help we might keep him on this earth a while yet."

But to Anne's increasing alarm Nathaniel could neither speak nor move in any way. Unconsciously she picked up his feelings of utter helplessness as she dabbed at the tears that ran freely down his cheeks.

"Do not distress yourself, my dearest Natty," she soothed. "You only have to rest now; then you will soon be yourself again." But soon afterwards, as she gently kissed him, she felt his lips suddenly slacken. Pulling away she saw his face change, become distorted into an ugly grimace, and knew without being told that he was having another attack.

"Oh! My dearest, dearest husband," she whispered sadly.

"Mama…Why…What…?" Julia could not seem to form the words to the question she wanted to ask.

"I think we should call for the doctor to return and John, of course we must ask John to come," Anne said calmly. "Will you see to it Harriet dear?"

"Oh! Mama!" Julia began to weep uncontrollably as her sister left the room. "What shall we do?"

"We shall pray Julia. We must pray that God will be merciful and let your dear papa stay with us." After all, she told herself. Nathaniel had always been a good man with a fervent belief in God's mercy. He would not be taken before he had time to truly enjoy the peaceful years due to him after a lifetime of work. No, God would not reward his faithful servant in such a cruel way!

"That was what I believed," Anne was to tell an old friend many years later. "But now I understand that God in his great mercy took my beloved Nathaniel from this earth before he could suffer another hour of frustration and pain. Within minutes of us kneeling to pray his soul had gone to its eternal rest. I was at his side when he let out his last breath, watched as his skin took on the stark cold of marble and, once the undertaker had laid him out, returned to sit with him until he was taken from the house to be buried."

She failed to mention that on watching his coffin being lowered into the ground her mind entered a black abyss from which, for a time, it was thought she might never ascend to take part in life again. So deeply affected by his death was she it was said that only at the point of burial was she forced to admit to herself that her dearest husband, the man who had been the most loving companion for over forty years, was gone.

And all this after being so strong amidst the continuous weeping and wailing of Harriet and Julia, the comforting of both them and John, the making of the funeral arrangements, the constant stream of commiserating callers. She was not even to weep after reading the notice in the *Chronique*, which announced,

> 'Sadly, last Friday night, after two successive attacks of strokes Mr. Nathaniel Westaway formerly of Don Street, but living near to Le Coie, in the Parish of St. Saviours for the last two or three years, passed away.
>
> Mr Westaway was aged 62 years and was often seen walking in the town, even up to two days before his death. After the late Mr Robert Brown he was the proud owner of many Jersey houses.'

"Oh! John! John!"

First Julia then Harriet went rushing down the stairs to greet their brother as a damp-faced maid took his cape and hat. Distraught with grief they flung themselves at him with an uninhibited show of affection. Though he put his arms about their shoulders he held himself stiff and did not respond to their desperate need of a comforting embrace. Harriet was the first to notice the lack of warmth and drew back and at this John put Julia aside too.

"What happened?" he asked, nudging them both towards the open drawing room door and closing it behind them all. Julia told him, her voice broken with convulsive sobs.

"Is Mama still with him?"

In reply only Harriet nodded as she gently pulled Julia away from their brother's side and led her to the fireside where she, placing her hands on her younger sister's shoulders, motioned her to sit down on a nearby chair.

"How is she?"

John's tone was so ordinary, his attitude so lacking of emotion, that both women felt a little nonplussed. But they would have been even more surprised had they seen their brother minutes after he had heard the news, had heard the loud moans of grief coming from behind the hastily slammed door of the front parlour in their brother's home. Had they heard the angry roar of, "Leave me be!" when their sister-in-law Anne Guillet rushed to his side or noticed how she continued to stand there, alarm etching deep creases on her face as he began to pummel the left side of his chest with his fist. Or even heard him muttering in torment, 'I do not understand. Why should it hurt so much now that you are gone? Why should I feel so much pain at the loss of a father who never once showed he cared for me, a papa from whom I could never win approval or any sign of affection? Oh! Papa…Papa! Why could you not at least have told me why I failed to win your love and respect?' If they had heard any of this they might have felt a little sympathy and perhaps, with added consideration, begun to understand why their only brother had acted so perversely over the years.

However, neither of them had been present to witness John's torment and so, presented with the cold façade that was his defence, misunderstanding once more turned to irritation.

"How do you think?" Harriet snapped.

"Mama is just sitting there beside Papa. She has not cried one tear as yet. She must cry John, really she must," Julia said, ignoring as usual the volatile tension between her brother and sister. "It would not be good for her to keep her grief inside."

At that moment the doorbell clanged loudly, startling the three of them, and they waited silently until the young maid, her face a little redder though no drier, announced the arrival of Mr Crow the undertaker.

"Surely the man is not cruel enough to come touting for business?" Harriet cried.

"He is here on business of course, but at my request," John informed her sharply. "Yet even I must admit the man is too prompt for I only sent word as I left Belmont Road. I should have preferred to have a word or two with Mama before he attends to Father's laying out. Indeed I shall keep the fellow waiting while I do so."

"Be gentle with her John," Julia pleaded as he strode towards the door.

He stopped and, looking aggrieved, said softly, "How could you think me to be otherwise at a time like this? It is very late and I doubt whether any of us will get much sleep tonight. I suggest you order some beef tea and when father has been prepared I shall come for you and we will all go up to see him together."

He went out into the hall to greet the man just as Jack, the husband of ten years to Bertha Dutot the housekeeper, came running up the stairs from the basement kitchen, a small bundle of hay, some string and a dark woollen hood in his hand.

"I'm sorry Sir," he apologised in addressing John. "I was just about to muffle the bell."

"Quite so," John agreed, then turning to Ebenezer Crow he took his hand and, before the man could offer condolences, said politely, "You must have left your funeral parlour as soon as you received my message. However I have not arrived here long myself so I would be grateful if you would allow me a few minutes with my mother and...my father, before you attend him. If you would kindly take a seat I shall return to take you up to the room."

Leaving the man to settle himself onto one of the carved back chairs that stood on either side of the ornate hallstand John climbed the two flights of stairs to his parents' bedroom. He found his mother sitting at his father's side as Julia had described. She was pale, almost as white as the arm of the dead man's hand she held to her cheek.

"Mama?" he called softly. And when she looked across at him he went to her side saying, "I came as soon as I heard. How was it?"

She accepted his kiss before she told him in her own words how Nathaniel had been found, of the second stroke and how he had fought to stay. But she did not mention the tears of frustration at his inability to either speak or move for she did not want this beloved man to appear weak in his son's eyes.

"Could you not have called me earlier?" John asked reproachfully.

"We had no idea it would be so sudden. Besides he would not have wanted any fuss."

'No, he would not have wanted any fuss. Neither would he have wanted me here,' John thought bitterly as at last he forced his eyes away from his mother and onto the body on the bed. He had been dreading the moment, fearing the sight of the familiar face frowning with vexation but was surprised at how utterly peaceful his father looked.

"Kiss him and make your peace John," his mother said, and going around to the other side of the bed he leant and placed his lips on the cold forehead, his eyes filling with tears.

"Oh! Papa, I loved you so much," he whispered.

"And he loved you too John," his mother assured him and, hearing this, he dropped his head onto his father's body and sobbed.

19

"NOT ST. SAVIOUR'S!"

Harriet, her normally gaunt face swollen and blotched from weeping, stared at her brother incredulously. The night had passed. No one in the house had slept, neither had John who had left at dawn and had just returned.

"Yes St. Saviour's. I have sent a message asking the Dean to call so that arrangements can be made for both the funeral service and the purchase of a plot in the cemetery."

"But you knew that we...that Papa has been worshipping at St. Mark's for some years now, ever since we found we preferred the teaching to that of the chapel. He would have wanted his final service to be held there. I also think he would have wanted to be buried in the cemetery in Green Street."

"Did he inform you of those wishes?"

Harriet shook her head reluctantly. John looked across at Julia who was huddled in a chair near the fire but she too shook her head. "Well unless he has left instructions with his solicitor to the contrary I will, as head of the family and Chief Mourner, have to make arrangements as I see fit."

"He might have discussed the matter with Mama," Julia offered. "It would be a kindness to ask her before you act."

"I have done so but they never discussed it. So as head of the family she has left it to me to..."

He was interrupted by the distinct but muffled sound of the bell in the hall, it having been wrapped in sacking by the thoughtful Jack. Once again they all waited for the gentle tap on the door.

"Beggin' your pardon Mister John, Miss Harriet and Miss Julia, but there is a Reverend person at the door," the maid announced, holding out the small silver tray on which the white visiting card lay. John was surprised that she was still crying openly and wondered, as he picked up the card, if any of his own staff would be as affected when his final day came.

" 'Tis the Dean," he informed his sisters without looking in their direction. "Ask him to come in, will you?"

William Corbet Le Breton hurried into the room, his hand outstretched to clasp that of John's.

"My dear Sir! Please forgive the early hour. I came as soon as I got your message."

"Good of you to come. I had not expected you so soon," John replied quietly.

"I can hardly believe it! Though I must admit to being a little perturbed at your father's poor state of health whilst we were together yesterday..."

"You were with Papa yes...ter...day?"

The outside shutters of the windows had been pinned close at an angle so that just a ribbon of daylight flowed through and, apart from the flickering coals of the fire and the glow from a lamp on the centre table, the room was in semidarkness. Therefore it was only as the Dean turned in the direction of the quivering voice that he noticed the two women for the first time. They were together in the shadows of the hearth – one sitting, the other standing protectively close to her side.

"I do most humbly beg your forgiveness ladies. I truly did not see you there..."

"My sisters...Harriet..."

John's voice rose on the mention of her name and Harriet bristled at the warning the tone held as he introduced her whilst at the same time he lit the wick to another lamp and placed it on the mantle shelf above the fireplace. 'How dare he!' she thought. 'As if I do not know how to be civil!' But to the man bending over her proffered hand and offering his condolences she said softly. "Thank you Dean Le Breton. 'Tis kindly of you to call."

"...And my sister Julia," John said. The woman remained seated but held out her hand.

The eyes that looked back at him were the most startling the Dean had ever seen, the skin on the hand he kissed velvety smooth. He forced himself to quell the familiar tremor of delight that ran through his body whenever he was near a beautiful woman and murmur the practised words of commiseration.

"You were with Papa yesterday?" Julia asked again.

"Yes, I..." he hesitated, unsure whether to mention the invitation and deciding to do so on the assumption that the envelope would probably be found when the pockets of Nathaniel's clothes were emptied. "I was about to call at the house with an invitation when I saw your father leaving the crescent. I caught up with him and together we went on to visit the new school they are building at Mount Pleasant."

"You said he was in a poor state of health but how did you come by that assumption? He was perfectly well before he left the house, was he not Harriet?"

"Yes Julia dear, he seemed in a finer fettle than he has been for some time. He was looking forward to his walk. Indeed he..." she gave a little sob and blew into her handkerchief before continuing, "he chastised me over breakfast, in his usual dear and jovial manner of course, for not taking more exercise myself."

John was solicitously holding out a chair and, having satisfied himself that Harriet too was now seated, the Dean lowered his lean frame into a sitting position before beginning to tell them about the happenings of the previous afternoon.

"Perhaps the climb was too much for him and the exercise compounded by the continuance of his walk. I am truly sorry that our acquaintance was so short for your father had the reputation of being a good and charitable man and I would like to have known him better. I can only rest in expectation that his worthy soul will be warmly welcomed into God's Holy Kingdom on Judgement Day."

"Amen," they all murmured.

The assurance that heaven awaited her beloved papa, even though she suspected it was an affirmation the Dean repeated to all parishioners who were known to be God fearing, was enough to convince Harriet that he was a suitable choice to conduct her father's final service. The vicar of St. Mark's would no doubt be quite irked at the arrangement but a large donation to the church funds would go a long way in appeasement. Putting her hand on Julia's to indicate that they should leave the room, she surprised both her brother and sister by saying, "John has need to talk to you about the service and interment Dean so we will leave you both and attend our dear mother. Should you have any need to learn of papa's favourite hymns and readings we will be happy to list them for you, would we not Julia?" Her sister nodded.

The two men left together, travelling up the hill in the Dean's trap to the cemetery where, calling on the sexton in his lodge, the three went on to search for a suitable plot. There were several pieces of ground to chose from and John took his time before settling on a large plot situated alongside the wall nearest to the Church. He felt that in choosing this site he would at last earn his father's approval. For it was close enough for the sounds of both the sacred words and music to be heard of a Sunday and sufficiently large for a number of family members to also be interred in the future.

As soon as this was noted the Dean invited John back to the warmth of the Deanery to discuss the final arrangements. Though the granite-stoned rectory stood a short distance away John declined, preferring the peaceful interior of the church instead. Therefore, with no relief from the bitter cold, for the church was as icy inside as out, the business was completed in a shorter time than either man could have imagined.

Still there was much to do, John reminded himself as he set off back down the hill and into town on foot. He had now to visit and ask four of his father's closest friends to act as pallbearers, a duty he knew all would readily agree to, regarding it as an important and final honouring of a man they all revered. In addition he had to speak with two others who might also expect to be asked but, being rather shorter in stature than the four bearers, he would need to suggest, in a manner which would not offend, that they walk alongside. Once these civilities had been attended to he needed to call into the undertaker's establishment and order black gloves and sashes for them all. Next was a visit to the Printing Press where, having ascertained a list of people from his sisters, the printing and delivery of invitations had to be arranged. Finally he had to call into the Stopford Hotel in David Place and speak to the proprietor about the provision of the funeral feast.

In his absence and with word of Nathaniel's death travelling fast, the mourning visits began with the first of what turned out to be a continuous stream of callers being admitted to the house from nine o'clock that morning. Some asked to be permitted to view the body and were taken up to the bedroom where Nathaniel had been laid out in the same double bed in which he had died. There, though they murmured comments such as, 'Aw! He looks every inch the man he was,' and 'As in life so he is in death eh?' the body they stared down on held little resemblance to the man they had known. For this stranger had his hair neatly combed back from his white, marble-like face, with a grey beard and sideburns that were neatly trimmed, whereas Nathaniel Westaway had always looked ruddy and weather-beaten, his hair and beard unkempt.

Anne sat at the side of the bed throughout, accepting their words of condolence graciously but rarely looking away from the face of the man she loved. She spoke just once when agreeing on how fortunate they had been to share over four decades of marriage but, apart from that, she was silent. After a while they made their whispered farewells and with a general sense of relief rejoined Harriet and Julia in the drawing room, where others were exchanging snippets of news and tittle-tattle, which was no bad thing in that it had the effect of temporarily averting the sisters' minds.

On the day of the funeral, at little more than a walking pace, a team of four black horses, each wearing a black velvet coat and halter decorated with large raven plumes, pulled the glass-sided hearse into a crescent lined with mourners. It was followed by two carriages, two gigs and a long line of assorted conveyances. When the hearse stopped outside of Number 1 John got out of the first carriage and made his way into the house, followed by the pallbearers. There was respectful silence from all around as Nathaniel's coffin was placed in the hearse and John led his mother and sisters to the first of the gigs which was empty. Once this was done John returned to the first carriage as the pallbearers, having seen the coffin safely enclosed in the hearse, got into the second. Only then did the long funeral cortège begin to make its way up the hill to the Parish Church of St. Saviour.

It had not been possible for 16 year-old John junior to return from his schooling for his grandfather's funeral so two of his brothers – 12 year-old Charles and ten year-old Nathaniel – accompanied their father in the carriage immediately behind the hearse, the pallbearers in a second. Then followed two gigs of womenfolk with the first carrying Anne, Harriet and Julia before a line of carriages, which joined in the cortège as it left the crescent. The remaining mourners, many in number, walked the journey on foot. There were men in frock coats, their top hats adorned in black ribbon and women in black gowns, capes and unadorned bonnets, amongst which were neighbouring tenants who had kindly permitted some of their household staff to trail behind with Bertha and Jack. Finally bringing up the rear was a large body of men who had worked for Nathaniel, every one wearing the black band of mourning on his left sleeve, including Donal who for ten years past had been inn-keeper of the popular tavern he owned in the northern Parish of St. John.

All these and more who had come from other parishes filed into the beautiful granite-walled church. They filled it until there was standing room only left in the porch. After the lengthy service they all stood aside to let the family lead the way over the short distance to Nathaniel's final resting-place in the churchyard. Few could actually watch the interment but they crowded silently around the paths nevertheless, as if they held against leaving until the very last minute. Neither could they all have been invited to the meal that was waiting at the Stopford Hotel for their great number came as a complete surprise not only to John but all the family.

Anne could not be encouraged to attend the meal so Harriet and Julia, who were not really inclined to do so either, accompanied her back to St. Saviour's Crescent. There the household staff, having returned rapidly whilst the burial was taking place, had opened up the shutters and curtains and prepared tea and cake in readiness.

So it happened that John stood alone to welcome the mourners to the meal in his father's memory. Shaking the hands of the men, a few of whom had been invited more because they were his friends rather than that of his father's, he could not help but notice a difference in their manner. There was a new look in their eyes, a look of respect. It was the same look he had seen whenever his father's name was mentioned. And he knew why!

Though he had never flaunted his money with rich living Nathaniel Westaway was presumed to be a very wealthy man. He was known to own a large number of properties, the exact quantity only being guessed at by anyone other than himself and his solicitor. Even John did not know exactly how many houses his father owned though, as the sole male heir, he expected to be made familiar with every one of them very soon. And there was money too, the amount again he could only speculate. And now it was all his, all his, or would be before another day was past.

Of course he had always known that one day he would be rich, had made various plans in his head about how he would spend his inheritance but they had been only daydreams. He had never felt seriously able to consider such plans whilst his father was alive. And he had always seen his father as being very much alive, constantly demonstrating his authority at every turn and closing his mind to every proffered suggestion.

Though he knew it was improper to think ill of the dead the rancour that had been festering for years began to fill John's being as he remembered his father's constant dismissal of good advice, his refusal to delegate. There were so many matters he could have helped with, if only his father had listened, if only his judgement had been trusted. Well now there would be no dissent, he told himself. No one would now argue against him for at last he was his own man, and a very rich one at that.

The feeling of bitterness was quickly replaced by one of great expectation as John thought of the future that lay ahead, yet not one of the guests would have guessed at the sudden change in his emotions as he solemnly continued to greet them.

Such was his gift at hiding his true feelings.

20

THE FOLLOWING MORNING saw John entering St. Saviour's Crescent a good fifteen minutes before the arrival of his father's solicitor. On being informed that his mother and sisters were in the family parlour he made his way to the first floor.

He found his mother sitting in a high-backed chair by a blazing coal fire and pausing only to nod in the direction of his two sisters, who were both perched on one of the window seats, he crossed the room to her side. He bent to kiss her cheek but at that very moment she bowed her head so instead his lips met the crispness of lace ribbon that fell over her forehead from her black cap.

He was immediately irritated but he forced himself to control his voice as he asked, "How are you today Mama?" and when she made no response he glanced enquiringly at his sisters. Both, he could see now, were still tearful. Harriet shook her head slowly before turning away to stare out of the window but Julia came across and putting her arm around her mother's shoulders said sadly, "We are going to walk up to the cemetery later to visit papa, are we not Mama?" But her mother made no comment.

An uncomfortable silence followed until John said, "I think father would have been satisfied with the funeral arrangements. Everything went off very well. The Stopford made a fine effort of the meal and I received many kind words on your behalf mama."

Still Anne made no move to either speak or even acknowledge his presence and he was almost grateful when Julia asked, "Did you ever expect such devotion to father John? We did not look to see but we felt the number of mourners far exceeded what was expected. Bertha says they numbered over a hundred."

"That may be something of an exaggeration but there was quite a crowd. I must write a note of appreciation to the Dean. I thought his address most appropriate."

"I am afraid I was too overcome to have much recollection of the service but what do you think Harriet?"

"As you say, John, it was appropriate and faithful to father's strong belief. I hope you will add our names to your note of appreciation. As to the mourners it was to be expected that the number would be large considering Papa's regard amongst the community. It was a great pity that John Junior was not in the island but Papa would have been pleased that Charles and Nathaniel attended, young as they are. It is just a shame that he did not see much of his ten grandchildren as he would have liked when he was alive."

Over the years Harriet had taken to speaking her mind, an unattractive feature which, though much accepted as part of her character by her parents and sister, did not endear her to many others, including her only brother. In fact John had come to receive each cutting remark as a barb, a barb intended to find a mark and therefore a mark that had to be defended by retaliation. He was therefore preparing a suitably trite retort when Julia said, "It has been kind of Anne to call so often and to be so considerate of Mama's and our welfare. Please tell her how much we appreciate it."

John smiled at his youngest sister, unconsciously acknowledging the way she had once again intervened to ward off the verbal disagreement which would inevitably have followed. She asked if he wanted tea or something stronger and when he shook his head she went back to her place at the window.

There followed another protracted silence during which John let his eyes roam around the room. It was not a room he liked. Even in daylight, with the shutters on the windows having been flung wide and pinned back by their steel rods at dawn that morning, it remained gloomy. The walls covered in dull green baize and relieved only by framed biblical quotations, faithfully embroidered by his mother and sisters, looked all the more dismal with the curtains, chaise longue, indeed every cloth-covered piece, being set against them in a darker hue.

Alongside the back wall the large familiar mahogany sideboard looked as frumpish as he had predicted it would and the sight of it caused him to remember back to the time when he had tried to advise his father to either sell or leave it where it stood in the more spacious parlour at Don Street. Suddenly he was back at the old family home, lending a willing hand to the loading of all his parent's furniture onto what became a succession of horse-drawn vans, but shaking his head in exasperation at the seeming immovability of this last piece.

"It is far too cumbersome to move papa. Why not just leave it for the future tenant to either use or dispose of?"

But his father had just frowned and after a minute's deliberation said, "It will not be left John. If it cannot be moved today I shall ride out to St. John's and ask Donal if he and his keg-carrying men will do it. Their combined brawn would soon shift it, I have no doubt."

And the mention of that hated name had spurred his tired limbs, giving him the extra power he needed. The piece at last yielded its position though it took all his strength and that of three other men to finally push it onto the back of the van.

'I will not think of the O'Reillys or any of my father's men today!' John told himself sternly now. 'It was enough that I was always made to feel inadequate beside them, that Papa had always favoured their work over mine. But never no more!'

Yet the inner voice of resentment made itself known again as he reminded himself that he need not have offered his help with the removal, that he could have left it to the paid men. 'But no!' The voice carped. 'Once again you offered help to your father and once again it was taken for granted. It was not even as if you had done it in expectation of the paltry coins given out to the men by way of gratuity. All you would have liked to hear was a word, one single word, of appreciation. Well, you are not likely to hear it now. Not now that your father has gone.'

Suppressed tears began to scorch the back of John's eyes as they continued browsing the room and stopped to rest on his mother's desk – 'Mon escritoire,' as she called it. It lay open with paper and envelopes in readiness, he imagined, for the writing of letters and notes in acknowledgement of the many messages of condolence she had received. His mother had a gifted way with words when it came to such writings, a talent he had once presumed to be a feminine trait but which, to his great surprise he had found that he, and not his sisters, had inherited.

He looked down at his mother, sitting so still as if oblivious of all that was going on about her. He presumed that this unexpected torpor was the outcome of her unreleased grief but found it nevertheless unnerving in that he was not used to this sudden change in her. It was odd how his feelings towards his mother had altered over the years. The need to bait her at every turn had dissipated long ago and had been replaced with something akin to regard, regard for her clear insights in the occasional debates that, though sometimes still earnest, rarely became heated now as they once would have done.

He bent down and, squeezing her clasped hands gently, asked, "Mama, is there anything I can do for you?" But she did not even blink her eyes in response.

Confounded, he straightened up and stared into the blazing coals as the thought suddenly occurred to him that she might never recover, but remain in this state until the end of her days. It was not unheard of in the elderly and she had reached the great age of 77 he reminded himself. She may need a great deal of care and attention.

'Still I need not make that my concern,' he considered now. 'Both Harriet and Julia are quite capable of looking after her. 'Twas a blessing indeed that neither of them had married but then, their single state might yet be a great drain on the pocket.'

As if picking up his thoughts Julia came forward and he watched as she fussed over their mother. Of his two sisters she with her handsome face and affectionate nature had been the most likely to find a willing suitor but for some reason she had remained unmarried. He wondered if he would have to remedy that situation if, as he suspected, his mother and sisters became his responsibility. He would be wise to marry his sisters off, let a future husband take over the added responsibility for their mother, though it would be difficult where Harriet was concerned. Her querulous and sanctimonious manner was as unattractive as her face. However if he could see Julia settled that would be one less responsibility. Yes, he would have to give the matter some thought.

"How are the children, John?" Julia asked. "We would love to see them would we not Mama?" Now down on her knees with her arms about their mother she looked up at him pleadingly. Yes, a visit from the children might be a good idea, he considered silently. He would have a word with Anne.

"Well of course the older boys are at school as you know but I shall have a word with Anne," he replied. "She could bring Charlotte and Susan one afternoon if you all feel up to it. Perhaps we could talk about when would be suitable at a later time. Charles will be coming by of course. Oh! Dear, I do believe that I forgot to tell you that he is to be taken on as apprentice to Anthony Enright, a master mariner, and will be leaving within the week for Liverpool."

"Oh! How exciting for him, did you hear that Mama? Charles is to be a seaman at last. Do you remember how he once told us that he was going to be the Captain of a ship one day? Why, we could well have another Horatio Nelson in the family!"

"Hardly," John said wryly. "Nelson was in the Royal Navy whereas Charles will be learning his trade on a merchant ship."

Julia did not need to be told that Admiral Nelson had commanded the Royal Navy for she was aware of the fact but she had not known that Charles was to do his time on a merchant ship. Still she did not retaliate at the chastisement but with reddening cheeks began to brush imaginary dust from her mother's skirt. Seeing this, John felt immediately contrite and was about to remedy the situation with some kind word when the sound of the doorbell distracted him.

When the arrival of the lawyer Jean Le Balastier was announced, John helped his mother out of her chair and led her slowly by the elbow back down the stairs. However, as they entered the drawing room he let Julia lead her to one of the high-backed chairs which were positioned facing the large chenille-covered table. Having then greeted the man and accepted his condolences he moved to the fireplace where he stood with his back to the flames and watched him accompany Harriet across the room.

It really was a case of appearances being deceptive, John thought as he studied Jean Le Balastier. Had he not learnt from his own notary that this man was a much-respected Solicitor of the Royal Court and senior partner in the firm of Le Balastier, Toudic and Toudic he would never have believed it, for he had the appearance of a most peculiar character. Beneath a loose-fitting black jacket the buttons of the man's waistcoat strained to hold against his corpulent belly, across which not one but two gold watch chains were ostentatiously draped. This feature alone would not be too strange were it not for his legs which bowed under the excessive weight from above. Clad in tight white breeches and strengthened at the ankles by stout boots, he was apt to walk with a waddle, which was all the more prominent now as he crossed the room, his rigid arms pinning scrolls of papers to his side. John could not help but wonder if it had been the man's very eccentricity that had drawn his father to seek his services in the first place. His father seemed to have had a leaning towards the strangest of characters, he mused, thinking back to the old yard keeper Thomas

Le Beau, a one time beggar who had the most grotesque gait.

Placing the papers on the table, the man spoke softly to Anne and Julia who had now taken their places on either side of their mother, his loose grey shoulder-length curls seeming to dance gently with each movement of his head. Yet as John went on to study the notaire's rotund, clean-shaven face, upon which he suspected a fondness for the likes of Spanish sherry had endowed the permanent flush, he was surprised to see what looked like sincerity in the pale brown eyes.

Ye Gads! A sincere lawyer? John nearly laughed at the preposterous notion. For every thinking man knew that all notaries were, by their very choice of profession, devious beings. Pretentious too. Not that he would ever voice his opinions now that John Junior was considering taking up the law, no, no. For even though his eldest son's own supercilious ways sometimes irritated him immensely, the glowing commendations in the academy's last annual report engendered a great pride. He regretted showing the report to his parents however, for the remarks of how he too could have achieved such recognition had wounded him greatly.

'I always hoped that you would have taken up the law and become someone of note in the island,' his mother had admitted.

'But there you are Mama, at the time we agreed the boy should choose his way and we have let him do so,' his father said, adding, 'Still, I have often thought 'tis a crime to waste a good education when you think of the poor souls who can but just put a cross to their name.'

John had closed his eyes as the painful recollection resurfaced only to open them again on hearing a soft cough. He found Jean Labalastier looking at him questioningly, waiting for him to take his seat at the end of the table. John did so, moving the chair further out from the table so that he might stretch his long legs as far out in front of him as they would go. It was the most comfortable sitting position for him but one of which his parents disapproved in that it was a pose of modern casualness. Suddenly remembering this he hastily bent them and sat straight up in the chair as they had always expected and was instantly annoyed with himself for the ingrained but now unnecessary act of submissiveness. It was this irritation, together with the cramping ache that was beginning to lock his knees, which caused him sharply to command, "You may begin!"

Jean Le Balastier, a mild-mannered man, was taken aback at this slight but tried not to let it show. Though his late client, a man who was ever polite and always a great pleasure to meet and talk with had not expressed so verbally he had surmised that his relationship with his son had not been an easy one. Now, given the young man's attitude, he understood a little more. There was a disdainful air about John Nathaniel Westaway that spoilt his handsome features, and there was no doubt he was a handsome man. What a pity, the lawyer thought, that looks and character rarely matched each other. But then, had it been otherwise, certainly in his own case, he might never have been fortunate enough to claim his dear wife who constantly assured him that she would not change his loving heart for the handsomest man in the world. Ah! His darling Ada! What man would he have been without her? He could hardly wait for the week to come to an end for then he would be finished with business such as this. For in seven days they would be away from the island and settled into their new home in Bordeaux anticipating their future grape harvests and wine making. Could any man be more fortunate!

He cleared his throat and rapidly brought his mind back to the matter of his late client's will and testament. He would need to put all his attention into the next hour or so. He was not looking forward to John Westaway's reaction one bit, no indeed. Picking up one of the scrolls he untied the ribbon that held it fast before carefully straightening it out on the table in front of him and beginning to read.

"In the name of eternal God, Amen. Knowing that life is uncertain...." At this both Harriet and Julia began to sob quietly and though he looked up momentarily to give them a sympathetic glance he did not pause and continued, "but that death itself is a certainty I, Nathaniel Westaway, being in perfect soundness of mind and living at 37, Don Street in the Parish of St. Helier in the Island of Jersey, do make this my last Will and Testament. But first I commend my soul into the hands of my Creator and Heavenly Father in the hope..."

Permitting his attention to drift away from the short sermon he suspected was going to follow, John glanced from the lawyer to the younger of his sisters sitting alongside.

He noted how Julia's eyes never left the lawyer's face as she listened intently to every word that had originally come from their father's lips and how every few sentences she muttered 'Amen' to the agreed hope for his eternal redemption. Yes, she was still a handsome woman, despite the present blotching of her normally smooth and pale skin, he agreed critically as he took in the violet eyes which seemed all the brighter for the shimmering of tears. Her dark curls, with just a mere glint of the silver which passing time could not deny, were caught up in a bun on top of which sat a fashionable flowing bow of lace.

Julia had always liked to follow the fashion in clothes, he remembered, and refused to dress plain even for the regular attendance of Church. Yet, of his two sisters she was the most devout in following their father's habit of reading from the Bible each day, but unlike Harriet she bore no trait of self-righteousness.

He looked further down the table, past his mother's bent head, to the outline of Harriet's pointed features as she too stared ahead at the lawyer. He had gradually relaxed his sitting position once more but she remained rigidly upright, her utterances of 'Amen', slightly out of unison with Julia's, being nevertheless loud and succinct. Her grey hair was pulled back into a chignon beneath a cap of darker grey cotton accentuating a face that was lined with disapproval. With such a forbidding countenance, it is no wonder she has few true friends, he thought.

At that moment the unguarded fire spat out a shower of hot cinders. Most fell before reaching the brass fender but one large piece landed on the Indian rug, which lay in front. Seeing this, John quietly removed himself from the table and, retrieving the tongs from the companion that stood alongside the hearth, picked up the offending ash while stamping softly at the scorch mark to stop it from developing further.

"Do I have your permission to continue Mr Westaway?"

All at once John felt himself back as a boy in church, observed by the vicar in the act of stretching out his feet and stamping on the beetles which wandered about the floorboards. The services were usually conducted in French but the minister had a nasty habit of reverting to English whenever he had occasion to berate anyone in the congregation for not paying enough attention.

"Yes!...Yes... Of course!" he replied, his cheeks beginning to blaze red as they had then. But just as suddenly he realised he was no longer that boy and that it was merely his father's solicitor who had spoken so he added, in a tone that sounded more sharply than he intended, "Get on with it man!"

His sisters swivelled around and stared at him aghast.

"John!..." Harriet began to exclaim indignantly before seeing him throw the offending ember on to the fire and realising what had happened, got up and rushed to his side. "The idle girl must have forgotten to replace the guard," she said, reaching to his right and picking up the steel shield to put it in front of the flames. "Thanks to you there does not seem to be damage," she conceded generously as she examined the scorch mark, "But the girl will be punished nevertheless."

Remembering how upset the maid had been over the past few days he was about to speak up on her behalf when Jean Le Balastier asked,

"Is everything all right?"

Resuming their seats, John explained and apologised for his rudeness.

"Then the apology should be all on my part sir, and I hope you will accept it for I am afraid I did not realise what was happening," the lawyer said. "But if I might continue?"

For once the heads of brother and sister nodded in unison.

"To John Nathaniel Westaway, my son by the grace of Almighty God and living at number 20, Belmont Road in the Parish of Saint Helier...,"

'At last!' John thought. 'Now it comes!'

"I bequeath my properties, they being the following. The five deeded properties in Don Street in the Parish of St. Helier..."

Excitement began to surge through John's body but, not wanting anyone to witness any unseemly elation he bent his head, pretending to study the crease of his trouser legs, pinching at them unnecessarily whilst nevertheless listening intently.

"A lot of two and another of three houses in the west of Rouge Bouillon known as..."

He had not thought his father owned those other properties in Rouge Bouillon! But then, he reminded himself, they would probably be properties adjoining the old brick field, bought up whilst the land was cheap, when no one else envisaged a time when the works were either played out or closed and desirable properties built in its place. 'My compliments to you Papa!' In his mind John saw himself clasping his father close, his hands clapping his father on the back before a wave of regret came over him as he realised he would never have attempted such a thing. His father would not have approved.

It was not the same in his house, no indeed, he thought now. His sons were not afraid to show their true feelings, or voice their opinions, for in his house there was another important difference and that it was that the women knew their place. Oh! Yes!

John brought his mind back to the moment and forced himself to pay attention as the lawyer continued to list properties. He had known his father owned some of those mentioned of course but others came as a pleasant revelation. A warm flush of satisfaction ran through him as he realised all the title deeds would be passed over to his solicitor that very day and that by the morrow he would be able to peruse them time and time again at his leisure. The inventory was long and he was not surprised to hear the man pause to take deep breath.

"And to my dear eldest daughter Harriet Westaway I bequeath the title deeds of the house and land in the Parish of Trinity, the title deeds of the house and garden in the Parish of Grouville…" John's head jolted upward. He stared incredulously at the lawyer.

Nervously Jean Le Balastier waited for the interruption he was sure would follow and hoped he would not begin to perspire. He always became even more unnerved when the pores on his face began to leak. "The five houses and land in Springfield Crescent, numbers one to five of Campbell Terrace," he continued, his voice wavering slightly. "…the four houses in Belmont Road being…"

'No, no. I must have misheard!' John told himself. 'Father would never have done such a thing as to leave property to Harriet or to be as vindictive as to give her two of the neighbouring houses in Belmont Road.'

'The land and three buildings pertaining to Wesley Street…'

John knew the street, and its occupants, well. Named after the Wesleyan chapel that had been built within its short length it was just a hare's breath from his home in Belmont Road. He also knew that his father had owned the land and properties, one of which was let out to a furrier. Indeed, he had already taken an opportunity of speaking to the man and arranging that the next quarter's rent be delivered to his office at the coal yard.

'And to my youngest daughter Julia, I affectionately bequest the following properties in St. Helier. The two deeded houses in Ann Street, the one in Dumaresq Street, the one in Church Street, the named Surrey and Palmyra cottages in Palmyra Lane, the house in Poonah Road, the three attached houses at the beginning of Belmont Road....'

So he had not misheard after all, his father had divided his estate. But surely this could not be legal? It was too preposterous! He was the sole male heir and as such should have been awarded all the properties along with the tutelage of his mother and sisters. It was a travesty of all the natural laws of succession, he railed silently. How could his father have done such a thing, more importantly why did Le Balastier not advise against the making of such unheard of bequests? He was obviously not as competent as everyone, the local notary included, was led to believe, otherwise he would have done so. Well he would get nowhere trying to prove incompetence on the part of a solicitor of the Royal Court but there may be bones to be picked within the bequests themselves and his own lawyer would be the best man for that task. Aw! But, at what cost? Lawyers were not cheap. Still, the will could not be allowed to stand as it was and a victorious outcome could more than pay all legal expenses.

John's well shaped lips which, unnoticed by anyone else in the room, had drawn into a fine line during his mental rankling, now relaxed so that he smiled with ease as Jean Le Balastier made to leave. He was retiring from the legal profession, he told them all, but he would see that all the heritages would be in the hands of John's lawyers before the end of the day. He trusted that all the papers would be found to be in order, he added in an aside to John, for as the sole male heir it would be his moral duty to see that the bequests were adhered to. Choosing his words carefully John assured him that he trusted his lawyers would oversee that all was rightfully carried out.

As soon as Le Balastier had left, John said he too would have to get back to work and made his farewells.

Reaching up to kiss him on the cheek Julia said, "We have been very fortunate in being the children of such an industrious Papa, have we not John?" But he merely nodded as Harriet, following to give him a cursory peck, interjected with, "That we have, that we have."

Once outside, John changed his mind about returning to his work immediately and decided to take a long walk instead. He needed to calm his thoughts, he told himself, so, on reaching the entrance to the crescent, he turned left and set off at a pace down towards the Spring Fields. When he reached the spring he turned right and strode past the low walls that enclosed the crowded pigsties, ignoring the men who were rolling the skins in the Tan Yard behind, and headed on for Town Mills.

Once at the mills he followed the branch in the road until he came to the junction that would take him over the incline to Rouge Bouillon. Only here did he begin to slow, deliberately forestalling the moment he would reach the top of the climb and look across at the elegant properties that were now his. Excitement was stirring within him and he let it grow amid dreams of the grand future that lay ahead. There would be no more scrimping, no more delaying of payments of the quarterly accounts. He would buy a carriage so that he could drive Anne and the children out into the country every Sunday from spring to autumn, that was except for when they were travelling. And they would travel, of that he was determined. He could do all he dreamt of now that he was a man of property, the owner of a list that would increase considerably by the time the lawyers had proved the illegitimacy of his father's will and made him sole beneficiary.

Aw! But he could afford to be generous, he thought benevolently now as he looked critically across at the elegant houses that had taken the place of the clay pits and those in the terraces round about which were built on the land his father had later bought. There would be certain, less grand, properties from the list that he could allot his sisters as an income for the remainder of their lives and so provide their independence. He could afford to do that. Pulling himself proudly up to his full height he walked on and headed for the centre of town.

John Westaway's home, Surrey Lodge in Belmont Road, was much simpler in contrast to those he had just viewed but, though he admitted to not liking it at first, he had come to have a great affection for it over the passing of time. Three-storeyed, with high walls on either side, it stood slightly to the left of the plot's boundaries and had been built during one of the island's lean periods when, rather than see his men out of work, Nathaniel bought up land and built for himself. The plot had been one of five that Nathaniel had purchased in the once cobbled and sparsely built thoroughfare and it had taken him several years to complete the area's reconstruction. The other sites now contained more than one house creating a mainly residential street which had once caused John to ask his father whether, with placing the house at such an angle, and in a single stance, his father had originally intended to add more dwellings to the plot.

'It had indeed been my intention,' his father had said whilst handing over the deeds, 'but that was before I realised how well set up it was for your business. Besides,' he had added, 'the land will always be there should you consider giving up the buying and selling of coal in the future and investing in property instead.'

The reason John had not liked the house at first was because he had dreamt of one on the generous style of his childhood home with rooms either side of the wide passage to the large front door. Surrey Lodge by contrast was a contracted building with a small front entrance to the side and the internal staircase against the wall just a few feet away. To the right of the narrow passage were doorways leading to both the elaborately furnished, but rather cramped front parlour and family living rooms.

At the end of the passage was an oblong-shaped kitchen which was just large enough to house a refectory table and the twelve wooden wheel-backed chairs that surrounded it and through the kitchen was the large scullery and cold room. These rooms, and the two storeys of bedrooms above, jutted out from the back of the house to lie between a long walled-in garden, a vegetable, fruit patch and water well, and an area known as the backyard. The garden, with its gate and adjoining two bed-roomed granite cottage, which, though tenanted, was still part of the property, faced onto Providence Street and continued back up alongside the house to make the corner where the street joined with Belmont Road. The vegetable and fruit patch was directly behind the scullery and the yard ran back past the right of the scullery and kitchen to the family living room. Through the door in the wall that ran the length of the yard was John's place of business – the coal yard. This in turn covered the area from the house to the corner joining Belmont Road and Museum Street.

As he entered the front door on his return home John found his wife, Anne Guillet, standing at the bottom of the staircase that led to the upper rooms. She was staring upwards in horror and following her gaze he saw that their smallest son was sitting astride the banister rail. He sprang forward instinctively as the whooping six year-old hurtled downwards and snatched the lightweight body up and away from the rail before it reached the foot.

"Alex!" Both he and Anne exclaimed in unison, he laughingly but she in fright.

"I did it Papa! I came slidin' down all on my own and I wassant frightened."

"But you gave your Mama a fright Alex," John said, noticing how the colour had faded from his wife's cheeks. He shifted the child onto his right arm so that he could draw her close with his left. "And frightening your mama is not a gentlemanly thing to do, is it now?" The little boy shook his head. "So what do you say to your Mama?"

"I'm sorry Mama!" the child said earnestly, leaning across to kiss his mother on the lips.

"And now you must promise not to attempt to slide down the banisters again until you are sure either I or your brothers are here to catch you. Do you promise?"

"Yes Papa!" the child said solemnly. Then, taking advantage of being in his father's arms without either of his two younger sisters clamouring to be in his place, he nuzzled his nose affectionately into the curly side-whiskers. John turned his head slightly to kiss the fine blonde curls and in the next instant the child had removed his father's top hat and placed it over his head. It fell right down over his eyes causing his parents to laugh.

"What shall we do with the rascal Mama?" John asked Anne. She smelt of baking and her dark hair held a dusting of flour, an obvious sign that she had dashed from the kitchen as soon as she realised the boy's intention. Yet there was no sign of the agitation she must have felt now as, entering the game, her almond-shaped eyes looked back at him with mock severity.

"I think the boy should be put to hard labour helping his big sisters Annie and Henrietta clean up the pastry table in the kitchen," she said.

"So be it little man," John said, whipping his hat away before placing the child down on the ground. "Just see you make a good job of it."

"Yes, Papa," the child promised as he scuttled happily down the passage, knowing that helping to clean up the pastry table meant being given the left-over scraps and perhaps a few currants or raisins.

"I do believe I shall need eyes at the back of my head, the speed with which that child moves," Anne said. "And to think he was so ill only a few weeks back."

"And bearing in mind how we feared for his life we must praise God for the return of such exuberance my dear," John said, looking down at her.

It was true, the boy had been struck down with a much worse case of measles than any of his brothers and sisters who had caught the disease at the same time. But, whereas the others had rallied well within the shared sick room, his temperature had risen to an alarming degree causing him to rant unnaturally. John had carried him into one of the other bedrooms where Anne and their eldest daughter Annie had taken turns to sit with him. It had been a very worrying time for, though this was the first serious illness little Alex had suffered, he had always been the more delicate of all the children, the others being of robust build in contrast to his dainty frame.

"I will never forget that distressing time, dear, but it would be foolhardy to be too lenient with his pranks because of that, don't you think?" Anne asked, unable to resist a smile as Alex's infectious laughter carried up the passage.

"And neither shall we be, but on the other hand nor must his boyish ways be stifled. I will have him grow into a man and not some fop, despite his angelic looks. Now my dear, I do believe I have time to look in at the yard before dinner is served." He sniffed the air appreciatively, "oxtail soup I believe?"

Anne nodded as she added, "with your favourite dressed mutton to follow. Then we have pork pie with turnips, roast…"

"Enough! Enough!" He laughed, unbuttoning his coat and slipping his hand inside to draw out his watch from the pocket of his waistcoat to note the time. "There is still another hour before I can indulge in that healthy repast madam so I implore you not to tempt either I or my poor stomach with thoughts of what is to come!"

Hanging his coat and hat on the nearby hallstand John happened to glance into the mirror at its centre and in doing so he caught Anne's reflection as she stood behind him. She was looking at him keenly and he knew instinctively that she was pondering on what might have occurred at his father's house. He knew her well enough to know that she would not ask, just as she knew he would never discuss such matters of his sole concern with her, even if she were so bold.

The two upper storeys of Surrey Lodge comprised a quaint arrangement of narrow passages, steps, staircases and inner connecting rooms which gave the house a character all of its own. There were ten rooms in total, eight used as bedrooms and two as water closets. The bedrooms all had fireplaces but, whereas gas light had been installed throughout the lower floor, these rooms were lit by candles, set into brass sconces on the walls.

At the top of the main staircase a narrow corridor led on ahead to the small rooms built above the kitchen and scullery but John did not take this route. Instead he followed the passage to the right and, avoiding the staircase that would take him on to the upper floor, he turned into the room alongside. Facing directly onto the road, it was a medium-sized room, which unfortunately appeared much smaller because of the furniture that occupied it. For the large brass bedstead, with its thick patchwork-covered eiderdown disguising the deep feather-filled mattress, dominated the centre and, with the dark mahogany furniture lining two of the walls, there was very little room to spare.

As he stripped off his clothes John was gratified to find the room was still warm despite the remains of the previous evening's embers having been cleaned out and the small fire relaid ready for the lighting at four. With haunting memories of the inflamed chilblains that infected his feet throughout his childhood winters he determinedly avoided the cold both for himself and his family. It was the reason he always insisted the bedroom fires were lit as dusk fell during winter and warming pans were put in the beds. These two habits did not always keep the chilblains at bay but with the additional wearing of thick woollen stockings during the day he believed the right precautions were being taken.

John had two best and two working outfits. Leaving the best that he had been wearing on the bed for Anne to put away he quickly donned the working suit hanging in readiness on the door of the armoire. Attaching the collar and cuffs to his shirt was a fiddle because of his sudden realisation of the passing of time, but soon it was complete and he was making his way back down the stairs again, pulling on the black cuff protectors over his sleeve ends as he went.

He was anxious to get to the yard now, eager to see that his earlier orders to his foreman Matthew had been carried out and to give further commands to cover his absence that afternoon. For on divesting himself of his best clothes he had resolved that he would change back into them again later. He would need to present himself well when calling on his solicitor.

John's Advocate was as surprised as his client at the contents of

Nathaniel Westaway's will relating to property, not only at the large extent of the estate but also at the bequests. That two-thirds had been bequeathed to women when there was a male heir caused him to question John as to his father's state of mind when it was written. John could only admit that he considered his father's thinking to be quite sound until he retired from his business, after which time he found him irritatingly slow in coming to decisions. Could it be that the Will was unsound, he asked.

The Advocate replied that in John's shoes he would be asking that very question. John said the notion had crossed his mind for he was quite nonplussed by his father's actions in dividing his estate and he would welcome any help and advice. The lawyer said he would prefer to talk with Jean Le Balastier before he made any recommendations but in the meantime he suggested John make himself responsible for collecting the rents on his sisters' properties until matters were settled.

Jean Le Balastier had left for France by the time John's lawyer sent his clerk with a request for a meeting so a letter had to be sent to which there was a long delay before the reply was received. In the interim Nathaniel's accounts were audited and a deficit of £3,750 was found.

Harriet and Julia were shocked at this revelation for they had always considered their father to be meticulous about his accounts but, called into the office of their brother's lawyer, they each signed an agreement to pay a third of the sum. On looking through their father's papers later, however, the sisters found proof that the deficit did not exist.

Though he did not enlighten them John's Advocate was already aware of the fact. "Let them take the matter to court which is their right," he told both John and later Pierre Le Sueur, the sisters' lawyer, when he called to discuss the matter.

Advocate Pierre Le Sueur, Constable of St. Helier, was troubled. It was obvious that delaying tactics were being used and he advised the sisters to get possession of their properties before going to court.

"No court would sanction any fraudulence so you have no fear that the agreement would not be annulled at a later date," he promised them. But, unfortunately, he died suddenly before he could represent them further.

It was nearly a year later that John, angered by his sisters' persistent requests to let them have their inheritances, directed his lawyer to action them for being in breach of the legal agreement they had signed where they had promised to pay the deficit on their father's account. Harriet and Julia attended the Court with their new solicitor, Mr Dallain, who presented the proof that the deficit did not exist. But the Court would not accept it because a year and a day had passed from the date the sisters had signed the agreement. Reluctantly they accepted they would have to pay but, they asked, when were they to be in possession of their properties.

Despite many meetings, when bartering and ceding of ownership of various properties were discussed, matters rolled on for another 11 months before Harriet and Julia were called before the Court to see their properties legally validated. Another six months were to pass after this before they received all the title deeds. They had still to receive the rents that John had collected on their behalf.

Naturally the sisters were both hurt and angry at their brother's continual dismissive behaviour towards them. Though they kept up appearances in front of others a point was reached where the three were barely on speaking terms. However, when they received the news that 15 year-old Charles had died at sea, whilst the ship on which he had been apprenticed was on route for China, both Harriet and Julia accompanied their mother to Surrey Lodge to pay their respects. He was their nephew after all, they told themselves, and this was not a time to hold grudges. They were gratified to find their generosity of spirit was well appreciated.

Time passed with repeated requests for John to pay the rents he owed them, time during which he resisted, claiming to have carried out repairs on the properties so no monies were due. In return they asked him to submit a statement of accounts but none was ever forthcoming.

Then Anne Guillet fell ill with consumption and, suspecting that John would be most distressed, they instructed their solicitor Mr Dallain to bide his time. After she died in 1856, two years after her son Charles, they called again at Surrey Lodge but were disappointed at John's coldness towards them. When 16 year-old Maria followed her mother to the grave the following year they did not call but wrote letters of sympathy, for by then they had been forced to serve him with an order of justice to produce the accounts. When at long last he conceded, they found he had deducted £1,000 as a fee for acting as their agent. They were furious but admitted defeat.

Anne too had become increasingly angry at her son's behaviour. When the bartering and ceding of the properties was happening she had feared the crescent would be lost so she bought it and on 15th April 1857 made her will, leaving the six houses equally between Harriet and Julia.

The following year John took out a Court action against each of his sisters for the original sums of £1,225 with much added interest for the years during which they had withheld payment. With the threat of prison for failure to comply they asked the Court to deduct the charges which were considered to be excessive. When the Jurats thought them moderate they took their appeal to the full court. After this failed they determined to drop all further proceedings and deposited £1,600 each with the Jersey Banking Company. They wrote to John saying that they thought it was a fairer amount than the excessive interest asked and gave him seven days in which to reply. He replied by increasing the amount of interest. By this time the month of April 1861 had been reached.

21

"JOHN! JOHN!"

Anne's voice, unsteady and feeble with age, failed to rise above the sound of the two men shovelling coal into the cart at the side of the yard. Nevertheless they looked up as she hobbled towards them leaning heavily on two walking canes. "Where is my son? Where is he?" she demanded angrily.

"Mama, what are you doing in here?" John asked coming out of the wooden shack he used as an office. "This is never the place for a lady, here...." He came to her and lifted her skirts which were dragging in the black dust. "You should have come to the house."

"And be put off as your sisters have continually been? Huh!" She retorted, hitting out with her canes so that he let her skirt drop. "You know full well why I am here John, so do not pretend otherwise. Only on your word could that denunciator Godfray call at the house this last hour under the impression that he could carry your sisters off to prison for a debt you know they do not owe. You have got to stop John, you have got to stop all this vindictiveness towards your sisters right now before you drown in the hell pit you are digging for yourself."

"And they are without fault? Huh!"

"No, I have never owned that, but you have had it within your power to settle matters long before now. Well, I have stood by quietly, praying that you, as head of the family, might come to your senses. And I might add whilst we are just the two of us, the one most in the wrong.... You need not shake your head for you know I am right..... However this latest, most outrageous act of threatening to imprison your sisters is too much."

"It was not an idle threat Mama. They will go to prison if they do not pay. As the law stands it is an offence to owe money and if the debt is not paid the debtor is thrown into jail until it is. The law cannot be changed on any whim of mine. All they have to do is pay me the money they owe."

"Bah! You cannot be serious! These are your sisters, your own kith and kin...."

"I am deadly serious Mama, let them make no mistake about that!"

"And make no mistake that I will cut you off completely, by word and deed, if you dare to go through with it!" she threatened. Then, on seeing his face blanch, she softened her voice to continue, "You know full well that your sisters have offered to pay you the right sum they owe but you have been hellbent in continually holding out for more. Why John? Do you need money so badly that you need to steal from your own family?"

"It is not stealing! The money is mine by just right and they will pay it!" John shouted angrily before suddenly realising that the men were witnessing the spectacle of mother and son in verbal conflict and would be gossiping about it to all and sundry later. "Get yourself back to own little domain, Mama dear," he hissed, "and the crescent you bought from your children to safeguard your own ends. Ha! But it did not take you long to come out of mourning and begin meddling, did it?" He shook his head before saying with a sneer. "And to think I was almost taken in by that mute act at the time! When it comes to deviousness Mama, it would be a rare man who could compete with you!"

Tears of indignation sprang to Anne's eyes as she glared at her son. "How can you be so cruel John? That was no act but a black despondency, which continues to afflict me from time to time and had you visited more frequently, you would have been aware of that fact. There has not been a single day during the ten years since..." He made to correct her but she went on determinedly. "I exaggerate only by three months and ten days to when it will be the tenth anniversary of your dear Papa's death but I repeat there has not been a single day since that I have not grieved his loss. Grief affects the mourner in many ways John, you should know that. I would hope none would be unkind enough to criticise you and the children for coping so well after the loss of Anne and young Charles and Maria."

An odd look crossed his eyes, and she tried to define it, tried to elicit from it some sign that under his cool exterior he had been greatly affected by their deaths. Yet surely he could not have remained unmoved? She asked herself. A deep feeling of regret suddenly overwhelmed her as she realised that she had never truly understood him, that in standing aside from the feuding between her three children and excusing his perverse coolness towards herself she had encouraged a breach which was now too wide ever to be mended. Still she had to try to reach some sort of understanding.

"As for buying the crescent, why would you begrudge me that? It is my home, the last home your papa built for me and I was in danger of losing it amongst all the legal wrangling that was going on between the three of you. May God bless your dear papa throughout his days in eternity for insisting on seeing that I had the wherewithal in my name long before he died, else I would not have been able to keep my home from your greedy..."

But he had stopped listening and had turned to watch the men lead the horse and cart out onto the road.

"John, this behaviour of yours..." she began again but now he had taken out his fob watch, glancing at it before looking in the direction of the departing men. He seemed to have already dismissed her, either that or he was ignoring her presence as if she was of no account. How could he act this way – he to whom she had given birth? There seemed to be no way of reasoning with him.

"Oh! John, John," she said sadly. "How did matters ever get to this point?" And when he made no reply she turned and walked slowly back to her waiting carriage.

He stood unmoving for some minutes after she had left before noticing the silence that hung about the yard. He was alone. Suddenly a heavy depression fell over him and he hugged his chest in an effort to ease the beginnings of a now familiar ache. 'How did matters ever get to this point?' his mother had asked.

'God alone knows,' he answered mournfully as he returned to the shack. 'God alone knows.'

Later, feeling the need to use the water closet he went through the gate at the far end of the coal yard and entered the backyard to his home. His two youngest daughters, Charlotte and Susan, were taking in the dry washing from the rope lines that spanned the entire length of the area. He waited whilst they made a parting between a couple of bedsheets, and gave a dim smile in response to their cheerful rhyme of 'In and Out the Windows' as he passed under to enter the scullery. The cook and housekeeper Mrs Mulberry was busy preparing the evening meal at the table and the maid adding coal to the grate as he hurried through but though the older woman asked, "Everything to your satisfaction sir?" he merely nodded in reply.

At the foot of the stairs he stopped suddenly as a memory came back to haunt him. It was of the day he learnt of the contents of his father's will and he had come home to find Alex sailing down the banister rail with a worried Anne at the foot. The memory came so plainly it was as if she was stood beside him and he could smell the very scent of her. Overcome with longing he gripped the rail and lowered his forehead onto it.

'God in heaven,' he moaned silently, 'when will this pain ever ease?' It was five years since Anne Guillet had been taken with consumption and the time had passed just as his mother had described with never a day or night going by that he did not not bring her to mind and long for her presence. Only after her death had he realised how much he had needed her, not just as someone to assuage his desires but also as a dear heart who loved him no matter what he said or did. Losing her had been his bitterest blow.

It had been easier for him to accept the loss of 15 yearold Charles who had died of a fever on board ship somewhere between England and China two years before Anne for, since leaving soon after his grandfather's death, the boy had not returned to the island. And sad though they all were at the time, it must be said that with only the very occasional letter to keep him in mind they had all become accustomed to his absence. Even his twin, Henrietta, who had been so close in spirit that she had sensed something was wrong long before the news reached Jersey, had not succumbed to her grief until the day their sister Maria died the following year to their mother Anne.

For 16 year-old Maria's death, coming so soon after her mother's and from the same illness, finally caused Henrietta to accept that three of her most loved family were gone forever and she fell into a deep state of melancholia. But John too, with his grieving for Anne intensified by the additional loss of the one daughter who had inherited the lively and warm nature of his dead sister Charlotte, suffered terribly. Unable to lower the manly façade he had built around himself by openly mourning he began instead to exhibit sudden rages at the smallest wrong any member of his family committed.

In addition, whenever their father was absent, John Junior, who had adored his mother intensely, took to constantly criticising Annie on whose unrehearsed but capable shoulders the maternal mantle naturally fell. Naturally Annie, in inheriting some of her paternal grandmother's strength of mind, stood her ground, which infuriated her domineering brother even more. Rows between the pair surfaced daily.

Had Nathaniel and James not been away this added turmoil would probably not have continued for in championing their sister they would have quickly taken their older brother to task. But Nathaniel was in the Royal Engineers and James had enlisted into the 13th Light Infantry so both were unaware of what was going on at home. The remaining brother – the slightly built, innocent faced and gentle young Alex – always left the house as soon as he felt trouble brewing and headed for the home of his aunts and grandmother where he knew, of all his sisters and brothers, he was the most welcome.

It was an almost insufferable time for all the inhabitants of Surrey Lodge, not forgetting young Charlotte and Susan. As the youngest of the family they had become used to a certain amount of petting from both parents but now their mother was dead and, in being so completely changed from the man he had once been, it was as if they had lost their father too.

They were not to know of course that amplifying their father's agitation was the ongoing business of settling their grandfather's affairs. Only the apprentice lawyer John Junior knew the full account, and that both because of his work practice and the fact that as the eldest he would in turn inherit his own father's estate.

"And it now appears that they are defying the latest court order," John complained to his eldest son as they walked through the empty, echoing rooms of a large house at the end of a terrace further along Belmont Road. "They refuse, would you believe, to pay me the interest on the money I was originally awarded through the courts nine years past but which through the generosity of my heart had let lie dormant."

John Junior snorted derisively. He knew of it all of course. It was he who had advised his father the money was still outstanding, that the maiden aunts had no right to it. But they would never get away with this latest claim. His father only had to stand his ground. The court had always ruled against them.

"So, tell me, what would you say if I were to make you a gift of this house in celebration of your 25th birthday?" his father said, changing the subject abruptly.

"I would say that it would be my greatest pleasure to accept," John Junior replied. It was also, John added as he handed his son the keys, a way of expressing his gratitude for all the advice and shared discussions that helped clear his mind towards all his legal dealings.

"It meant greatly to have you agree that by all rights of inheritances I should have been the sole heir of your grandfather's estate," he told him. "I also appreciated your sincere commiseration when after full search the lawyers found that nothing could be done about the injustice and that I had to concede to the relevant deeds being finally handed over to your aunts. But were they grateful? They were not! The devil take them!"

"You must simply insist that they pay you the full amount Papa."

Suddenly the fight went out of John and he felt a great weariness overtake him. "Aw! But son," he confided, "I have come to be heartily sick of it all."

It was true. He had seldom enjoyed a moment's peace since his father's death thanks to the bedevilment of his sisters. Even his regular visits to the graves of his dearest Anne and Maria, who lay above his father in the large plot he had bought in St. Saviour's cemetery, were sullied by his sisters' bitter acrimony. For there, on the very path he had to walk and only a few feet from the grave, his sisters had bought another plot. On it they had put up a monstrous monument in memory of their father.

'Erected by two mourning daughters,' the engraving glaringly announced. As if the headstone he had put up had not been good enough! It was the epitome of all the ugly bitterness that had sprung up between them.

John had been a frequent visitor to his parents' home whilst they lived in Don Street but the visits decreased once they were installed in St. Saviour's Crescent. His father would often stop by the coal yard on his way to or from town and, on leaving, ask him to call on his mother and sisters. John always promised that of course he would but he rarely did. He had been very busy, he replied when asked why he had not done so. And he had spoken the truth. For new coal suppliers were now competing for business and with a large family to support he needed to keep his yard open for longer hours in order to gain a reasonable income.

And even though that income improved greatly after his father's death, permitting him to employ a foreman to run the yard, he still did not visit. But this time it was simply because he did not wish to. And it was all his sisters' fault, he told himself. If they had not been so doggedly persistent in demanding possession of their inheritance in the first place, thereby causing him to avoid meeting up with them at any cost, he might have visited his mother more often. It was their malicious ways that kept him from her side.

"Threaten them with prison!" John Junior had said, breaking into his father's thoughts. "Nothing like the threat of a term in prison to bring debtors to heel I've always thought!"

John stared at his son's face without seeing the natural puffiness of the cheeks, the bushy sideburns and drooped moustache of the same texture that had once been his father's, but seeing only the cold pomposity in his eyes.

"I could not see my own flesh and blood put in prison!" he gasped.

"It would never come to that," John Junior assured him. "Take it from me, they would crumple at the thought of it and you would bring all this sheer effrontery to an end once and for all. If they persist in deducting the interest from the sum they owe you then threaten to put them in prison until they pay in full."

It was an outrageous suggestion but his son was right, John thought. Such an action might bring the ongoing *roman-fleuve* to an end for once and all.

But four years passed before he acted on that decision. Four years during which he continued to avoid his sisters in the hope that they would come to their senses. Years during which he began to walk another path in the cemetery when visiting the graves of his dear Anne and Maria, keeping his eyes firmly fixed on their names rather than risk being moved to anger by the sight of the mocking commemoration to his father.

For anger, he had learnt after an incident when he had struck out at Alex and caused a terrible cacophony of crying and screaming to erupt amongst his children, was a most destructive force. The anguish and fear on their faces, all that he loved most in the living world, had shocked him to the core. Breaking down, he hugged them to him and told them he was sorry. His tears encouraged theirs so that soon they were all hugging each other and crying copiously. The action allowed the family's immense grief to finally erupt and dissolve but John did not see it that way. He thought it was his terrible behaviour that had caused such suffering and vowed never to let it happen again.

With John Junior happily installed in Elizabeth House, further along Belmont Road, and Annie confidently running the family home with the help of the cook and kitchen maid who had been employed in addition to the two general helps they had always kept, peace was restored at Surrey Lodge. The home leaves of Nathaniel and James were each joyously celebrated and three trips taken to undergo the exploration of London, Edinburgh and Paris. Then there had been the unexpected visit to the island by Her Royal Majesty Queen Victoria and Prince Albert when Annie, Charlotte and Susan had rushed up to join the crowds at Victoria College with their father, Alex and John Junior. It was not the most organised of occasions but they were all delighted to have a close view of the Royal couple.

Outside of the family island life continued to evolve. The previous nine years had seen many changes including the town drainage scheme masterminded by the late Advocate Pierre Le Sueur, Constable of St Helier, successfully installed beneath the many streets of the town, including Belmont Road. John agreed with leading men of the time in describing the scheme as 'the greatest of all blessings'.

'It was a pity,' many added when attending the elaborate funeral of the 41 year-old lawyer, 'that he had not lived to truly enjoy the fruits of his labour.' Pierre Le Sueur it was who had been Harriet and Julia's Advocate.

The family had also come to appreciate the postal service as a way of rapid communication with folk either in the island or away and regularly used the pillar-box close to the Rectory in David Place, which was nearest to their home. Anthony Trollope, a Surveyor's Clerk employed by the Post Office, had introduced the roadside letter-boxes into the island during the year of Nathaniel's death when they had been the first to be seen in the United Kingdom. The States were very proud of this innovative feature.

A Petty Debts Court and Police Court had been created, as had a paid police force within the town. The cost of the force was borne one-third by the States and two-thirds by a rate on the householders of St. Helier, a charge about which most, having complained bitterly at first, soon came to accept as inevitable.

A great fire had destroyed the hospital and there was a public demand for one 'of the English style' to replace it. This would mean housing the paupers, poor-law children and lunatics separately from the sick, the tending of all four groups together creating grave concern.

The problems of the poor were, as ever, present but, whereas Anne, Harriet and Julia continued to treat them with Christian compassion John and his family tended to dismiss the majority as 'deserving of their condition'. It was a popular belief amongst the more prosperous settlers, a class system which had quickly spread amongst the more fortunate of islanders.

It was throughout all these events that the ongoing legal wrangling between John and his sisters continued and on receipt of the letter from his sisters saying that they had deposited what they thought was a fair amount with the bank, and did not intend to pay him any more, which caused him to finally call an end to it all.

"I have instructed the lawyers to make good the threat of prison if they do not pay the full sum," he told John Junior.

"About time too," his son replied. "Do you realise how much court time they have been able to monopolise over the years? I have been quite embarrassed by our relationship, I can tell you, and though the Jurats have dismissed their every application it is our family name that is being bandied about. This farce should have been ended long before now."

Yet it was another six months until John Junior forced him to act.

"Enough with the dithering Papa. Stand back and allow the law to take its course. Despite what you think the aunts will soon capitulate once they have a sniff at the rotting cells!" He had promised.

Yet regardless of the determined front he had shown his mother earlier on the 11th of October 1861 John Nathaniel Westaway was not proud of the way matters had turned out. Although he did not care very much for them, these were his sisters after all.

22

"Well, what did you think of the sermon?" Anne asked on the following Sunday as, handing both Julia and Harriet one of her walking canes to carry, she stepped between them and linked a hand through each of their nearest arms. Together like this the three went out through the church gates and turned left into St. Mark's Road.

Julia bent her head forward and, looking across at her sister, gave a little smile. Harriet grimaced in return.

"Well?" Anne asked again before adding, "And what is so comical about that question pray?"

"Nothing Mama dear," Julia said, trying to look serious.

"Now Julia, behave!" Harriet warned, a playful gleam suddenly appearing in her eyes. "If you had been giving the sermon as much attention as Mama, instead of staring at that Madame Tricot's new bonnet, you would have been able to answer that question!"

"Staring at new bonnets, even if they are extraordinarily stylish, does not affect one's hearing," Julia answered, "but I suppose had I closed my eyes I might have dropped off to sleep and then I would have missed the subject of the sermon altogether and need to be reminded."

"And did you fall asleep Julia? That would have been very unusual of you."

"Not me Mama!" Julia laughed outright now. "But someone very close to me."

"Really, who?"

"You!"

"Oh! Julia, how could you suggest such a thing?" Harriet said sternly. "Mama may have had her eyes closed but she was listening and thinking, is that not right Mama?"

"That is perfectly correct! So tell me what did you think of the Reverend's understanding of the parable of the Prodigal Son?"

"Oh! Mama!" Julia said, hugging her mother's arm closer into her side. "And I thought you had taken a little sleep."

"Well I cannot say that I truly heard all of it, that sing-song voice of his is better than a lullaby sometimes, but I heard enough. So?"

"Step back Mama!... Julia!" Harriet suddenly warned as the wheels of a passing carriage ran through a large puddle in the gutter, spraying water up and outwards and just missing the skirts of their coats. "Heathen!" She muttered angrily.

"Harriet! And on the Lord's day too. Really!" Anne admonished. "Well?" She persisted as they fell into a unified pace once more. Then after a few minutes had passed and there was still no reply she said, "Oh! For goodness sake! I might as well talk to a cat for all the response I am getting from you two!"

"We do not wish to discuss it Mama," Harriet said firmly.

"We? You speak for Julia?" and turning swiftly to her younger daughter Anne asked, "You do not want to discuss the sermon either?"

"I think Hattie would rather not discuss the principal of the parable Mama, neither would I." Then, leaning her head towards her mother's, Julia said softly, "I know it must upset you deeply to have your children at war with each other like this Mama. But it would take a saint to forgive John and welcome him back into the fold after all that he has done. Though we try to be devout Christian women neither Hattie nor I are destined to be saints."

"But..."

"Butt! Butt! Butting is what nanny goats do. Is that not what dear papa used to say?" Julia said. Anne gave her a sad smile and bent her head towards her younger daughter.

"Your dear papa must be turning in his grave at what is going on between his children," she said.

"Oh! Mama, please do not say such a terrible thing. We could not act in any other way with John behaving so fraudulently and the courts aiding him in his crimes," Julia replied.

"Perhaps if you just paid up the money... After all, to go to prison..."

"Oh! It was never meant to come to that!" Harriet said confidently. "That threat of the denunciator on Friday was pure humbug. We would have been in prison by now had it been otherwise. No, mark my words, soon we shall find that the money that has been waiting all these months will be quietly credited into John's bank account and we shall hear no more."

At her confident assurance a false sense of security fell over them so it was a shock therefore when the denunciator Godfray arrived at breakfast time the following morning. Brandishing a warrant which entitled him to take both Julia and Harriet to the prison immediately he allowed them no time to finish their meal as he ordered them to pack a few belongings.

"You said it would never come to this!" Julia hissed as they made their way up the stairs.

"And I never thought it would!" Harriet snapped. "John's talent for treachery has surpassed even my expectations. Well, he shall not win. Even with this act of duplicity he will find that I will not cower. You do not have to join me Julia. I will not blame you if you prefer to pay him and be done with it, but I shall not. Prison will not be pleasant but for me it will be a martyrdom of principal."

"How can you think I will let you go to prison alone when we have been joined in this together all along? Though the thought of it is quite abhorrent I am of the same mind as you and would not pay him, not now, not ever."

"What is it? Has that man come? Will you be going to prison?" An anxious Anne staggered out from her bedroom which, in deference to her age and disability, had been moved down from the room she shared with Nathaniel to one on the rear of the first floor.

"Yes Mama, we are going to prison," Harriet said bitterly as she passed by to climb the next flight of stairs to her room. "This is what the Mister John Westaway has brought his family to."

But Julia paused to reach for her mother and taking hold of her arm said, "Where are your canes Mama? You know you should not walk about without them."

"Bah to my canes! Tell me you will reconsider and pay John."

"No Mama," Julia said firmly. "We will not." Then when she saw the tears appear in her mother's eyes she drew her into her arms and soothed. "Now you must not upset yourself Mama. John will soon relent and in the meanwhile you are not to fret about Hattie and I for we will be together. We have spoken to Bertha and Jack who are, as we have always known, slaves to your every wish, so we in turn will try not to worry about you. Jack has promised to come to the prison every day and when he does we shall give him a letter for you. It will be like it is when we have been away on our travels" she ended, sounding almost jovial.

"Do not take me for a fool, Julia dear, and do not fool yourself. Though the prison was reformed after Elizabeth Fry's visit all those years ago it is still the most awful place and, despite your innocence, the stigma for having been placed there will remain with you both for the rest of your lives. I will never forgive your brother for allowing this to come about and I want you to know that though I wish you too had acted otherwise I am very proud of you and will be always. Please remember that."

"Thank you Mama. I love you," Julia said brokenly.

"I love you too," Anne told her. "Now I must finish my dressing so that I will be presentable when you leave. Where is that man by the way?"

Realising that her mother was referring to the man Godfray, Julia said he was in the drawing room.

"You should have told him to wait outside in the carriage," Anne said, turning away.

Suddenly the household bustled into activity as Jack searched out travelling valises and took them upstairs whilst Bertha, shaking her head in disbelief that this kind of thing should happen to the honest and good Misses Julia and Harriet, hurriedly made up a basket of food. At the same time she ordered the new housemaid Betsy to fetch the bolsters and counterpanes from the sisters' beds and when Jack returned she instructed him to help the girl pack them into neat paper parcels on the kitchen floor.

Upstairs, Julia and Harriet were having difficulty in deciding what they should take with Harriet being by far the more practical and including writing materials, clock, candles and matches amongst a set of fresh garments. Julia had to be reminded that she would not have a need of her prettiest clothes or lace handkerchiefs, things she had a great liking for, but nevertheless Harriet smiled indulgently when she insisted on taking her special Bible. Large, bulky and leather bound with a metal clasp, it had been given to commemorate her twenty-second birthday, the inscription inside reading, 'the gift of her beloved father.' At the time it had been a gift of her choice since when she had endeavoured to study it as an almost daily ritual, for it contained added notes and observations that she found most useful in fully understanding the scriptures. Harriet knew that though her young sister had another Bible, a smaller one with a matching Book of Common Prayer that she carried to church twice each Sunday, this was special in that it was also a constant reminder of their dear papa.

Though it seemed like an interminably long wait for the lawman Godfray, to the sisters it seemed like only moments between the time he arrived to when they were saying goodbye and urging the small, tearful party which had collected on the doorstep to 'be steadfast in your prayers for us.' The drive through the town also seemed short and all too soon they found themselves within the gates of Newgate Prison, hauling their two bulging valises, bedding and food basket into the grim looking building. However, once inside, they were put to wait alone for a long hour in a narrow darkened room containing several tables and chairs, whilst all their belongings, having been taken from them, were searched.

"Miss Harriet an' Miss Julia Westaway?" The slovenly woman who appeared suddenly in the doorway pronounced their names in a slightly derisive tone. Not knowing what was expected of them they just stared at her until she ordered, "Get yerself out 'ere, the Turnkey wants yer."

"How dare...!"

"Harriet, shhh!"

"He don't like bein' kept waitin' so if it please yer ladyships to follow me," she said pointedly to Harriet before leading the way into a much smaller room. There sitting at a tall desk, similar to that used by the clerks in many businesses and offices, was a gaunt-faced man with sunken eyes and cheeks that blew in and out in time with his rumbling breath. He barely glanced at them as he recorded their names and ages and the words 'indebted to Mr John N. Westaway' in his ledger but when he did look up it was with an indifferent stare as he said, in a breathless and laboured tone, "You will be expected to make your beds and sweep out your cell every morning, one half-hour being allowed each meal time for the cleaning of your pots and pail in the yard. You will take whatever exercise necessary at that time. You will rise at the seven o'clock bell and eat at eight. All meals will be fetched from the cook-house and eaten in your room. You will be permitted visitors between the hours of nine and eleven o'clock in the morning and two and four o'clock in the afternoon for which you will be called from your room. Dinner is at noon and supper at six. You will be ready for the bell at all times. Lock-up is at eight o'clock in the evening. You will be able to receive clothing and necessary goods which will be first inspected by either myself, or a member of the Prison Board, but no

food or liquor. Any benefactions will be distributed as I see fit. All
bedding and linen brought into the prison will be fumigated but may
be hung to air in the open whenever the weather permits or the Matron
deems necessary. You will be required to attend divine service when
performed unless prevented by illness or other reasonable cause. Any
disobedience of either my orders or rules and regulations of the prison
shall be visited with such privation and punishment as may be lawfully
correct. The Matron here will now take you to your cell in the Debtors
Ward."

"And what of our belongings?" Harriet asked him, while returning
the glare of the woman now eyeing them contemptuously.

"Your bags are there, take them," he said, flicking his hand in the
direction of a corner on the opposite side of the room.

"And our bedding…?"

"And our basket of food?" Julia added.

"As I said your bedding is to be fumigated. As for the victuals that
will be distributed as the board sees fit," he said waving them away.

Without another word they picked up their valises and, following
the Matron out of the office, hauled them along a corridor the exit of
which was barred by a door faced in studded metal with a bolt top
and bottom. The bolts were drawn back but, taking a large key from
the bunch hanging on a chain at her waist, the Matron placed it in the
additional lock and turned it. She then pulled the heavy door open to
reveal a narrow passage lined with similar doors, one of which gaped
wide. Once through the main door the Matron locked it behind them
before leading them through the passage and unlocking the door at
the further end. As the sisters passed the open doorway they peered
in and saw what looked like an occupied cell but there was no one to
be seen.

On the other side of the further door, which once again the Matron
locked behind them, was a flight of stone steps which took them to an
upper passage laid out exactly like the one below. All the doors however
were closed. Stopping at the fourth door along on the right she
unlocked it and, opening it wide, stood aside for the sisters to enter.

"It is…" Julia began, her voice coming out in a shocked whisper.

"Not as bad as expected!" Harriet, though panting under the weight
of her large valise nevertheless ended her sister's sentence spiritedly
as she passed by on her way through the thick wooden door to the

cell. Dropping the bag to the floor she glanced around the dim interior as if inspecting a room at an inn, her nose seemingly oblivious to the foul stench that held Julia back from entering.

On the left-hand wall, wedged between tall rickety cupboards standing like drunken sentries, two stain-covered palliasse beds hung one above the other on thick chains. Directly ahead, high above an unclothed table and two chairs, a small barred window was set deep into the granite wall, a long rope dangling from a metal loop at its centre. Also on that wall, at head height, two small niches had been carved out and caged with wire to enclose candles, the cold wax from which spilled out into imitations of miniature frozen waterfalls. Lastly, on the right, another table with a chipped jug and basin on top of it, flanked a small, ash-filled fireplace. "Indeed, it could be much worse" she announced finally.

An appalled Julia looked back at the Matron now observing them both with unconcealed amusement. "Do you have to lock us in?" She asked nervously. Being closed, all the other doors in the narrow passage took on a terrifying sight with bolts top and bottom of their studded metal façades. Though now open she knew the other side of the door to their cell was the same and suddenly she dreaded the thought of being interned behind it.

The woman nodded before saying, "Yer should be grateful 'tis only after the last bell. If yer were on the lower ward yer'd be locked in earlier." Then, after regarding them for a few minutes she added finally, "Well, yer 'ad all the rules told yer by the Turnkey so it just abides wiv me say, welcome to the Newgate Inn me proud ladies!" She chortled to herself as she made her way back along the narrow passage.

"When are we to eat?" Julia called after her.

"When I ring me bell!" was the reply before the door banged shut and they heard the sound of the key being turned in the lock.

For a while the two sisters stared at one another in dismay as, as in a thick fog, an eerie silence closed in around them. Then suddenly they were in each other's arms, holding each other tight, in a wordless embrace.

"We should unpack," Harriet said at last, turning away and walking towards the table. "It is best if we get accustomed to everything as soon as possible."

"Oh! But Hattie, it is just too terrible" Julia gasped. "The smell...the squalor...that woman.... Do you think we will be able to bear it after all?"

"Now, now Julia. Where is that intrepid soldier of yesterday? That valiant woman who consistently warned me not to yield under the onslaught of legal cannon fire?"

"In truth I did not think John would permit things to go this far."

"In truth neither did I," Harriet agreed, "but I shall never forgive him for it and neither should you."

"Oh! Rest assured there is nothing John could do now to redeem himself in my eyes," Julia said, returning to the passage where she had left her valise. Dragging it into the cell she now looked about properly. However, unlike her sister, her first action after placing it down was to follow her offended nose. On doing so she quickly located the culprit beneath the lower hammock.

Reaching inside her cape she took an embroidered handkerchief from the small drawstring bag hanging from the waist of her dress and, pushing it to her face grabbed the handle of the pail with her free, gloved hand. Then, averting her eyes from the foetid contents, she carried the pail into the passage at arm's length before placing it down away from the door.

Re-entering the cell she made her way to Harriet's side where she opened the window by pulling on the rope. "It defeats me how you can abide this smell," she said, winding the rope into a figure of eight around the nearby cleat.

"I suppose because it is the same smell as came from the hovels mama and I once used to take soup and bread to. Mama taught me then how important it was never to show distaste and I do believe the advice must have stayed. We will soon get used to it," Harriet told her before changing the subject with, "tell me which cupboard would you like to use?"

Julia did not care and said so. Quietly she joined her sister in emptying the contents of her own bag and placing all but her large Bible away out of sight. Moving the jug and bowl to the floor she put her Bible on the middle of the small table alongside the fireplace, stroking its cover almost tenderly as she did so.

"I hope one of us can remember how to light a fire," Harriet said suddenly, poking at the embers in the grate. "Not that we will have to worry about that today for we have no means of feeding it. We shall simply have to keep our capes on for the time being. We must put a bucket of coal and some kindling on the list for Jack to bring. I shall begin the list now."

Julia, having seen her sister take the writing paper, plume and ink from her bag earlier, watched her sit down at the table under the window and begin to write, before turning away.

"I think I should sleep down here, with you being much taller," Julia commented, sweeping her hand over the crude mattress on the lower bed before gingerly sitting on it. The hammock swung slightly under her weight, clanking the chains and forcing her to plant her feet firmly on the ground in an effort to remain steady. She tried to sit upright but with the plank of wood to the upper bunk just above her head she was unable to do. She leant forward, her elbows on her knees. But even through her many voluminous skirts she could feel the straw filling of the palliasse and, under that, the unforgiving wooden support, so she stood up again.

Suddenly they heard the heavy passage door being dragged open, followed by the clanging of a hand-bell. "Prisoners Westaway, yer dinners is awaitin' yer pleasure," the Matron's voice rang out mockingly.

She was waiting at the open doorway, her hands on her hips in a gesture of impatience. They hurried forward and followed her back down the stairs and through numerous passages to the cookhouse. There, under the gaze of several pairs of curious eyes belonging to other female prisoners they were each given a tin tray, plate, cup and spoon and told to collect their meal. It was an unappetising mess of ox-head soup thickened with oatmeal, potatoes and vegetables and a lump of bread, accompanied by a cup of weak tea.

On taking them back to the ward the Matron paused to unlock a door at the side of the passage on the lower floor that the sisters had thought was another cell but saw instead that it led through a smaller passage into the yard. They would be allowed half-an-hour before she returned to lock both it and the door to the upper ward again, the woman said. Both doors would be opened at every meal during which time they would be expected to take their exercise, wash their pots, fetch water and – she added referring to the offending article she had seen lying in the upper passage – clean out their pail. At this Harriet wanted to protest that the pail was not theirs but had been left by the previous prisoner to occupy the cell but the woman turned away too quickly and was soon locking the door they had all just passed through behind her.

Silently Julia and Harriet took their seats at the small table under the window of their cell and listlessly spooned at the food. The mess, from which steam had risen when they had been in the kitchen, had become lukewarm during the walk back to their cell. It was also quite vapid.

"Oh dear," Julia murmured as she thought longingly of the breakfast of herring roes on potato cakes that she had left unfinished on the table when the denunciator came to arrest them earlier that morning.

"I think it would be permissible to leave the rest under the circumstances," Harriet said finally after they had eaten a fraction of what was on the plate. "Let us get rid of all this before that harridan of a woman gets back."

It was only as they left the table that Harriet remembered that they had not said Grace before beginning to eat and, to a relieved Julia, decided to wash out the pail as a personal penance. Julia said her penance would be to eat every morsel of the next meal no matter how terrible it was and Harriet replied that she might prefer to empty the pail a comment which, despite her growing despondency, made Julia laugh.

The yard was long and narrow and enclosed in part by prison buildings and the remainder by a high wall. The air was bitter cold but there was a refreshing smell of the sea, a natural phenomenon seeing that the entrance to the Prison faced the sand dunes, Harriet said as they gulped it in.

As they crossed the yard to the far end where the well and pit were to be found she told Julia that though she had temporarily lost her bearings she now realised that the building they had come from was the addition which overlooked Gloucester Street.

" 'Tis a pity we cannot look out of the windows of our cell for we could have passed many an hour watching the comings and goings of the street. But then we must be grateful that it was built to hold debtors apart from the worst of criminals and for that we must thank Elizabeth Fry," she said. "You would have been too young to have been told about her visit in '33 Julia, but Mama and I were introduced to the Quaker through Mama's good work with the poor, though of course we never enquired about her religion nor considered visiting the prison ourselves. But we learnt from Mrs Fry's own lips how appalled she had been at seeing the conditions here and how she was going to speak up about it on her return to London. At that time men, women, mothers with children, murderers, thieves and debtors were all put together and one can only imagine how terrible it was with several prisoners to a cell, no beds, little food, one pail between all..."

"Oh! Do not go on!" Julia pleaded.

"Well, it must be said that without her intervention these conditions, bad as they are, would have been much worse had her recommendations not led from an English Home Office enquiry into the prison reform. I have to own that I did not approve of the woman's work at the time I met her, even though we were later to hear it earned the admiration of our dear Queen, but now I can only be thankful. For without her intervention we would have been put amongst real criminals and not separated as we are now by being in the Female Debtors' Ward."

Harriet had been talking throughout the short walk to the other side of the yard and also while she removed the wooden cover from over the pit and had tipped the remainder of their meal, and the contents of the pail, into the foul smelling abyss.

"One can only imagine the strangeness of Mrs Fry's life," she continued as she then accompanied her sister to the nearby well and watched as their utensils were washed in the basin Julia had carried from the cell, after which she rinsed out the pail several times. "One day amidst the splendour of the Palace in the company of our dear Queen and the next amongst the common criminals in jail."

"We will be counted amongst the common criminals from now on," Julia remarked soberly.

"Ah! But we know we are not and must stand our ground against anyone who dares to suggest otherwise," Harriet told her, as suddenly the bell rang out. Looking back across the yard they saw the Matron at the door and hurried towards her.

"Oh dear, just look at the pair of us," Julia said as she blew wayward wisps of hair from her face and felt water from the dripping pots seep through the skirt of her gown. Harriet's gown was not only wet but stained, strands of hair springing untidily from the bun at the back of her head. Though both women had removed their bonnets and capes on entering the cell neither had thought to put on their house caps. "And that woman is taking a great delight in our discomfort," she whispered, having noticed the look of wry amusement on the woman's face. "What say you that we spoil her fun by not letting it show?"

Harriet nodded and they both smiled gently at the woman as they approached. However, their ruse failed when the Matron nodded to the far end of the yard and barked sarcastically, "Yer like invitin' the rats to yer abode do yer? Well we're not partial to them 'ere so get yerself back there and draw the lid over the pit. And yer'd better make it like a bat outa hell 'cos I've yet to have me meal and with me stomach feeling as if me throats cut I'm likely to be nasty!"

Julia made to return but, while scowling at the woman, Harriet held her sister back before saying that she would go and began retracing her steps. At this the Matron gestured impatiently that Julia was to make her way back to the cell alone but Julia refused, urging Harriet to hurry instead. Thankfully the woman did not press her but seemed content to watch Harriet begin to scuttle at the plea and smirked minutes later in return for the thunderous look she received. Watching the pair, Julia realised that her sister had taken on yet another enemy and her heart sank further at the thought.

"Let us not antagonise her unnecessarily,"she begged as, once back in their cell, Harriet ranted against the woman's manner. Having wiped the pots they were now rubbing at their skirts with the cloths in an effort to dry them too. "Come, let us brush each other's hair. That is always calming, is it not?"

Later, a certain peace having descended, Julia settled at the small table to read her Bible whilst Harriet sat at the larger one to write a letter to their Mama. It was a short letter, mentioning nothing of their unhappiness or discomforts but saying instead that they had been offered their first meal, taken in the sea air whilst walking in the yard and that, whilst she was writing, Julia was studying her Bible but sent her most affectionate love. She then set about the list of things for Jack to bring.

At three o'clock they heard the door to the passage being pushed open before the Matron's voice announced. "Prisoners Westaway, yer 'ave a visitor."

Harriet picked up the list and the letter to their mother. "It may be Jack but whoever it is let us put on a brave face," Harriet whispered as they followed the woman back down to the long room in which they had sat on their arrival earlier that morning. It was Jack.

" 'Tis a bit early but your mama is fretting that there might be things you need," he said.

"There certainly is, God bless her," Harriet said, handing him the list.

"How is mama?" Julia asked.

"Badly," he said. "She wanted to come with me."

"Oh! Do not let her!" they chorused.

"Look after her Jack," Harriet said giving him the letter.

"You can rest assured me and Bertha will do that Miss Harriet, but I don't know how we can stop your mama against coming once she's made up her mind."

"Just try, Jack," they asked as he left.

It seemed they had only been back in their cell a short while before they were called out to return to the same room. However by this time the visiting hours were over and they were to collect their bedding. No longer in tidy bundles, it had been thrown on one of the tables. Gathering it up they draped it over and around their shoulders to carry it back to the ward. It smelt strongly from having been fumigated but a smell they were familiar with, being part of the household cleaning regime.

Their next and final meal of the day was at six o'clock in the evening and it was no different to the one they had at dinner, being ox-head soup thickened with oatmeal, vegetables and potatoes and a cup of weak tea.

In a whispered aside Julia said she hoped the basket of food they had brought with them found grateful mouths. Harriet said she doubted whether it would have gone further than the Turnkey, to which Julia said the poor man looked as if he needed a good meal so perhaps they should be glad that it went to a good cause.

"At the unhealthy state of him I suppose it would be thought of as uncharitable to consider that it might be a lost cause?" Harriet asked as they returned to their cell.

"Now Hattie!" Julia chided with a grin, before saying the Grace.

Neither sister relished the thought of eating the tasteless mess but once they began they ate all that was on their plates and would even have wished for more, due to the immense hunger that had overtaken them.

It was almost dark when they went outside to do, what were to become their thrice-daily chores but there were four lit lanterns to help show the way. To their surprise they found that this time they were not alone. There were two other women carrying out chores in the yard who, the sisters ascertained, occupied cells on the lower floor. One, a widow with a family of six to feed, was in debt to the butcher and baker and the other, an heiress who had mismanaged her legacy, owed money to a milliner. They were a complete mismatch of circumstance and yet, in sharing a cell and working together in the cookhouse to earn money to pay off their debts, they had become friends.

The lower floor, the sisters learnt, was for prisoners reduced to short commons where their creditors paid only three pence daily for their keep. This meant the food rations were extremely meagre and, had they not been taken on to work in the cookhouse, they would be locked in for part of the day as well as the night. Working in the cookhouse had two advantages for it meant they were able to work wheezes for extra rations and be out of their cells until the last meal had been served.

"I believe you have fireplaces in your cell and room to move about," Marie Ann, the heiress said. When Harriet failed to comment Julia felt she had to nod.

"Long time since I sat by a fire," the woman complained.

" 'Tis bitter in our cells," Nell, the widow said.

"They sounded so envious I lost the will to admit we did not as yet have the coal for the fire," Julia said when they were back in their cell.

"It seems we shall have a lot to be grateful for after all," Harriet said, lighting a third candle and placing it on the table. They sat there discussing the other two women, judging the competence of the heiress and commiserating that the children of the widow had been taken from her and placed under the auspices of the poor law, until the final bell rang.

'That final bell,' Julia was to confess to a close friend Philippe Baudain many years later, 'signalled the very worst part of each terrible day. For it told us the Matron was on her way to lock us in behind that thick metal-faced door.

I am not ashamed to say that the very first time I watched the door being shut and heard the key turn in the lock I clung to Harriet in a misery of terror and tears and she,who had been so brave until then, was equally so. It felt as if we were being interred alive in a burial vault. And, even though from the following day we had the glowing embers in the grate and the night candle to cheer us, we continued to dread being incarcerated. It was far worse than the disrespect from the Matron, the lowly chores, the tedious monotony of the commons, even the scarcity of the victuals of the short commons that made me so ill. The incarcerations, the hours of which were increased from the nights to most of the days once John reduced us to short commons, were the very worst of all that and especially so once we no longer had the fire and night candle.'

Julia and Harriet had been in prison for sixteen days when John, who had been paying ten pence daily for each of their keep, reduced them to short commons. During that time Harriet had written him several long and bitter letters protesting their innocence and castigating him for his treatment of them.

In one she wrote: 'We have been struggling for the last ten years to wipe out the stain you had put on our father's affairs and would have succeeded but for the unjust judgements rendered in your favour by that corrupt court.' In another: 'You have dared to put us in jail although we have numberless times offered to pay you those sums which, as God is True, you know we do not owe one penny of.' Then in conclusion: 'We hope you are as peaceful and happy out of jail as we are in it.'

She was not to know that each letter, enforcing both hers and Julia's resolve not to weaken or withdraw from the fight, was to alienate her brother all the more. Nor was he to suspect that it was his lack of response that goaded her into writing the long epistle to the Editor for publication in the daily paper, the *Chronique*. 'Having been incarcerated in prison by Mr J.N.Westaway since Monday 14th October,' Harriet's letter began, 'and fearing that it might be thought that we were imprisoned for a just debt which we refused to pay, we now feel fully justified in stating the facts.'

She then went on to explain in great detail the difficulties they had experienced in trying to obtain the inheritances left them by their father. It was a long letter, leaving nothing out as she stated all that had happened over the years. Without once referring to John as her brother she complained bitterly about his treatment but even more acrimoniously about the Courts which had abetted their own gender.

After condemning the Jersey Laws and Courts for acting against women and subjecting them to many wrongs and injustices, Harriet ended the letter with an appeal to all heads of families. 'For the wellbeing of your widows and daughters, it behoves you to exert yourselves to get the existing law which gives the Principal Heir such arbitrary power, as he now has, changed.'

The publication of the letter caused quite a scandal and John and his family, who were freely walking the streets where Harriet and Julia were not, took the brunt of it. Though Harriet had not named him as her brother the relationship was common knowledge amongst townspeople and many felt that, whatever the rights of the case, John had gone too far.

Charlotte and Susan arrived back to their home from a shopping trip in tears. "Oh! Papa, there were women talking about us behind their hands..." Susan began. "Then we heard one say the most terrible things about how you have condemned Aunt Harriet and Julia to prison. Please say it is not so," Charlotte finished.

John, who had been immensely angered by the publication of Harriet's letter but temporarily undecided as to what to do, was now provoked into furious action. Unused to discussing such matters with his daughters he curtly explained that it was not he who was at fault but their grasping, sanctimonious aunts. Then, leaving them abruptly, he went to his lawyers where, furious at the notoriety that now surrounded them all, he arranged that the fee he was expected to pay for each of his sister's imprisonment be reduced from ten pence to three pence daily on the 1st of November.

Suddenly life in the prison, which had settled into a dismal but settled routine, became quite unendurable for the two sisters who had until then been remarkably stoical. They were removed to a cell on the lower passage without the means of a fire or adequate candlelight and their rations severely cut to two meals of watery gruel without either meat or potatoes and only one slice of bread a day. The daily visits from Jack were curtailed and their biggest dread, that of being entombed in their cell during the night, was increased to include six hours of the day. This also meant they were no longer able to pass the occasional time of day with the two other female prisoners, something they had unexpectedly come to enjoy, and resented the fact that the women were locked up for less time.

Within three days of being in the lower ward Julia became so ill that Harriet, not faring well herself but fearing for her sister's life more, called for their solicitor and arranged to pay all that their brother John demanded.

"But never let it ever be said that we forgave him," Julia said bitterly as, surrounded by their belongings thrown untidily onto the pavement outside the prison, they waited for the carriage to take them home. She was leaning heavily against Harriet and looked as sickly as she felt. "And neither he nor any of his family must ever profit from us again."

"Well, I cannot wholeheartedly agree with you there, Julia dear, for I have it in mind to make my will at the soonest opportunity."

Julia looked quite surprised.

"Well, I think one shilling would be quite generous in the circumstances, do you not?" Harriet said, hugging her sister close to her side.

And despite herself, Julia grinned.

Anne, who had not been to see them at their insistence, was shocked by their thin, sickly appearances and took charge on their arrival back at St. Saviour's Crescent, ordering them both to bed where Julia remained for several weeks and Harriet for two. As soon as she had recovered Harriet called on their lawyer to arrange that the debts of the women Nell and Marie Ann be paid and by Advent the two sisters were able to attend the weekly services and Christmas masses with their mother.

Over the weeks the three talked at length and Anne confessed that on the day they were taken to prison she had written to John and told him that she no longer considered him to be her son and wished to have nothing more to do with him. However, not wanting to inflict a father's sin upon his children, she would be pleased to welcome any of the children should they care to visit. Julia said that though it would be very difficult should she and John ever meet she doubted whether she could bring herself to talk to him. And though she too would never wish to see his sins inflicted upon his children she would rather leave all her money to the poor than let any of them inherit a penny from her. Harriet said that she ought to write her will and testament then, as she had done. Anne agreed that would be wise. Her will had been written for some time.

When Anne failed to wake on the 30th January 1862 the sisters, in overlooking the fact that their mother had succumbed to weaknesses attached to the great age of 88, blamed her death on the terrible trials and tribulations that John had inflicted. Conventions called for him to be notified and they did this by having a clerk from the office of their mother's solicitor call on him with the added information that all the necessary arrangements had been made.

Anne had left no instructions as to her funeral wishes and much to the barely disguised resentment of both Harriet and Julia, custom demanded that the funeral cortège be led by John and his sons John Junior and Alex. To his credit John did not question their insistence that the service be held at St. Mark's Church or the interment beneath the monument close by Nathaniel's last resting-place though neither word nor look was exchanged between them during the entire proceedings. Only Alex, having returned from London where he was apprenticed to a stockbroker, lingered to take his aunts' hands and offer them comforting words.

Neither, to their surprise, did John question the contents of his mother's will which she had written five years after his father's death, when she had bought the crescent in the midst of her children's battles. Therefore they were never to learn how he felt about their equal inheritances of her monies and property.

Julia and Harriet were visiting Paris when 23 year-old Henrietta died the following April. Though they had not seen or spoken to their niece for some years Alex had told them, at the time of his grandmother's funeral, that she had never fully recovered from the melancholia that beset her after the deaths of her twin Charles, her mother and sister Maria. Julia had intended writing to her, to tell her how she and Harriet fully sympathised, having been deeply affected by their parents' and her grandparents' death, but had let time pass without doing so. When the regular weekly visits to St. Saviour's churchyard were resumed she laid a posy on her niece's grave by way of regret.

23

The early morning hours of Thursday March 17th 1870

JOHN WAS SOMEHOW loath to prepare for sleep and continued to lie fully
clothed on his bunk, his mind alive with thoughts and memories. He
was returning to the island on the paddle-steamer *Normandy* after a
week in England visiting daughter Annie and her husband at their
home, Netherton House at Sidcup in Kent. It had been a good and
happy visit even though the four children of Frederick Hedger, who
had been a widower at the time of marrying Annie, were boisterous in
the extreme. Frederick was a charming man and they had shared many
good conversations. John thought the man and his children well suited
for Annie's affectionate and caring nature.

The pair had married in St. Saviour's Church the previous summer
and though John had been sad at the thought of losing Annie from the
family home he had provided her with a happy day to look back on
before Frederick took her to meet his children in England.

He thought back to that warm day in August and smiled at the
memory of how happy and young she had looked in her white organza
dress and bonnet decorated with sweet peas, so much younger than
her 32 years. As a fine needle-woman, she had sewn the dress herself
and, carrying a bouquet of lilies, his heart had been greatly touched
when, on coming out of the church, she had led her new husband along
the path to the right and placed the lilies on her mother's grave. He
never walked that path himself, preferring always to use the rear gate
into the churchyard and so avoid the mental anguish caused by passing
the monument his sisters had erected, but dear Annie held no such
torment in her heart and for that he was glad.

Whilst he had been with the young couple during the last week
they had announced that they were to have their first child. He had
been so pleased that after kissing them both he had given a short speech
on how they should take pleasure in every fleeting moment. As he did
then, he said, and would continue to do by visiting them frequently in
the future so that he could experience the joy of watching his first

grandchild and, he hoped, further grandchildren grow.

Suddenly John's reverie was broken by a hasty shout of "Hard to port!" followed by a warning blast from a whistle. Just seconds later there was a shattering blow to the starboard side and, with the heavy sound of crunching wood ringing in his ears, he was thrown bodily against the side of the cabin as the vessel heeled over. As it righted itself he was tossed from the bunk onto the floor just as a further tremendous crash dashed him about once more. Badly bruised, he stumbled awkwardly out of the cabin as the vessel was hit yet again, this time nearer the stern. With an intense feeling of trepidation he joined the bunch of dazed passengers and crew making their way to the bow of the upper deck.

Dense fog prevented sight of what had caused the collision but John gave this barely a thought as he listened to the Captain summoning the remaining passengers to join them on deck. John had come to know and trust Captain Henry Harvey, as did many of the passengers who had sailed with him during the seven years he carried them to and from the islands and Southampton on the *Normandy*. He knew from the man's tone that the vessel was in grave danger of sinking, long before the order was given to 'Man the lifeboats!'

The main lifeboat and its davits had been carried away with the second collision, which only left the two on the port side, a cutter and jolly boat. Ordering them to be lowered the Captain then used the megaphone to urge the now invisible ship that had hit them, to send boats to their aid.

Most of the women and some of the men, having waded through rising water from the bow, got into the boats. John followed a group into the cutter but, when he caught sight of the partly dressed young woman leaning against the bulwarks in a dazed state, he clambered out again and hurried to her side.

"You must come!" he said, taking off his jacket and wrapping it around her. It was almost too late, the cutter was drawing away. He had no other choice than to throw her into it but was gratified to see her caught by the other passengers.

There were 22 people in the cutter and nine in the jolly boat as they pulled away but Harvey did not stop to count as he urged them to return as quickly as possible to take the remaining passengers and crew off.

From a quick glance at the Captain's face John knew instinctively that the ship had only minutes left. Yet somehow he was filled with calm as he waded back through the now waist-high water which had prevented four nervous women passengers from leaving the dry bow and taking to the lifeboats.

"Do not worry, help will come" he said as he reached their side, but his words were lost amid their screams as the water sucked them all down.

It was the following day before news of the disaster reached the island and it became known that 34 passengers and crew of the *Normandy* had been lost after it had come into collision with the three-mast, square-rigged steamer *The Mary* in thick fog. None of the names were known until the survivors were eventually brought into St. Helier when there were great scenes of anguish from those who learnt of the loss of their loved ones. The distress was tremendous. In Guernsey Victor Hugo, a regular contributor to French newspapers, wrote that it was a catastrophe, that the island was in mourning with flags being flown at half-mast. So it was in Jersey, with dramatic accounts also being published.

Julia and Harriet first heard the news of the ship's sinking by word of mouth and were greatly shocked for they had travelled to Southampton on the *Normandy* themselves several times and were acquainted with the iron-framed, two-funnel paddle steamer. It was only when they read the newspaper accounts the following day, however, that they learnt that John had been on board and was one of those listed as drowned. Indeed, reports were quick to name him as a hero, praising him for giving up his place in the lifeboat to a young lady. Though one newspaper gave her name as Miss Clara Godfray, while another as Miss Albina Falle, the latter to whom it was added that he handed his jacket as a protection against the cold, there was no doubting the fact that he was gone. It was difficult to take in, so hard even to believe, but it was true. The sisters were stunned into silence.

"It is perhaps a wicked thing to say under the circumstances but at least we no longer have to cross the street rather than walk on the same pavement as him," Harriet said at last.

But while the sisters could not bring themselves to weep for the loss of a brother who, by his cruel treatment, had killed all the love they once had for him, a great host of others went into deep mourning.

When he was informed John Junior collapsed with grief and Susan and Charlotte, John's two daughters still living at home, were overcome too. Alex, who was in London, took leave from his work and went to Sidcup from where he, Annie and Frederick travelled back to the island to stay for a while at Surrey Lodge. Only Nathaniel and James, Lieutenant Nathaniel of the Royal Engineers being in Ceylon and Captain and Adjutant James of the 13th Light Infantry in South Africa, remained temporarily unaware of the tragedy.

Some of John's friends at the United Club where, having been Vice President for some time John had been made President only two months before, openly wept. The clubroom was draped with emblems of mourning as a token of the deep grief felt by all the members and note was made in the Minute Book. Five days later a long and sincere letter was sent to John Junior, himself a member, confirming how much his father's loss had been felt not only by them but the general public. The island had been deprived of an esteemed citizen and they a valuable friend and worthy President, it said. That he showed such noble and calm courage in saving the lives of passengers at a most perilous moment would be 'a memento of his sterling worth as a Christian and testify more than words can tell of the character of your honoured parent,' it added.

When he replied, John Junior thanked them for their great expression of sympathy and recalled that at the club's last annual dinner there was much talk of how deeply they had all been affected by the former President's death. 'I remember turning to my father and saying that when providence took him away from serving you I trusted that his absence should be as strongly felt. Little did I imagine how soon you would be called upon to deplore his death.'

Many lips were singing John's praises, from the highest to the low. When the possessor of a long memory recalled the scandal of when his sister denounced him from the prison, vindication was instant. Surely there was more to the family story than met the eye? it was asked. Had the gentleman not seen that his mother was given a decent funeral even though rumour had it she had disowned him? Besides it was wrong to talk ill of the dead, especially a hero such as Mr John N. Westaway, so we will hear no more.

That John had become a popular and well-respected public figure before the tragedy was acknowledged but he was now also an exemplar who had saved two young women by seeing them into the lifeboats. It was only natural that when, five days after the tragedy, a public meeting was held at the Lyric Hall in the presence of the island's Bailiff to open a relief fund for the widows and orphans, a call was made for two memorials. One was to be for John and the other for Captain Harvey.

When reports of the enquiry, held at Greenwich on Monday 4th April, were published, the findings of the assessors, who laid the blame with the *Normandy*, were hotly contested within the islands.

For it was stated that while crossing shipping lanes the *Normandy* suddenly met with a cloud of thick fog and was too late to either slow or cut her engines before coming into collision with *The Mary*. *The Mary*'s crew insisted that their masthead light was showing and she was blowing the fog whistle. Yet the look-out crew on the *Normandy* neither heard the whistle, nor saw the green masthead light. All they saw was a red light, usually indicating a yacht, which under the becalmed conditions would not have been moving and so a collision would have been averted.

The captain of *The Mary* was on the bridge and heard the sound of paddles moments before seeing the green masthead light of the *Normandy*, which was then about three ships' lengths away and immediately took evasive action. At the same time the crew on the *Normandy* saw *The Mary* and did the same but it was too late.

While there was much argument as to who had run into whom the assessors found against the *Normandy* who, in crossing the shipping lanes, was under obligation to look out for other shipping.

However, it was what happened directly after the collision that was the most upsetting – The Mary failed immediately to send out boats to the stricken *Normandy*, despite the pleas from Captain Harvey and survivors who reached the ship minutes later. Had this been done, it was considered, the fatalities would have been far fewer.

Survivors' evidence given at the enquiry were once more repeated within the islands, details of the findings were argued over and many unsolved questions asked as people tried to make some sense of the tragedy.

Meanwhile, The Independent Order of Foresters in Jersey, of which Captain Harvey was a member, decided they would be responsible for his memorial and plans were drawn up for an obelisk. When, the following year, the Harvey Memorial was unveiled at the chosen site on the Victoria Pier, one of the local newspapers commented that the names of both John and a Mr H.W.Kinloch had been omitted. The Reverend Minister of St. Simon's Church quickly responded by saying that this monument was not a tribute to the *Normandy* but to the brave Captain and crew members who lost their lives in the collision. A public monument was soon to be erected to honour, 'our brave and much respected townsman, John Nathaniel Westaway', he added.

The voluntary subscriptions for the erection of a monument in John's memory were to far outweigh expectations as funds rapidly appeared. 'Mr Westaway was one of our leading fellow citizens' the citation began. 'He was a public spirited and liberal, just and most honourable man. Hence the general sorrow with which the island community heard of his death. The last act of this useful and honoured life was one of rare selfless devotion. Hence the spontaneous desire that was quickly expressed to pay public honour to his memory.'

It was decided that his memorial monument should take the shape of an artistic fountain and that the work should be entrusted to the eminent Frenchman, Monsieur Robinet. Another four years were to pass before the sculpture was installed on the Albert Pier and if the length of time taken had been criticised all was forgotten at the sight of it. For set in the centre of a large circular trough an octagonal column supported a circular bowl in which an open-mouthed dolphin wound itself around an anchor. An oval bronze plaque depicted a cameo of John and underneath another plaque with the words 'In commemoration of the gallantry of John Nathaniel Westaway when the S.S. *Normandy* foundered 17th March 1870'. There were gasps of admiration by all who were present and many women wept as, with a hand signal from the Constable of St. Helier to an unseen official, water spurted from the fish's mouth. There were many speeches and Advocate John Junior, one of the specially invited guests along with Annie and Frederick, Alex, Susan, Charlotte and James, who was on leave from the 13th Light Infantry, gave an additional short oration of appreciation on their behalf. That finished, cups were handed around and all took a drink from the crystal clear water.

The cameo was such a good likeness of their father that had it not been out of reach Annie, Susan and Charlotte would have liked to stroke it lovingly.

"What a handsome man he was," someone in the crowd murmured.

"Indeed, indeed, and an ever loving papa too," Annie said.

"If only brother Nathaniel could have been here," James said, sounding as if he had a blocked nose. James had broken his nose when diving off Dublin Pier to save a man from drowning, a feat for which he had been awarded a gold medal. It had been many years since he had met up with his brother, the Lieutenant Nathaniel, and found it hard to believe he never would again. They had been such pals and despite only meeting up occasionally due to their service postings, they had kept up with each other's exploits by letter. It had been very difficult to accept his death while on duty in Ceylon, only one year after their father and three years before the ceremony.

The two maiden aunts, Harriet and Julia, were not present, neither was Emma Tregear, John Junior's new wife.

How long John Junior had known Emma Tregear before he married her he was never to publicly admit but it would have been at least three years. Emma had come to Jersey from Plymouth to work as a house servant and given birth, in 1863, to an illegitimate son, John. Nine years later, in 1872, she gave birth to another son, Henry Charles, to whom John Junior gave his name. They were married when the little boy was two year-old when at the same time John Junior legitimised the 11 year-old John. If any of John Junior's sisters or brothers were aware of the elder boy's true parentage they did not discuss it. Neither did they question why he did not marry Emma, a sweet girl though not of his class, until their child Henry was two year-old, for no one ever questioned John Westaway Junior.

In the four years since his father's death John Junior, having inherited his father's estate, sold various properties and began to look around the island for a large plot on which to build a new home more in keeping with the new status he was working towards. His legal practice was very successful and, following in his father's footsteps, he had been voted in as President of the United Club but still he remained unsatisfied. What he wanted now, he decided, was one of the top legal positions in the island, that of Solicitor General to the States, and for that he would need to be appointed by the Crown.

To hold such a position he felt he could not possibly remain living in the very ordinary 33, Belmont Road so, after a great deal of searching, he chose a plot of enviable position on the south-eastern coast and had a most beautiful house built up on it. With stunning and uninterrupted views it was accessed from a long drive in the centre of which was a large outcrop of stone, known locally as the Witches' Rock. He was told that to destroy this manifestation would bring about ill-fortune and, though he would not profess to be in any way superstitious, he insisted it was left undisturbed and named the house 'Rocqueberg' after it.

John Junior felt he had attracted more than sufficient misfortune when, the previous year, two of the three banks into which he had deposited his inheritance failed. He had still not rid himself of the hollow feeling in the pit of his stomach on discovering that the large sum he had deposited with the Jersey Mercantile Union Bank had simply vanished. That someone he knew and trusted, a Jurat of the Royal Court and Managing Director of the bank, Joshua Le Bailly, was guilty of fraud and embezzlement was shocking enough but, to his mind, the sentence of five years penal servitude was simply not sufficient. He would have had the man hung, drawn and quartered for the devastation he had caused.

Yet unlike others, John had not been bankrupted, even with the collapse of the Jersey Joint Stock Bank where he also lost money, for he had been wise enough to divide his accounts three ways. Still his assets were such that, if he was to maintain standards, he needed to sell Surrey Lodge and the now disused coal yard and settle his two sisters somewhere else. After all, he considered, he had been more than generous maintaining them in the old family home up to the present but he could not let them stay there indefinitely. But he could not go about the matter until James returned to his troop for both James, and the late Nathaniel, had thought fondly of their young sisters and would never have sanctioned such a move. Still he would not have to bide his time for many weeks.

Whereas his three brothers – Nathaniel, James and Alex – had inherited their father's height and good looks, John Junior possessed neither. With his unkempt sideburns and upper lip hair his face resembled that of his grandfather, except that the hair on the back of his head was short and swept back as was the fashion. Neither did he display any of the roughness of skin, which identified his ancestor's trade. However, where his grandfather had been of narrow build, a characteristic his father and brothers had also inherited, John Junior was shorter and inclined to be stout and, though his forehead was high, his brown eyes were small, giving him a deceptively ordinary appearance.

Yet there was nothing at all ordinary about John Junior. What he lacked in appearance he made up for in self-importance, a pomposity nurtured by those who did not possess his great intelligence and impressive knowledge of local law.

His ambition to become Solicitor General to the States of Jersey was realised in the summer of 1879 by which time he had settled into Rocqueberg and was the father of three children, 16 year-old John, seven year-old Henry and two year-old Emma Beatrice. It was not long before he earned the reputation of being highly articulate in the Court and, though he did not acknowledge his aunts in any way or they him, the pair had begun to read newspaper reports of his cases with interest. For, they had albeit somewhat begrudgingly to admit, his line of reasoning was very persuasive.

Julia had just finished reading her nephew's legal arguments in the case of Le Feuvre versus Le Feuvre in the *Jersey Press* during the evening of 8th October when her eyes drifted across to another column. She gave a sudden gasp before muttering, "Oh dear! That cannot be right. No, no…Oh dear…Oh dear!"

"I do wish you would not do that Julia! It is most irritating," Harriet said sharply, her insides complaining bitterly of the hearty meal she had eaten less than thirty minutes before. Having left the housemaid to clear up the dining room the sisters were now in the parlour, the furniture and decoration of which had not changed since their father had originally built the house. Julia was at the fire but Harriet was sitting in what had become her usual place on the window seat. The daylight was fading and, unable to focus clearly on the open book in her hand, her eyes were on the business of people in the road below where, despite the early evening hour, it seemed everyone remained busy. It had been a long time since there had been a purpose to either her days or evenings, she told herself. Her brain felt dulled and her whole body ached in revolt at the lack of activity. It all made her feel very much older than her 65 years.

"Oh! But Hattie, it is just so hard to believe…Listen! 'It is with deep regret that we announce the death of John N. Westaway, her Majesty's Solicitor General, which took place at 6 p.m. this evening. It appears that after pleading very eloquently and with a good deal of energy in the case of Le Feuvre versus Le Feuvre...' I had just finished reading the account when my eyes drifted..."

"Do stop wittering and either get on with reading the newspaper or pass it over to me!" Harriet interrupted harshly.

"Of course dear, now where was I? Ah! Yes...'It appears that after pleading very eloquently and with a good deal of energy in the case of Le Feuvre versus Le Feuvre at the Royal Court the Solicitor General proceeded to the Victoria Club where he ordered luncheon...'

"United Club!" Harriet interrupted again and when Julia looked across questioningly she added, "you said the Victoria Club!"

"That is what it says...'proceeded to the Victoria Club'."

"Must be a misprint then unless he has divided his loyalties, for he was president of the United Club the last I heard...No matter...Go on reading!"

'He ordered luncheon and whilst it was being prepared went to the lavatory to wash his hands. Whilst there he fell on the floor and was immediately conveyed to the Committee Room where Doctors Godfray, Cronier and Le Quesne were soon in attendance on him and they unanimously pronounced his case utterly hopeless. Mr Westaway's family were immediately communicated with and Mrs Westaway, Miss Westaway his sister...'

"That would be Susan of course, with her having been living with John Junior since he sold Surrey Lodge."

Then seeing the look of fierce irritation on her sister's face Julia hurriedly continued,

'and Mr Westaway Junior shortly afterwards arrived. The deceased gentleman remained unconscious up to his death when he quietly expired in the presence of his family.

Mr Westaway was appointed Solicitor General only a few months since in the room of the late Mr G.H. Horman who also, strange to say, died very suddenly.

Previous to his being nominated Crown Officer Mr Westaway enjoyed an extensive practice as an Advocate of the Royal Court possessing a number of clientèle. As a pleader both in civil and criminal cases he had no superior in the island and in consultations he was facile princeps. Much sympathy is felt for Mrs Westaway and her family in their sad bereavement…'

Julia folded the paper slowly as she added, "It will not only be sympathy that woman will need when the will is read out for as his father's son she will have no hope of being fairly treated."

"The sins of the father shall be visited upon the children…" Now it was Harriet who was muttering.

"Pardon?"

"So many early deaths of John's line, it is God's punishment on the evil doer…"

"Yet some would question the punishment that makes an eternal hero."

"It was the people who made John a hero, not God!" Harriet retorted.

"What a loss… Such instructed, distinguished…and brave nephews."

"Really Julia, you do prattle so! What was brave about John Junior?"

"I was not thinking of John but of Nathaniel and James and dear Charles who would have risen to the rank of Sea Lord had he lived…"

"There you go again, saying the silliest things! Charles was a midshipman. Who but God knows what he would have become had he not drowned?"

"Nathaniel and James excelled themselves so there is nothing to say that Charles would not have done the same. Besides we do not know that he drowned for we only heard that he was buried at sea somewhere between England and China," Julia responded spiritedly. "And we cannot deny that though he might not have distinguished himself in the field of battle, John Junior had the finest of brains…. It just remains with Alex now…"

Alex was a stockbroker in London and advancing well, according to the reports he gave of himself whenever he visited his aunts. Both he and Susan, their youngest niece, were the only two of their brother's children to visit.

"I fear Alex will never truly apply himself, he never did even when at school so he is not likely to now that he is a man. He was rather like you in that respect Julia. You could have done much better had you applied yourself to your lessons instead of always thinking of your appearance…!"

Julia took a deep breath as she clenched her fingers into a tight fist. Harriet had become so irritating of late, their conversations never travelling far without her interrupting to peck away at one or other of her failings. She knew she should walk from the room but she could not control the anger that was rising inside. "Considering you believe I could have done better at my schooling I think I have since redeemed myself in business, for who has profited most from our father's legacy may I ask?" Julia bristled.

A gentle knock at the door ended the verbal battle of wits before it became so loud as to be heard in the basement kitchen. Bertha put her head around the door before opening it wide. She entered the room and closed it gently behind herself.

"Have you heard the news Miss Harriet…Miss Julia?" she asked, looking from one to another.

"About our nephew the Solicitor General? Yes, Julia has just read the news from the evening paper. They did not waste time in publishing his death," Harriet said as she moved her stiff limbs in the direction of her mother's old éscritoire. "And neither must I dally over writing our notes of condolence. Perhaps you would send someone to post them once they are done?"

Bertha said that of course she would but in the meantime would they like her to bring them each a small tot of brandy? And answering for both Julia and herself Harriet replied, "No thank you."

"I will have one thank you Bertha," Julia said forcefully. She had no particular liking for brandy but she would not have Harriet answering for her. Really she was taking too much upon herself! When the brandy arrived she ignored her sisters loud 'tut' of disapproval and, letting the newspaper fall to the floor, took the small phial in her hand and sipped at the glass slowly before leaning back in her chair.

The room grew quiet save for the sounds of the nib of Harriet's plumed pen as it either scratched the vellum or the side of the ink well after being replenished. Julia did not share Harriet's talent for writing letters, especially those of condolence, so she was always pleased to leave the task to her. And with Harriet occupied she would have time to think. She liked to think. Harriet called it daydreaming and though she had to admit there were times when her mind drifted amongst pleasurable thoughts it was not always like that. Sometimes her mind could think on quite serious matters, such as the notion that was beginning to eat away at her now.

John Junior was dead but there was no sorrow inside her as there had been for her other nephews and nieces who had preceded him. Yet of all ten of them he had been the one she had loved most dearly as a baby, had spent hours rocking his cradle and singing lullabies to. How old had she been then...fourteen going on fifteen? Too old to run all the way from Don Street to Vine Street in such an unladylike fashion yet she could not have helped herself, so keen was she to reach her brother's home. She liked to get there in time to help Anne Guillet dress the baby in his starched white *broderie anglaise* trimmed gowns, a coat and bonnet on top, before they all set out for walks across the Lower Park, taking turns to push his perambulator. And even after Annie was born three years later and the twins Charles and Henrietta the following year, by which time the family had moved to Surrey Lodge, John Junior remained special to her, toddling to greet her with his arms wide and calling her 'Ju-Ju.' Oh! The sheer love in those chubby arms that wound around her neck!

What had caused that early adoration to fade? Had she been such a bad aunt? She asked herself this as memories arose of the numerous times she bought generous gifts of toys and later schoolbooks, not only for John Junior but for all her other nephews and nieces too. She only stopped giving when they failed to thank her, a decision which coincided with a decrease in the children's visits to the house. She had missed their excited chatter, their joyful ways, but they had to learn that bad manners would not be tolerated. The fault of course had lain with her brother who should have been a better disciplinarian but then, when it came to John's faults, that was the least of them.

As the years passed however, incidences occurred which made her regret not having got to know her nephews and nieces better, especially the two youngest girls.

At one event, in the autumn of the year John drowned, she and Harriet had come upon Charlotte and Susan at the opening of the Jersey Railway Company's line from St. Helier to St. Aubin. They had met up whilst waiting to board the new train from the crowded platform of the West Park Station, and been truly warmed by the way the girls had kissed them both before thanking them for their kind cards of sympathy over the loss of their father. Julia had been so touched she suggested that they share a carriage but John Junior appeared at that moment, having been at the kiosk buying his sisters' tickets. After a cursory greeting, followed by an equally brisk farewell, he ushered them further along the platform.

He ushered his sisters away again when they all met up amongst the crowds at Noirmont where the fête was in full swing and that time there were looks of genuine regret on the girls' faces. Over the next few weeks and months they had remembered those looks and hoped for a visit but it did not happen and they could only conclude that John Junior had ordered against it.

It had been many years since their eldest nephew had been pleasant to them so, though they would have preferred it to be different, they were not entirely surprised at his behaviour. However an incident, which occurred the following summer to the inauguration of the train service, was to banish all hope of civility between them.

It happened when Julia was invited to join the official party seeing a group of forty paupers off to a new life in Canada. She had been invited in deference to her generosity in providing new clothes for the paupers' journey and, not being too surprised to find John Junior had also been invited as a member of the legal profession, she was determined to be courteous. However to her utter chagrin he totally ignored her, even when they were so near amongst the group at the pier head that their shoulders touched, and even during the time when the Constable of St. Helier included them both in conversation. It was the most pointed of slights and she found herself growing increasingly angry.

As Julia walked closely behind him on their way back to their waiting carriages she hissed loudly, "My goodness, John Nathaniel Westaway Junior, it seems like only yesterday I helped to change your swaddling rags and here you are with your pretensions as if the smell was still under your nose. Well, it must be admitted you did make rather a mess as a babe, and so slow were you that I am still left wondering if you have yet learnt to use the chamber pot!"

He neither looked around nor hesitated in his pace but the stiffening of his back told her that he had heard every word.

When she related the incident to Harriet, who laughed long and loud at her temerity, Julia added that her decision against leaving her worldly goods to any descendants of John's held firmer than ever. She was going to leave it all to the poor.

It had been a long time since she had heard Harriet laugh, Julia thought as she stared into the flickering coals. She had never possessed a great propensity for fun but at least there were times throughout their lives when she had been quite amiable, even during that awful time they were both incarcerated she had been good company. They had also enjoyed some very pleasant holidays together after Mama died when they had visited the Loire area of France, the Pyrenees, Paris, Rome and London. She would never forget that particular visit to London when they saw Her Royal Majesty Queen Victoria riding in her carriage. Harriet had been equally excited.

"Hattie, shall we take a holiday in the spring?" she asked suddenly. "It would be good to see new sights. You could choose where we should go."

"How would these old bones manage the walking we would be obliged to do?" Harriet replied sourly.

"We could hire carriages."

"Then my back would ache from the sitting."

"We could be sure to take additional cushions."

There was such a long silence from the other side of the room, with not even the sound of the quill's nib scratching its way across the writing paper, that Julia was forced to turn and look enquiringly at her sister. Harriet stared back.

"If I thought for one minute my stomach would not object to the foreign food I would ask that we consider a trip through the Loire valley of France. There was an interesting piece of writing in the *Chronique* only a few days ago mentioning a picturesque town called Vendôme."

"We could take a large sachet of stomach powders with us," Julia said, her hopes rising. "And over the months ahead you could work out a map from the atlas of all the interesting places that we should see. What do you say?"

"I say we should certainly think about it," Harriet said in a much brighter tone than she had used for weeks.

Sixteen year-old John Tregear Westaway called the following morning, having been directed to give his great aunts the news of his father's death, unaware that at the very time of his visit Harriet's letters to both his mother and Aunt Susan had been delivered and were being read. He had walked all the way from La Rocque and seemed quite grateful for the cake and tea he was offered. His father's funeral, he told them between mouthfuls, was being arranged by his aunt Annie's husband, Frederick Hedger and the island's Bailiff, Jurats and Court officials would be in attendance. The service will be at St. Saviour's Church with the interment in the family grave. Neither his mother nor his aunts would be attending he added, which they took to be a verbal notice that they would not be expected to do so either.

The lad had grown a lot since they had last seen and spoken to both him and his mother Emma the time they happened to meet when their two carriages threatened to collide in one of the country lanes of St. John's one Sunday afternoon four years before. At that time Henry had resembled a three year-old cherub whilst John had been a mischievous boy of 12. Now he was tall and thin, with dark features and lustrous hair much reminiscent of his mother. Henry, they were told, was attending the College whilst he, John, was in his final year. But no, he replied when asked, he did not think he would follow his father into the law. As yet he had no idea what he would like to do, a statement which caused Harriet to comment, 'Huh! We heard that from your grandfather John Westaway when he was your age!'

In his will John Junior had appointed a board of guardians to manage his estate and a pregnant Emma Tregear found she was not to make a single decision without taking it to them first. The years that followed were extremely hard for her after the board decided it was necessary to sell Rocqueberg, the specially built home that she and John Junior had both been so proud to inhabit. John's affairs were in such a poor state that from that time onwards Emma and the children were moved from place to place, and in varied accommodation from rooms to houses, before finally going to live in Kent with Annie and Frederick Hedger.

The next time Julia set eyes on John Tregear Westaway was 13 years later. The year was then 1892 and it was early in the month of July when she received a visit from her solicitor Phillipe Baudains saying that her great nephew requested to see her. Though shocked with the speed with which the request had come about she knew instantly what the visit would be appertaining to and agreed on the insistence that he, Phillipe Baudains, also be present.

On the 20th of April that year Harriet died, having suffered painfully and long from carcinoma of the bowel. Julia had been warned that the wording of her sister's will, made some twenty or so years previously, would not stand if challenged by a hereditary member of her brother's line. For at the time of her death Harriet still owned eight properties originally willed her by her father and the Jersey Law of Inheritance decreed that, being of the female gender, she was not free to leave these to anyone of her choosing. They, or the sum of their value, had to revert back to the male descendants of her father's line. The sum, after the properties had been sold, amounted to £2,392.19s.8d.

There was a slight resemblance in the man John Tregear Westaway to the lad who had come to inform her and Harriet in 1892 of his father's death but Julia would not have recognised it had she met him in the street. He arrived at the house in the company of his wife and, though noticeably surprised to find great-aunt's solicitor present, spoke quite affably, though with an odd accent. He was over on a visit from New York, he said, and having been informed that he had inherited from his great-grandfather's estate wished to leave his kindest regards with her before returning to America.

Julia asked him if he knew anything of his family's history and he said he did not. Though she could not detect whether he was telling the truth or not she went on to tell him that his inheritance had not been the true wish of his great-aunt Harriet but had come about because of the injustice of the island's laws. She told him that her brother, his grandfather, had both her sister and herself imprisoned over a false claim which had led them both to vow that none of his family would ever benefit from them again. The fact was verified in her sister's will where she bequeathed the princely sum of one shilling to her brother. She never changed the wording even though he preceded her for she wanted his descendants to know the odium she felt.

"I am telling you this so that you should not expect any further inheritances," she said. "Do you remember much of the French language you would have spoken whilst you were here in the island?"

"A little," he replied.

"Well, hopefully you will understand enough of the contract you hold which states that you have received a one time payment."

As soon as the couple had left Julia turned to Phillippe Baudains and asked him how she could ensure that there would be no claim on her estate in the future. He advised her to sell any all her father's inheritances and to keep only what she had come about by herself.

"It will pain me to do so but I shall take your advice," she said. She always took his advice for she knew that, as the trusted and dear friend he had become over latter years, it was given most sincerely and with only her good at heart. Long ago she had told him all that had happened within the family from the time of her father's death. Though being of the legal profession he had been aware of it, hearing it from her lips made it all the more moving. "I want that the poor should inherit," she insisted.

"Then I should think deeply as to your wishes after your demise and write a new will," Phillipe added. Phillipe Baudains was not a fanciful man but, although he would not openly admit it, he had become slightly unnerved at seeing John Tregear Westaway again. For notwithstanding that the man lived in America he had the uncanny notion that it would not be the last time they would meet. On greeting each other they had both silently acknowledged the fact they had met before when John had come of the age to administer his father's estate and Phillipe had been one of the appointed guardians of John Junior's affairs along with Frederick Hedger and others. Phillipe had not felt easy in mind about the man then and he did not feel easy in mind about him now. As to what cause he really could not say.

24

~ *Nine years later* ~

Thursday September 19th 1901

"THE DOCTOR'S 'ERE," Elizabeth Curwood's guttural Jersey accent was deep and coarse.

"Yes, I watched him cross the road. How are you today Doctor Bois?" Julia asked, moving her glance from her housekeeper to the man who had also entered the room. She had been looking out for him from the window of the upstairs drawing room, as she did most mornings. "Would you serve us tea and cake Elizabeth?"

"I really should not stop too long. I have many patients to call on today," he said.

"Ah! But I warrant none pay your account with as much speed as I do. It will not hurt them to wait ten minutes." Julia, sitting with her feet up in the specially widened window seat padded with cushions, indicated a nearby chair. She was wearing her favourite blue dress. It was a trifle faded now and especially tapered by the dressmaker to fit her much diminished frame but, with her sparse white hair giving her face an ashen look, the colour enhanced the blue of her eyes. She knew it was so because Elizabeth had told her and Elizabeth was not given to compliments.

The doctor dithered and she hoped he was not going to say that he could not stop. She patted the seat encouragingly. Once he sat and took tea she might keep him for an hour or so. She did so enjoy company. It took her mind from her weariness.

"Well, are you stoppin' or wot?" The housekeeper, having picked up the basket containing a small sleeping puppy from her mistress's feet, turned to glare at him, her eyes mere slits. Her skin was remarkably clear for a woman of her age, which was halfway through the fifth decade and her dark curly hair, held atop with a small lace bow, held not a sign of grey. Her eyes too, when opened fully, were dark and bright. But her domineering and uncouth character overshadowed these attractive features.

"Of course he is!" Julia said determinedly. "And do ask Charles to turn on the fountain."

"Well just you see that you don't overtire yourself," the housekeeper said with sudden gentleness, fluffing up the cushions behind Julia's back before she left the room.

As soon as the door closed behind her the doctor said, "I really do not know why you continue to employ that one, especially with the notoriety both she and that drunken brother of hers reek upon this house."

"Elizabeth looks after me like no other has ever done before," Julia said, temporarily forgetting Bertha and her husband Jack who had followed one another to the grave some twenty or so years before. She was thinking of the several incompetent housekeepers who had come and gone before Elizabeth Curwood applied for the post. "And as for Charles," she continued, "though I abhor his drinking habits, as he well knows, he is a first-rate electrician and I can put faith in his workmanship, which is more than I can say for those who come off the ships each day, claiming to be artisans. Do you know of another crescent of houses that have such modern conveniences as this? No! And for that reason alone I would not be without him. Ah! Look! The fountain is playing, how I love that sight! I had it placed at about the spot where my dear papa fell before being found to have suffered an apoplexy. Did I tell you?"

She did not realise that she had, in fact, told the story many times nor did she notice that, in knowing that he was about to hear more of the recollections she regularly repeated, the doctor was glancing critically around the room as he took his seat. He was noting how clean and tidy it was, that there was a heavy smell of beeswax indicating the wooden furniture had been recently polished and, in the midst of the chenille-covered table, a bowl was piled high with fresh fruit.

Unknown to Julia the doctor had been asked to be keenly observant during his daily visits. Rumours were circulating the town that she was being badly treated by the woman Curwood, and there was great concern for her welfare. However the entire house, as far as he had seen, was kept cleaner than most he entered during the course of his day, the clothing of its elderly mistress always very presentable. All the fruit and vegetables that came into the house were bought free of blemishes and bruises and the fish and meat fresh to the day. The meals were well cooked and daintily served and, most important of all, the woman paid diligent attention to his instructions as to the medication that he prescribed for his elderly patient. Try as he might he could not find fault with the housekeeper's care of her mistress.

Yet perhaps it was the woman's very manner that founded the rumours, he asked himself. The surly, coarse and common Elizabeth Curwood had taken it upon herself to be very protective of her mistress, guarding her from those visitors she thought unsuitable and even ousting others from the house should they act or say anything untoward. She had disposed of two physicians before he was asked to call so he knew he had to tread carefully if he was to maintain his watching brief. One maintained that her tone was often bullying towards her employer yet though he had heard it to be brisk, to the contrary he had often heard it soft.

No, to his mind the intemperate Charles Curwood, who lived in the house along with his sister, was the greatest cause for concern. His drunken rages were such that the police were often called and the furious rows with his sister at those times alerted the whole neighbourhood. There was even a time when it was necessary to place Miss Westaway under the protection of the police and another where she was forced to prosecute him for smashing the front door with a flowerpot. Yet to everyone's surprise, when the case came before the magistrate she had spoken up for him, paying the fine to secure his release.

"...and it was all so gay! Oh! You look quite distracted doctor! Am I keeping you?"

"No, no. I was listening to your reminiscing of the decorations in the crescent for the Queen's Diamond Anniversary. As you say, they were very gay. I remember commenting on them as my wife and I passed by."

"Harriet and I once saw her Royal Majesty riding in her carriage through the streets of London, she had a stern look but oh! How proud we were to have seen her so close. It is a great thing to be so loved."

"It seems the whole world mourned her passing. I doubt if the King Edward will be as well revered though they say he has a charming manner and at ease with all of his subjects, those that he meets of course."

She stared at him in confusion as he looked away from her to open his medical bag and began delving into it. Had the dear Queen died?

Surely not? Yet…yes of course! How could she have forgotten the people openly weeping in the street, all the shop windows dressed in black…?

"Do you think I would have forgotten such a terrible thing?" she asked crossly. The doctor gave her a strange look before he replied. "No, no, and I would never have suggested such a thing."

Suddenly there was a sound of a clanging bell from the street below and she turned to look out of the window.

"Oh! Do look doctor," she exclaimed. "There must be a fire up the hill, see the appliance racing away? I wonder where the fire is?"

He got up and leant across her to look down at the road beyond the narrow garden in which the water fountain played. The horse-drawn fire wagon from the small sub-station situated beside the lower end of the crescent was racing past, water splashing over the sides of the swinging pails, the fireman next to the driver clanging the warning bell.

"Let us hope it is not too fierce and no one is put in danger," he said, moving away again just as Elizabeth Curwood came in, carrying the tea tray.

"Was that the fire wagon I heard?" she asked. Then, before either of them could reply, added, "Probably some rascals playing with lighters in a hayloft no doubt. Well now Doctor, how do you find your patient today? Did you tell the doctor you're not sleepin' too well, Mistress?" she asked, handing Julia a cup of tea with a finger of cake in the saucer.

"I sleep very well, I always have slept very well," she answered and seeing the conspiratorial look that passed between her housekeeper and doctor she repeated adamantly, "I always have slept very well!"

The tea was hot and strong, just as she liked it. The cup and saucer was so pretty too, such delicate china. It tinkled together as her hands shook. She did so love delicate china. Elizabeth and the doctor were watching her closely as she drank, she wished they would not do that. It made her hands shake all the more.

Elizabeth picked up the piece of cake and held it towards her mouth. "Try a mouthful," she said. Obediently she took a small bite. It was delicious. It reminded her…"Did I tell you Mr Whistler took me down to the Troglodyte Caves up at the Five Oaks last week, Doctor?" she asked, spitting out a few crumbs with her words. Elizabeth leant forward and wiped her mouth with an embroidered serviette. "I had been many times before of course but they remain of great interest, don't you think?" She went on. "The dear man often requests my company when he wishes to use his photographic equipment to advantage. We use my carriage of course, for he cannot possibly afford to run one of his own. He says that he would like to go to Grève De Lecq tomorrow, the fort provides so much action for his pictures. I will rest in the tea-rooms on the road below until he finishes. I do enjoy the currant buns from that establishment. They are almost as good as yours Elizabeth."

She wished Elizabeth and the doctor would not exchange sidelong glances like that, it was so impolite. And Elizabeth had no need to help her hold the cup, she was quite capable of doing so without spilling. But oh! This tea was refreshing.... Just like the tea she enjoyed that afternoon they took the carriage ride to Gorey. Do you remember Mama? I was wearing the prettiest of bonnets and a gown of deep blue and you said you had rarely seen me look so pretty....

"Well, she looks very well," she thought she heard the doctor say. "She probably sleeps on and off during the day?"

"Speak up!" Julia commanded. "I cannot abide people who mutter."

"I was just saying how well you look today," the doctor said.

"And so I shall remain under your care. You are much better than Doctor Bentliff, he was getting such a fuddy-duddy. Still he and his wife will be aptly suited for the running my crèche. I did tell you of the large nursery we are opening in the Royal Gardens?"

Before the doctor had time to even nod in reply she had turned away and was now pointing to the pavement below. "My goodness! Look at that ridiculous hat Mrs Partridge is wearing. Has she not read the fashion magazines?"

"That is not Mrs Partridge," said Elizabeth, who had leant across her to see, "It's that uppity Madam Noel, the fishmonger's wife. Thinks she's the cat's whiskers that one does."

"Really? She is the image of Mrs Partridge in that hat," she murmured.

"Is she still being bothered with beggarsome callers?" The doctor asked Elizabeth.

"Not since I started giving 'em the old heave-ho! Cheeky buggers trying to wheedle money out of a defenceless old lady. The religious ones are the worst, and that one that runs the children's home out east. I told 'im, 'e ought to count himself lucky that she's been so generous all the past years. I told 'em all to bugger off. Load of thieves some of them. Do you know we caught her nephew Alex having nicked a hundred pounds after one of his visits and still the dear lady went on to pay his hospital bills until he died last December? Felt sorry for him she said because he didn't do as well as his brothers. Dare say I've got a bit of a name for myself because I speak as I find but someone's got to look after 'er interests. And it's no good you thinking you might 'ave something coming to you either. She's left all her money and property to the poor, has had it written down in her will for years."

"Blessed are the poor for they shall inherit the earth....," Julia began to recite.

"I believe the quotation is, 'Blessed are the meek for they shall inherit the earth.'" The doctor interrupted.

"That is what I said," Julia snapped. "Aw! Come now Elizabeth, when are you going to pour the good doctor and me a cup of tea? Our throats are quite dry."

Elizabeth held the cup to her lips. She took a sip and then another before shaking her head to signal that she had drunk enough.

"Did you see Emilie Le Breton at the new theatre last week doctor?"

"The opening of the new Opera House took place last summer and yes, I did go to see the play. Lillie Langtry is a most beautiful woman and clever actress..."

"Why she gave herself the name of Lillie I do not know," Julia scoffed. "Emilie is much the prettier do you not think? She would not remember me but I knew her well as a child. Such a harum-scarum and yet she could be quite the young lady when beside her father opening church bazaars and the like in her mother's place. What a handsome man he was! I never could bring myself to believe all the gossip, could you? Her poor mama, such a frail lady but then with those robustly energetic children..."

Suddenly she leant her head back against the cushions and said, "I think I shall take a little nap now. I am very tired. Do you think you could help me into my chair by the fire Elizabeth?"

"There, I warned you not to tire yourself out," Elizabeth Curwood said as she lifted Julia bodily away from the window seat and carried her across the room to the fireplace. There was hardly any weight to her at all, even fully clothed. "As you see for yourself doctor, she never stays bright for long."

"I look forward to seeing you tomorrow, Doctor Bois. I shall watch from the window as usual. I always recognise your step, it is very distinctive," she told him as he left.

But Julia recognised neither him nor his step when he returned to the house at four o'clock the following morning on the insistence of a distressed Elizabeth Curwood.

"Oh Papa, I am so glad you have come," Julia muttered weakly as soon as he reached her side. Then without another word she fell into a deep sleep from which she left the world nearly two hours later, at twenty minutes to six.

25

JOHN TREGEAR WESTAWAY, having been notified of his great-aunt's death, arrived in the island from America two months after her burial in St. Saviour's churchyard. He was confident that he would be entitled to claim a great part, if not all, of her estate. It came as a shock therefore to discover that his great-aunt had disposed of all the properties that he might have been entitled to under the Jersey Law of Inheritance. Not only that but, apart from some minor bequests, none of which were in his name, she had willed the bulk of her estate, a great fortune, to the poor.

It was grossly unjust, he protested to the solicitor who had acted for him in claiming his share of his great aunt Harriet's inheritance. The fortune could not have been made but for the original heritages from his great-grandfather's estate, heritages that, by Jersey Law, should never have been shared but should all have gone to his grandfather. It made a mockery of all that the island's justice stood for! Why, even that common woman Curwood and her brother had benefited, £1,000 wasn't it? And a mere carpenter £1.2s.6d. for his lifetime, well not only for his lifetime but after his death throughout his wife's lifetime. How could this be right when flesh and blood receive nothing?

Phillipe Mourant Richardson agreed. However, he added, as it was known that Julia Westaway was feeble-minded and under the influence of the housekeeper, who viciously abused her, there was every reason that the will would be revoked. Court records could be found to show that the woman's brother was violent by nature and prone to drunken rages. His great aunt was probably under duress when she made the will and this could all be challenged. But to gather evidence, make investigations and later challenge the will would incur much time and expense. Did he want him to proceed?

John Tregear Westaway asked how long he considered it would take? The solicitor replied many months, perhaps a year or maybe two but he would try and keep it within a year and a day when, unless he can prove otherwise, the named beneficiaries could legally receive their bequests. Could he leave all the business in his hands while he returned to America, John asked. Certainly, Phillipe Richardson replied, but he would need his account paid on a quarterly basis. John, living on the money he had been able to accrue from hard work during his lifetime, could see it dwindling fast and said he would have to think about it.

That evening, after a stroll about the town, he stopped at the Soleil Levant Inn and ordered a tankard of ale. The innkeeper was an inquisitive man and John was one easily persuaded to talk, so it was not long before he was discussing the reason for his return to the island.

"Miss Julia Westaway you say? Tut! Tut! Dreadful business…. That Charlie Curwood never could hold his ale. The poor old dear never stood a chance with his witch of a sister watching over her. A prisoner in her own house she was. Drunks the pair of them were, him and his sister. Robbing her blind I was told while denying good and honest church folk alms. And the foul language on them! Aw! You should have witnessed the drunken brawls…. Well I've seen some in here as you can imagine but their fights were heard for miles around they were. Had the police there every week. No decent lady should have had to live alongside that. Disgraceful, that's what it was!"

John Tregear Westaway made up his mind there and then. With the innkeeper's gossip still ringing in his ears he called into Phillipe Richardson's office first thing the following morning. His great-aunt had been much abused in both mind and body, he said. She could not have known what she was doing when she made her will. It was his duty as a Westaway to see that her tormentors were brought to justice and her fortune remain within her family where it belonged. He hoped that a successful outcome would not be too long in arriving. The solicitor said he was confident that it would not take long but there again, with such a fortune at stake, there was bound to be a bit of a tussle.

That 'bit of a tussle' was to prove one of the greatest legal battles the island had ever seen and the years rolled by with frustrating regularity as lawsuit followed lawsuit in the pursuit of justice.

First there were the charges against Elizabeth Curwood, that she was a vulgar, domineering woman, uneducated in either schooling or nursing and addicted to drink and bad language. She had entered Julia's service in the summer of 1893 it was learned, two years before Julia made her last will and testament. Was the fact that Julia bequeathed her, a mere servant, £1,000 and the brother a carriage and

£100 not proof that it must have been made under duress? Accusations followed accusations, incidents of her abusive behaviour recounted with both brother and sister vilified.

The housekeeper's champions suddenly spoke up from the most unexpected quarters. Doctor Bentliff stated that though he had no reason to admire the woman, with her having the audacity to dismiss him from the house, he could only speak with honesty. She always followed his advice to the best of her ability, he said, and though she was coarse she could also be most gentle with her employer. Doctor Bois admitted the same. They and other witnesses claimed that though Julia was aware of all Elizabeth Curwood's weaknesses she would not hear of being without her servant as she treated her with more kindness than anyone else had ever done. The detractors were finally found to be those who were unsuccessful in trying to obtain money from Julia.

The case then turned to Julia's state of mind when she made her will and several witnesses were called. Her solicitors – Phillipe Baudains, Peter Falla and John Thelland – all maintained that she was of perfectly sound mind and was quite capable of dismissing Elizabeth Curwood if she suspected any coercion at the time she made her Will. Roger Eykyn, her stockbroker and old friend, said she was an astute investor and had made no secret of the way she intended to dispose of her wealth. Others admitted she was self-willed but was also impulsively generous.

Mr Lander, the artist from whom Julia commissioned the oil painting, 'Assise d'Heritage', for £400 as a gift for the island's States, stated that he visited her frequently. Though he was often lucky to get away within two hours he never wondered about her mental condition as she always seemed perfectly normal. Another witness said that she was sharp and shrewd in business.

On the other hand Mr Whistler thought her mental powers feeble and that it was trying to listen to her during the afternoon drives in her carriage. Mr Hagell, the Superintendent of the Dr Barnardo's also had tired of her company though he still accepted gifts for the Home. The same was said by the Reverend Skegg who visited no less that eighty times during the three years following Harriet's death and received gifts of objects worth several hundreds of pounds.

Doctor Bentliff spoke up for her brightness of mind. Doctor Bois could only say that he found her conversation to wander, though he admitted she was coming to the end of her days.

The content of Julia's Will was repeated time and again. Apart from minor bequests she had left the bulk of her estate, estimated to be around £100,000, to provide a crèche for babies, a fund for the *pauvre honteux* of the twelve parishes and another to provide clothing and books for Protestant elementary schoolchildren.

It was a vast fortune for which two local solicitors battled valiantly on behalf of their clients. On one side there was Philippe Richardson who was arguing on behalf of his client John Tregear's legal right of claim as a Westaway. On the other Phillipe Baudains was pleading that Julia's wishes should stand. The legal arguments continued unabated for nearly five years until, in desperation, Phillipe Baudains requested that the case be sent before the Privy Council.

At the end of February 1906, after many months and hours of deliberation, a declaration arrived from Buckingham Palace. It stated that the Privy Council had advised His Majesty the King that on the evidence put before them they had found Julia to have been in sound mind when she made her last Will and Testament.

It was not known how John Tregear Westaway received the news of his defeat but Phillipe Baudains, having been Julia's close friend and confidante for many years, was seen to shed unmanly tears of relief.

THE END

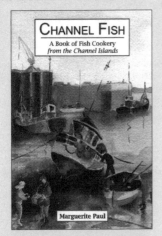

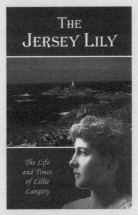

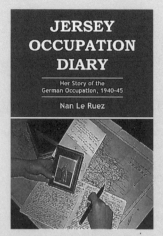